LEMON TART

OTHER BOOKS BY JOSI S. KILPACK

Her Good Name
Sheep's Clothing
Unsung Lullaby

Culinary Mysteries
English Trifle
Devil's Food Cake
Key Lime Pie (to be released Fall 2010)

Download a free PDF of all the recipes in this book at
josiskilpack.com or shadowmountain.com

LEMON TART

A CULINARY MYSTERY

JOSI S. KILPACK

SHADOW
MOUNTAIN

The Library of Congress has cataloged the earlier edition as follows:

Kilpack, Josi S.

   Lemon tart : a culinary mystery / Josi S. Kilpack.

     p.   cm.

  ISBN 978-1-60641-050-9 (pbk.)

   1. Cooks—Fiction. 2. Single mothers—Crimes against—Fiction.

3. Murder—Investigation—Fiction. 4. Kidnapping—Fiction. I. Title.

PS3561.I412L46 2009

813'.54—dc22

                                             2008037662

Printed in the United States of America

Alexander's Print Advantage

10 9 8 7 6 5

To my mother—Marle Schofield—for all the good things,
baked and otherwise

CHAPTER 1

The first police car went by at 9:23 according to the clock on the microwave. Sadie leaned forward, but the black walnut tree in Jack and Carrie's yard obstructed her view to the west. She scowled at the tree and went back to coring the last of the apples she'd spent all morning making into applesauce. She waited for the police car to turn around in the cul-de-sac and pass by her window on its way out. That's the only reason police cars ever drove into Peregrine Circle.

Except this time.

A second police car sped past less than a minute after the first, and Sadie stopped thinking about apples altogether. Living in the house on the corner, Sadie considered herself a sort of sentry standing guard over Peregrine Circle—her lack of view to the west notwithstanding—and her curiosity was piqued.

After putting the last of the apples into the pot and setting it to simmer, Sadie removed the jars that had just finished processing and put them on a dish towel next to the sink so they could cool properly. She then rinsed her hands and dried them on the hem of the Colorado State hoodie she wore—a birthday gift from Breanna last year—and turned off the Paul Simon CD that had kept her company all morning. Before stepping outside, she inspected herself in the small mirror she'd hung by the front door. She frowned at her reflection and removed the stretchy headband that held back her hair. She ran her fingers through her hair in an attempt to shape it into some semblance of order. Usually she was quite well put together, but today she was canning which meant she hadn't showered, which meant she hadn't blow-dried her hair, which meant the chunked-out sections hadn't been lifted and flipped to perfectly frame her face. But she didn't have time for that right now, so she gave her hair a final finger comb, coaxing her bangs to the side as best she could, grabbed her jacket, and pulled open the front door.

Her flip-flops smacked against the front steps beneath the frayed hem of her work jeans—paint-splattered denim washed so many times they felt like flannel. Never mind that the knees were nearly worn through or that she'd had to sew one of the pockets back on after an unfortunate incident involving a chain-link fence last summer. The jeans were comfort themselves and the perfect company for a day spent putting up applesauce.

She reached the sidewalk and shot another hateful glance at the tree as she approached it. Someday she was going to accidentally chop it down or light it on fire or something.

When Sadie and her late husband, Neil, had designed the house twenty-seven years ago, Sadie had insisted on a big window above the kitchen sink and facing the street. She liked to watch the comings and goings of the neighborhood, and with the inordinate amount of time spent at the sink since then, doing all the things a mother of two uses a sink for, the window had been a good investment. Sadie's baby brother, Jack, and his family, had bought the lot next door a few years later and the black walnut tree had been a housewarming gift Sadie wished she'd considered with a bit more care back then. She hadn't expected the tree to grow so big as to block much of the view she had insisted on. However, it didn't take long to walk past the tree and see which home had been the cause of alarm.

Anne Lemmon.

The two police cars were parked next to the curb. Sadie increased her pace and cut across the cul-de-sac—looking both ways, just in case.

"What's happened?" she asked an officer posted on the front walk next to the mailbox decorated with little lemon decals—Anne loved capitalizing on her last name even though she spelled it with two M's. Before he could answer her question, another officer, older—but not by much; thirty-five tops—came around the side of the house. His eyes locked onto hers and he came toward her.

"Do you know the occupants of this house?" he asked when he reached her. The name on his gold badge read Malloy. She swore there was a TV cop with the same name, but she couldn't remember which show.

Sadie nodded. "Anne Lemmon and her two-year-old son, Trevor. Is everything okay?" Anne and Trevor had moved into the Tillys' rental house about nine months earlier. She'd come from back East with practically nothing but her determination to change the wild ways that had landed her as a twenty-five-year-old single mom in the first place.

Both of Sadie's kids were away at college, and Sadie had taken early retirement eighteen months ago in order to care for her father who'd been diagnosed with colon cancer. Dad had passed away last December, and since then Sadie had enjoyed mentoring Anne—helping to quell her own loneliness—and they'd developed a wonderful friendship despite a nearly thirty-year age difference. Sadie was proud of the way Anne had taken to the changes in her life.

"Two-year-old son, you say," Malloy repeated, writing something down in a little notebook he held in his hand.

"What's happened?" Sadie asked for the second time.

"I'm afraid I can't give you that information, ma'am," he said, his tone blank and unsympathetic.

Sadie looked at Anne's front door, wondering what could have mustered this amount of attention. A third officer came around the corner of the house—he was chubby, with thick legs and a neck that disappeared between his head and shoulders.

Don't you have to be in good shape to be a police officer these days? Sadie wondered. Apparently not.

"It's locked up tight. We'll have to bust in—"

"Shut up, Harris!" Malloy yelled as he spun around, silencing the other man who seemed to have just noticed Sadie.

"I can let you in if you like," Sadie said, smiling sweetly and ignoring Malloy's gruffness. Surely the officers would give her more information if she helped them—and she *desperately* wanted more information.

Officer Malloy lifted an eyebrow. "You have a key?"

"Of course," Sadie said, her smile widening. "Just last week I let the furnace repairman in while Anne was at work. I retired a year or so ago, see, and even though I substitute now and again I'm home more than anyone else."

Every family in the circle had asked her, at one time or another, to keep their spare keys and she'd eventually put them all on the same ring that she always kept in her jacket pocket. Well, everyone had asked her to keep a key except for Mr. Henry, the house just next to Anne on the west side. All the same, Sadie knew he kept his spare key in one of those fake rocks you can buy online. She'd spotted that rock within days of his purchase.

She pulled the smiley-face key ring from her pocket and took a step toward the house, excited to be part of whatever they were doing.

"You'll need to wait out here," Malloy said arrogantly, stepping in front of her to block her progress. He was only a couple inches taller than her five-foot-six, and although she had a smaller build, she was strong thanks to three visits a week to the gym. If she wanted to, she could probably take him. But instead she reluctantly separated Anne's key from the others and handed it to him, the other keys dangling on the ring. He didn't even say thank you, and she frowned at his bad manners. The chubby cop hurried to catch up with Malloy and the two men climbed the steps.

The officer who'd been posted on the walk came to stand next to her and together they watched Malloy unlock the door, get into position, and then push open the door.

"Garrison police!" Officer Malloy yelled, taking Sadie by surprise and making her jump just a little. She looked at her guard, glad he didn't seem to have noticed her reaction or at least was too polite to smirk about it. By the time she looked back to the door, Malloy and the chubby officer had disappeared inside.

It was a long wait as she imagined what could have necessitated three police officers to investigate Anne's house. She really wished she knew what was going on. Officer Malloy finally came out after a few minutes and said it was all clear. As he descended the steps, he spoke into the speaker clipped to the shoulder of his uniform. "There's nothing here," he said. "What *exactly* did the tip say?"

When he reached Sadie's position on the sidewalk, he said, "I'd like to ask you some questions about Ms. Lemmon." He pulled a tiny notebook out of his shirt pocket just as something crackled on his walkie-talkie that Sadie couldn't understand. She'd always wondered about those tiny police notebooks. It seemed as though they'd fill one every single day, and she imagined boxes and boxes of filled notebooks shoved into closets at the police station. She hoped they recycled.

"Just a minute," he said to her before turning away and talking into the speaker again.

She looked toward the front door, and tucked a lock of hair behind her ear, her anxiety growing as her imagination ran away from her. So the police had received some kind of tip. Had there been an accident? Was Trevor okay? Anne's car was still parked in the carport. But the officer said the house was empty—how could that be?

Malloy was still talking on his walkie-talkie when Sadie noticed a familiar smell. She sniffed the air a second time. *Lemon tart*, she thought as she identified the aroma.

Anne was baking!

Sadie immediately relaxed, all the horrible possibilities taking a backseat to simple common sense. Nothing had happened to Anne at all; the tip that brought the police to her house had been some kind of mistake. Sadie smiled to herself and took a deep breath, almost feeling foolish for letting her mind run on ahead as it had.

"Um, officer," she said, tapping Officer Malloy's arm, eager to share her discovery with him. He scowled at her and took a step away, continuing his conversation on the speaker. He seemed to be having some kind of argument with a dispatcher—something about the whole thing being a waste of time and wanting permission to write up the tip as unsubstantiated.

Sadie couldn't make heads or tails out of what the fuzzy voice coming from the walkie-talkie was saying. She looked at the front door of Anne's house again. Everyone knew that once you could smell whatever had been set to bake, it was nearly finished. Was she really expected to stand out here while the tart burned?

Her guard went to get something out of his car, and Sadie assumed the chubby officer was still inside the house. She shifted her weight from one foot to the other, her anxiety growing again. Taking a step toward the house, she thought better of it and retreated, tapping Malloy on the arm again. He didn't even look at her, but took two steps farther away from her.

Fine, she thought as she headed up the steps.

"Hey!" she heard Officer Malloy call out as she reached the door. But she was too far into this to go back now.

"Lemon tart!" she shouted back, then quickened her pace and hurried into the kitchen, not wanting him to catch up and stop her. "Can't you smell it?" she yelled over her shoulder, flying past the chubby officer, Harris, who was standing in the living room writing down notes.

Sadie had shown Anne how to cook all kinds of things over the last several months, but Anne had been particularly studious about learning to bake the perfect lemon tart—she'd wanted it to become her signature dessert.

"She's baking," Sadie explained when she reached the stove.

Harris was right behind her and reached around her to grab the handle of the oven. He seemed to be repeating what she'd just said in his mind—as if he knew the difference between a lemon tart and a quiche.

On second thought, he might, Sadie thought after taking a second look at the belly hanging over his pants. He had a certain appreciation for food, it seemed. Sadie quickly put her hand on the door to keep it closed. "Every time you open an oven you lose five minutes of baking time," she said to Harris, her eyes narrowed.

"Let go of that, Harris," Malloy said from the kitchen doorway. Harris dropped the handle, looking flushed and uncertain. Officer Malloy turned to Sadie—his face was red too, but she doubted it was for the same reason as Harris. She lifted her chin in defiance and tried to stand as tall as she could, bringing herself almost to eye level with him.

"I told you to wait outside," he said, his eyebrows pinched together and his eyes angry. She couldn't be sure but he seemed to be pulling himself up taller too—perhaps to look down on her a little better. She was not impressed.

"And let the tart burn?" she asked with exaggerated incredulity. What she wanted more than the salvation of the tart was to look around the house herself, but for the moment she kept her eyes locked on Malloy's, not wanting to appear the least bit intimidated. She had at least twenty years on this kid and she wasn't the type of woman who let herself be pushed around.

He let out a breath as if she were a child and that got her back up even more. He might know how to investigate some tip and enjoy bullying the neighbors, but Sadie knew Anne and she knew this house. If something wasn't right, she'd be the one who would notice—not him. He narrowed his eyes and took a deep breath. Sadie mimicked his expression, narrowing her eyes even more.

"Please return outside," he said slowly, calculating. "Harris, turn off the oven."

"Turn it off?" Sadie said in disbelief, stepping back to block the oven door. "No way."

Malloy's expression faltered and she saw his uncertainty, which only strengthened her resolve.

"Excuse me?" he asked as if he hadn't heard her correctly.

"Most people vastly underestimate the satisfaction of good homemaking skills and I won't have anyone sabotage Anne's attempts. There are"—she turned her head to look at the timer—"three minutes left. This oven will not be opened a minute sooner."

"You're interfering with a police investigation," Officer Malloy said as he took a step toward her, his jaw clenched.

"And you're interfering with a woman's kitchen." Sadie lifted her chin even higher—partly because he was now only ten inches or so from her face. Malloy seemed to be trying to find a reply, but she continued before he had the chance. "You said yourself it was all clear and that whatever tip brought you here was unfounded," she said. "And Anne wouldn't have been baking if she weren't going to be right back. In case she isn't, I'll remove it." Yet even as she said it, the unease in her stomach grew. There were too many questions in her mind now.

Why would Anne put a tart in the oven and then leave? Sadie had been at her kitchen window all morning, how could she have missed Anne leaving? Why was the house locked up if she were only going to be gone a few minutes? What about Trevor?

The officer clenched his jaw even tighter; she thought she heard his teeth grind as he seemed to consider her words. "Harris, make sure she doesn't touch anything but the oven. McKesson and I will widen the exterior sweep."

Apparently Malloy was in charge because Harris folded his beefy arms and glared at her while Malloy went back out the front door.

While the tart finished baking, Sadie looked around the kitchen and the part of the living room in her range of vision. Everything looked normal—right down to the lemon-themed placemats on the table. The sink held an assortment of dishes, the counters were mostly cleared, and Trevor's shoes were by the back door. She'd hoped to get some idea of what had brought the police here, but she was starting to admit maybe Officer Malloy had been right—everything looked clear.

When the timer dinged at exactly 9:40, Harris wouldn't let her open the drawer next to the oven to get a set of hot pads. Sadie had to pull her hands into the sleeves of her jacket to keep from burning her fingers as she removed the tart. He also wouldn't let her find a cooling rack, so she was forced to set the pan on the stovetop, which was not the optimal way to cool baked goods. She kept that information to herself, however.

It's perfect, she thought as she set the tart down. The crust underneath the bronzed filling was golden brown, and pride welled in Sadie's heart to realize how far Anne had come. About the only thing Anne knew how to make when she had moved in was Belgian waffles—an odd item to perfect, but at least it meant she had some basic culinary knowledge. Now she was well on her way to becoming a superior cook. But the worry for her young friend returned as Sadie looked at the steaming confection. No one worked this hard on a lemon tart and treated it like it was any old frozen pie. Something was very wrong.

She turned to Harris to share her suspicions—but he was looking out the patio door, watching something. Sadie followed his line of vision and froze when she saw the other two officers gathered around something in the field of weeds behind Anne's house. Harris hurried out the back door and Sadie followed. She was stepping over the threshold when she heard Officer Malloy say, "Tape off the area. I'll call homicide."

Mom's Lemon Tart

*Jack's favorite!

Crust
1 cup all-purpose flour
1/3 cup powdered sugar
1/2 Pinch of salt
cup (1 stick) cold unsalted butter (cut into smaller pieces)

Preheat oven to 425 degrees. In a food processor or mixer, combine ingredients for crust. Pulse together until a dough starts to form in clumps. Press into greased tart pan, making sure to cover bottom and sides evenly. Pierce the bottom of the crust with a fork and place in freezer for 10 to 15 minutes.

Place tart pan on a cookie sheet and bake until crust is a golden-brown color, approximately 12 minutes. Remove from oven and let cool.

Filling

5 oz. cream cheese

1/2 cup granulated sugar (Breanna likes an extra 1/4 cup sugar in the filling)

3/4 cup fresh lemon juice (about 2 large lemons—**DO NOT** use concentrated lemon juice)

2 large eggs

Zest from one lemon (get zest from lemon before juicing)

Reduce oven temperature to 350 degrees. Mix cream cheese with electric beaters until smooth. Add sugar. Mix until well blended. Add the eggs one at a time, mixing thoroughly after each egg. Stop and scrape bowl halfway through. Add the lemon juice and zest and mix until smooth.

Pour filling into tart crust and bake on cookie sheet for 20 to 30 minutes or until filling is set. Let tart cool on wire cooling rack. Cover and refrigerate until well chilled.

Use whipped cream as an optional topping. It can be piped on in stars or served on top with each piece. For extra flavor in the whipped cream, add a teaspoon of lemon zest.

CHAPTER 2

Sadie made it to the top of Anne's back patio stairs before the word "homicide" finally sank in and her feet would go no further. She had forgotten to breathe and when her brain realized it, she took a deep breath that sounded like a vacuum sucking up a tablecloth.

Officer Malloy was walking toward the house, talking into his speaker-thing, and the sound of her desperate breath caught his attention. He hurried up the steps of the patio, catching her as she fell backward. They landed in a jumbled heap, but he'd kept her from hurting herself.

"Wha-at, what's out there?" she mumbled as he straightened himself and helped her up, leading her to a patio chair. She tried to look over her shoulder at the field but he quickly turned the chair so it faced the sliding glass door of the house instead of the backyard. She could barely register what was happening. *Homicide?* she said in her mind once more. That meant they'd found a body. The chill in the autumn air became decidedly colder and her hands began to shake.

"I'm sorry, Mrs. . . ." Officer Malloy trailed off.

"Hoffmiller," she said, choosing to focus on a fall-themed wreath Anne had hung on her kitchen wall—she could see it through the glass of the door.

"Mrs. Hoffmiller. Is there someone I can call to come and help you back home? A friend? Your husband?"

"I'm a widow," she said automatically, her foggy thoughts beginning to clear. There was Ron, her boyfriend, though the term sounded juvenile and besides, they were engaged. But Ron was at a real estate convention in Denver all week—he couldn't come. She turned and looked at Officer Malloy. "Who's out there? Is it Anne?" She swallowed the threatening tears. "Trevor?" she squeaked.

Officer Malloy quickly shook his head. "Not the child," he said.

"But Anne? She's out there? She's dead?"

Malloy took a deep breath. "The body will need to be identified for us to be sure."

Sadie tried to stand, but Malloy's hand on her shoulder pushed her back into the chair. "Not you," he said, sounding more irritated than sympathetic. "Next of kin."

The tears started to fall then, but she didn't even try to brush them away. This was Anne he was talking about—a girl trying to find her way. A friend. A neighbor. A mother. "I don't know of any kin, certainly no one local. I can identify her as well as anyone else," she said, her voice shaking as she rubbed the two stones of her mother's ring on her right hand. The feel of the smoothly cut stones—one diamond and one amethyst, her children's birthstones—helped her find her center once again and she pushed down the shock. "The sooner you know if it's her, the sooner you can move forward, right?"

Malloy hesitated, but finally nodded.

"Besides," she added. "It might not be her." Though she knew that was a ridiculous idea. The police had received a tip of some kind and found a body. What were the chances that a completely unrelated murder had taken place behind Anne's house?

Murder.

The very idea made her knees wobble—she was glad she was still sitting. *Then again, maybe it wasn't murder,* she thought as she took a breath and followed Malloy down the back steps. Maybe it was some kind of accident. Accidents happened all the time. Why, her friend Gale had a neighbor who'd gone out Christmas morning to set up a new satellite dish. His metal tape measure had crossed the electrical wires leading to his house. Killed him instantly. Though an accidental death would still be tragic, at least it would be less disturbing. Accidents were normal, practically expected. That had to be it. Some kind of accident.

They met Officer McKesson, who was blocking the body from view. Harris was wrapping a band of yellow tape around the perimeter of the house. Sadie heard a siren in the distance growing closer.

"She's going to identify the body," Malloy said. Officer McKesson hesitated, but after a few moments he moved aside. Sadie closed her eyes, letting Officer Malloy lead her the last few steps. The brittle grass and weeds of the field crunched beneath her feet once they left the back lawn.

"Okay," he said quietly. "Are you sure you want to do this?"

In answer to his question, she opened her eyes.

Anne's pale blue eyes stared at nothing, her blonde hair tangled in the weeds, and her mouth hung slightly open as if she were about to say something. Her head was at an unnatural angle to her body and her face and neck were a bluish-purple color. It looked like there was some matted blood in her hairline.

So it had been murder.

The thought hit Sadie like a cold bucket of water and she forgot to breathe again. Anne's arms and legs were sticking out in odd directions and her clothing was torn as if she'd put up quite a fight. *Good for her,* Sadie thought, wiping at her eyes. *Good for her.*

She looked away for a moment to get control of her emotions and noticed Anne's purse in the weeds not far away, the top of a sippy cup barely visible. Anne was always trying to avoid taking a separate diaper bag by cramming Trevor's things in her purse. Sadie stared at the cup and thought of the little boy with sandy blond hair and bright blue eyes. If Anne was here, like this, where was Trevor? It was almost too much to think about.

"Is this Anne Lemmon?" Officer Malloy asked, reminding her that she was supposed to be making an official identification.

She looked back at Anne's broken body—one of Anne's hoop earrings was missing and she wondered if that was important. Sadie sniffed. "Yes, that's her," she said, her voice shaking. She leaned down, wanting to straighten out Anne's head or pull her shirt down so her stomach wasn't exposed to the autumn air. She was dead, but was it necessary that she look so uncomfortable?

Officer Malloy pulled her up. "You can't touch her. We'll need to take photos and measurements of the crime scene."

Sadie nodded and gratefully turned away, though it felt like a betrayal somehow. It made her feel horrible to not want to look at the evidence of how Anne's life had ended.

"Can you get home on your own?" Malloy asked as they walked away from the body, toward the driveway.

Sadie watched the grass bend beneath her shoes. The grass was going dormant and was a muddle of brown and yellow and a few determined green blades.

"I'm fine," Sadie lied, numbness taking over.

"Because this is still considered an active crime scene, we'll be patrolling the neighborhood and canvassing the area. When you get home, lock your doors and don't leave. A detective will be coming around to ask you some questions. You might want to call someone to be with you."

Sadie stopped and turned to face him. "So I'm just supposed to go home? Do nothing?" How was that possible?

"I'm sorry," Officer Malloy said. "That's all you can do."

"I'll try," Sadie said under her breath. Doing nothing was not her strong suit.

"What?" the officer asked.

"Never mind."

CHAPTER 3

Sadie went home, locked her doors as instructed, and sat carefully on a kitchen chair as if too much movement might break them both. She stared at nothing as old ghosts moved in to haunt her. Most days she avoided such thoughts, but her defenses were down and the multitude of her losses began compounding.

She felt her muscles tense as her husband's face came to her mind. Oh, how she missed him. Neil had died of a massive heart attack nineteen years ago at the age of forty-one—leaving her a widow with two young children to raise. There was a history of heart disease in Neil's family, but he'd taken such good care of himself and no one had expected he would die so young—certainly not Sadie. Ten years later Sadie's mother had been killed in a car accident. And then, not quite a year ago, her father, who had lived with her and the children since her mother's death, had died of colon cancer. At least she'd had time to prepare for Dad's passing—not that the sting of finding him cold and gray one December morning had been any easier because of the expectation.

In some ways, the tragic turns of Sadie's life had aged her— she'd always felt older and wiser than other women of her generation simply due to the fact that she'd had to be centered, self-sufficient, and able to fill multiple roles. However, because of the twists of fate she'd endured, she also understood the fragility of mortality better than most, and she took full advantage of the life she had.

She knew many women her age who felt they had done their time chained to the kitchen sink and were convinced that other success would make up for the monotony of cooking and cleaning. She also knew women who lived only to take care of the other people in their lives, insulating themselves from the real world by disregarding their own ambitions and giving up their own life for someone else's.

Sadie was none of those women.

At fifty-six it was hard to accept that she was officially considered a senior citizen—she certainly didn't feel *old*—and she went to great pains to not look or act old either. Life was as much an adventure as it had always been, and she spoiled herself whenever she felt like it. She loved learning new things and relished her relationships. She'd been the one left behind enough to know that life doesn't last forever, so she made the best of every day she had.

Perhaps she should be used to loss by now, or the joy she found in life would have made up for the heartache, but that wasn't the case at all. Making the most of her life never filled in the voids left from losing the people she cared about. But neither did she expect it to.

Poor Anne, Sadie thought as her fingers felt across the nubby top of her ring. It was so wrong that just after deciding to change her life, to make a real future for Trevor, she was gone.

Sadie's eyes shifted to focus on a watercolor Trevor had painted for her a few weeks earlier and her fingers stilled on her ring. The blue and red of the picture seemed to be a mocking tribute to life. She could still see how his face had lit up when he'd given it to her—a true treasure in his toddler mind. She put her arms on the kitchen table and laid her head against them as she began to cry. She wished Ron were there, and yet if he was, she'd be embarrassed to break down like this. It was probably better he was away so she could sort out her thoughts and emotions in private.

Only a few minutes passed before she ran out of tears. Sarah Diane Hoffmiller was not the kind of woman to give into sorrow. She'd learned early on that it didn't do any good and today she had apples to sauce.

Still wiping at her eyes, Sadie stood and restarted the CD player. Grateful she had something to keep her hands and her mind busy, she traded her jacket for her candy-stripe apron and headed for the apples she'd left to simmer earlier. They were certainly done by now. Neil's mother had taught her many things, including how to make homemade applesauce. Sadie's own mother cooked out of duty, not joy, but Neil's mother was an amazing cook who not only blessed her family with the best meals two hands could make, but also had fun doing it. Her mother-in-law's gift had become a legacy Neil and Sadie shared, which Sadie then passed on to her own children after he died. There were few things that compared to the joy of cooking a delicious dish and sharing it with the people in her life. It was therefore a relief to know the apples wouldn't sauce themselves and that, for a moment at least, she could lose herself in the task.

A knock at the door startled her some time later, and she looked up from the pan of boiled apples she was in the process of mashing. The Paul Simon CD that had kept her company all morning had started over again and her favorite song was playing. It bothered her that someone was interrupting her—and then she thought about what had happened to Anne. And she was irritated about a little interruption?

As she approached the door, she heard what sounded like arguing, but as soon as she began pulling the door open the voices stopped. Two men stood on the doorstep and it didn't take Sadie long to determine they were the detectives Officer Malloy had told her would stop by—the badges they both held out gave it away.

"Please come in," she said, wiping her hands on her apron. She hadn't replaced her headband and tried to smooth her hair a bit as the two men followed her into the living room and sat on the couch in front of the big picture window. She smoothed her apron as well, her hands resting on her rather substantial hips and reminding her that no amount of pressing was going to iron them out. Oh, well, she'd spent thirty years trying to make peace with her figure, now wasn't the time to dwell on it. At least she didn't have any mascara smudges to worry about since she hadn't even thought about makeup today.

"You're a Paul Simon fan?" the older of the two detectives asked when she went over and turned off the CD.

"Love him," Sadie said with a smile, pleasantly surprised by the comment and grateful for the distraction. "I think he's one of the most underappreciated musicians of our time. However, I don't hold with his antiwar beliefs." She liked to make that clear. If nothing else, Sadie was a patriot.

"Same for me, on both counts." He smiled slightly, and she noted that she liked the look of him—a broad forehead and a clean-shaven face that didn't look old enough to match his silver-white hair. Late fifties she guessed, leading her to assume he must be like Jack—prematurely gray. She actually thought gray looked very nice on older men, and on a few women as well; however, she couldn't imagine being comfortable with it herself. Then again, she might simply like the pampering that came with getting her hair and nails done once a month. Either way, she wasn't about to find out just how gray her own hair really was. She'd been coloring it for almost fifteen years and preferred being a brunette.

Sadie sat in the chair across from the two men on the couch, curling her feet underneath her and trying to decide what to do with her hands. She was tempted to wrap her arms around herself in search of comfort, but then decided on clasping them in her lap instead. The pleasant air faded as the severity of the situation set in. Was it cold in here or was it just her? She looked longingly into the kitchen.

The men didn't look like the detectives on TV. The one who had recognized Paul Simon was dressed in jeans and wore a black turtleneck under a buff-colored jacket. His badge was clipped to his belt. The other detective didn't look any older than the police officers at Anne's house, his blond hair not yet faded with age or wintertime, blue eyes, and one of those dime-sized beard things in the center of his chin. Sadie hated those silly beards. Men should either have a full beard—like Ron—or none at all; none of this spotty facial hair that was such the rage. Yet, even with the stupid beard-thing, he could have fit right in on a beach somewhere, except he was dressed in a dark blue suit—tie and all. The formal attire and hard line of his jaw gave him a severe look that made his partner seem even warmer by comparison.

"My name is Detective Cunningham," the older one said, and as she looked at him she realized there was something familiar about him beyond his eyes that looked very much like Sean Connery's and his hair that was so similar to Jack's. He waved briefly toward his partner. "This is Detective Madsen."

Sadie nodded and looked at Detective Cunningham again. "Do I know you?" she asked.

He nodded and gave such a slight smile that she wondered if she had imagined it. "We met a few years ago when you headed the Senior Center Health Fair—I was one of the speakers."

"Oh, yes," she said, smiling back and nodding as she made the connection. "You talked about crime prevention for the elderly. It was a wonderful presentation." Sadie and her father had both found it very informative, even though she was still several years from her AARP card back then.

Detective Cunningham nodded. "I appreciated the thank you card and homemade bread you sent afterward, it was delicious."

Detective Madsen cleared his throat—the universal cue to change the subject—and they both went quiet. Sadie stole another glance into the kitchen as she heard the first watery rumblings from the stove. She'd already put the water bath canner on to boil in preparation to process the jars of applesauce once they were filled.

"Are we interrupting something?" Detective Cunningham asked.

"I was making applesauce." She looked into the kitchen again, fidgeting in her chair. "Well, actually, if you don't mind, I ought to turn off the canner." She stood up and hurried into the kitchen. But once there, she saw the washed jars on the counter and the pot of semi-mashed apples waiting for her on the counter—reflecting her neglect of the task she'd spent all morning preparing. She turned toward the detectives. "Is there any way you could ask me questions while I work on this? I'd hate to have to reheat the water in the canner. I've got another dozen and a half pints to put up today."

"Uh, sure," she heard Detective Cunningham say.

"Thank you," she said with relief. Detective Madsen, however, scowled as he followed Detective Cunningham into the kitchen. They both pulled out chairs at the kitchen table. Sadie picked up her masher, dripping with partially mashed apples, and began mashing again. It took all her strength to press through the quarts of soft apples until the masher hit the bottom of the pan. Then she would pull up with a *schlumping* sound and press down again—over and over until the apples were properly sauced.

Detective Cunningham began by asking about Anne's background. While she mashed, Sadie told them everything she knew, which wasn't much: Anne had moved from back East, didn't that mean New York? She had rented the Tillys' house nine months ago; Trevor's birthday was September sixth; and Anne would be twenty-six in January or February—Sadie wasn't quite sure.

"Why did she move here?" Detective Madsen asked. She looked up in time to catch a fleeting look of annoyance on Detective Cunningham's face, but it vanished quickly; she wondered what she'd done to upset him. She stopped mashing for a moment in order to assess the consistency of her sauce. She liked a smoother applesauce, not chunky, so she kept mashing, hoping it wasn't her wanting to work on the applesauce that created the tension in the air. She didn't see how it made any difference so long as she answered the questions.

"I only know that she wanted to change her life and felt Garrison was a good place to do it." With Fort Collins an hour to the west and Denver an hour south of that, Garrison certainly wasn't any kind of metropolis, and most people out-side Colorado didn't even know it existed despite its early his-tory as a major stopover for the Union Pacific Railroad. These days it was growing out of its agricultural foundations and gain-ing a reputation as a quiet respite far enough from Denver to enjoy peace and tranquility, but close enough to catch a plane when bigger horizons called. She finished mashing the first pan of apples and moved it to the counter. Then she slid the sec-ond pan from the back burner, took a deep breath, and started all over again; her shoulders were already burning.

"Can I help you with that?" Detective Cunningham finally asked, standing as he spoke. Sadie blinked and blew the hair out of her eyes. Was he serious? She didn't wait around to allow him to reconsider. Leaving the masher in the pot, she hurried to the pantry and pulled out another apron. It was dark brown with white lettering that said "If Mama ain't happy . . . give her chocolate!" She handed it to him once he'd slid out of his jacket and with a smirk, he tied it on and moved to the pan. He was a big man and seemed to fill the kitchen in just the way a man ought to. Sadie pulled a ladle out of the drawer and, after putting the canning funnel on the top of the first jar, started putting the already mashed sauce from the first pan into the jars that she'd lined up on the counter. Canning went so much faster with two people.

Detective Madsen rolled his eyes and scribbled some notes in his little notebook.

"Does Anne work?" Detective Cunningham asked.

"*Did* she work," Detective Madsen corrected.

Sadie snapped her head around in surprise, but Detective Madsen was looking at Detective Cunningham, not her. She quickly blinked back the tears brought on by Detective Madsen's stark reminder of Anne's death. Then she looked warily between the two men and wondered what she was missing.

"She worked at Albertson's," Sadie replied slowly, still trying to pin down the undercurrent in the room but knowing for certain that she did not like Detective Madsen. "She was a cashier—but she had a job interview last week and was really excited about it. It was for an office job—a receptionist or something like that."

"Did she hear back on that job?" Detective Cunningham asked.

"I don't think so," Sadie said with a shake of her head. "I'm sure she'd have told me if she did. I helped her with Trevor a couple days a week."

Detective Madsen frowned at the answer, but hurried to ask the next question, cutting off Detective Cunningham, who then shut his mouth and clenched his jaw. His mashing intensified.

"And do you know anyone who might have a grudge against Anne? Her . . . ex-husband or boyfriend? Someone she was afraid of?" Detective Madsen asked.

Sadie looked between the two men again as understanding dawned. *I'm not the problem,* she realized—and neither was her applesauce. There was something going on between the two of them that had started long before this conversation. She felt herself relax a little, grateful to know she wasn't the one to blame for the extra tension in the room.

"No," Sadie said, shaking her head and filling another jar with the rich golden sauce. "Trevor's dad isn't part of their lives." She looked up at Detective Cunningham. "All I know about him is that he pays her child support—enough so she could rent the Tilly's house instead of an apartment. She doesn't talk about him, but that's why she came here—to start fresh. I think he really broke her heart, if you want the truth of it, and she needed to find a new life."

"But you don't know his name?" Detective Cunningham asked almost before she'd finished speaking. He had a deep voice; her father would have described it as baritone, with a smoothness that surprised her. She wondered if he was a singer—her church choir was always short on baritones. Was Detective Cunningham a church-going man?

"I don't know anything about him or anyone else in her life before she came here. She kept her past very private."

"Was she dating anyone?" Detective Cunningham asked, sending a sparring look at his partner.

Sadie shook her head. "No, she told me she was waiting for Mr. Right. She seemed more interested in caring for her son and for her home than in men. But I have to tell you, I wondered if there wasn't someone."

"Who?" Detective Madsen asked, leaning forward as if desperate for the gossip. She really disliked him.

"I told you, I don't know. There were just times when she'd quickly get off the phone, or ask me to watch Trevor without telling me where she was going. I didn't press," she explained. "It was up to her how much she told me, and if there was someone in her life, which I'm not certain there was, she's entitled to her privacy." Though now Sadie realized there would be no such entitlement. The police would dig and dig until they learned everything they could about her. It seemed so unfair, poking and prodding into her personal affairs.

Detective Madsen's face was hard as he made some notes and then began asking her about today's events, anything Sadie had seen and why she'd run into Anne's house after being told not to. Saving the lemon tart didn't seem to impress him any more than it had impressed Officer Malloy, but she pretended that the rescue was her only motivation for going inside. Detective Cunningham kept mashing, allowing Detective Madsen to take the lead in the interview.

"What were you doing that kept you at the sink *all morning?*" Detective Madsen asked.

"Making applesauce," Sadie said with a bit of a chuckle as she waved her hand over the pans on the stove, the jars, and the bowl of apple skins ready for the compost pile. Wasn't it obvious? But Detective Madsen didn't smile and she cleared her throat. She hated the accusation she felt in every word of every question he asked. "There is just as much enjoyment to be had in self-sufficiency as there is in a weekend trip to Denver or shopping for the perfect pair of shoes. Homemade applesauce is most certainly worth the effort." It wasn't until the end of her explanation that she realized how defensive she sounded, so she smiled to soften her words. She'd learned long ago that you could say nearly anything so long as you smiled.

Detective Madsen looked at her as if she were some kind of loon, and she shifted her weight. "So you were at the sink all—"

"How does this look?" Detective Cunningham broke in, lifting the masher and stepping to the side of his pan. She moved in his direction and looked at the golden mixture.

"Very good," she said appreciatively. "Would you mind filling these other jars while I put the full bottles in the bath?"

"Bath?" Detective Madsen asked, seemingly annoyed by his own confusion.

"Water bath," Detective Cunningham answered, smiling in a very superior way at his partner. "To process the jars of applesauce." He turned to Sadie. "My wife used to make the best applesauce you've ever had—she put ginger in it. Have you ever tried that?"

"Ginger?" Sadie asked slowly, her eyes flicking quickly to his naked ring finger, which still showed a definite tan line. She filed the information away for later without stepping out of the moment. "I've never thought of that but I bet it's absolutely delicious." She put a finger on her chin and opened the spice cupboard. "Ground or fresh ginger?"

Detective Madsen cleared his throat again.

"I'm sorry, what was the question?" Sadie asked. She decided to add the ginger to another batch, not wanting to upset the younger detective.

"I asked why you were at the sink all morning long."

"I started washing, peeling, and cutting apples about 6:30. While the first batch cooked, I worked on preparing the next one—it's a rather intensive process."

"And what exactly did you see?"

"I saw Mr. Henry leave for work at 7:25. The Bailey kids walked up to the bus stop around 7:40. Then Steve and Mindy Bailey both left around 8:00—in separate cars. Carrie went out around 8:05, probably to the gym; she's been trying to lose weight since Jack left her last spring." She stopped, hating that she sounded like such a gossip and feeling like she was airing out the family laundry in front of strangers.

"You remember the exact times?" Detective Cunningham asked, pausing in his jar-filling and looking at her in surprise.

Sadie shrugged, feeling as if she ought to be embarrassed—but she wasn't. "I pay attention," she said simply as she began twisting the rings onto the tops of the jars, finger tight, and setting each jar on the rack suspended above the now bubbling water. "Those things happen every day, well, except the applesauce—that only happens for a few days in October."

"Applesauce," Detective Madsen muttered with derision, scribbling in his notebook some more. Detective Cunningham continued filling jars; though he made a fair amount of mess in the process, she was still grateful for his help. She knew not all men were as acclimated to a kitchen as Neil had been and she tried not to hold that fact against them. Detective Cunningham seemed content to let his partner continue the interview, but his face still showed his irritation every time he looked at the younger man. Sadie wondered again what the problem was between them. Weren't partners supposed to be friends? Cagney and Lacey were, but maybe it was different for women.

"Home canning is a dying art," she said simply in response to Detective Madsen's mutterings. Carrie's car drove past her home, quickly hidden by the black walnut tree, and Sadie furrowed her brow. Detective Madsen caught the look.

"What?" he said, standing to look out the window over the sink.

"Oh, Carrie just drove by. She started a new job last week so I'm a little surprised to see her home."

"You said she went to the gym." He watched her face closely. "Not work."

"Yes, the job is from 9:30 to 4:00 so she goes to the gym first, then goes straight to the office. Maybe the job was only a week long—she works for a temp agency, filling in at different places." She would have sworn that Carrie told her it was a three-week assignment. But then again she didn't know the specifics of her sister-in-law's life the way she once had. When Jack left, things had changed between them. They were still friends, but it was awkward and they both seemed to be waiting for Jack to come home and put things back the way they used to be.

"You didn't see anything unusual this morning?" Detective Madsen asked, interrupting Sadie's thoughts. She looked at him again and went back to putting the jars into the canner.

"Other than the two police cars in two minutes, no," she said with a shake of her head. "Detective Cunningham, would you mind lowering this rack of bottles into the canner?"

Detective Cunningham nodded, wiping his hands on his apron as she moved out of his way. He held the rack nice and level as he slowly lowered it into the pan.

Sadie smiled at his precision. "You're welcome in my kitchen anytime," she complimented him when he finished and put the lid on the huge pan.

He chuckled silently and she hoped she wasn't giving him the wrong idea—she was dating Ron after all—but neither did she want to appear ungracious about his help.

"You didn't see anything else out of place?" Madsen asked again.

Sadie set the digital timer stuck to the fridge and pushed the start button. "Jack and Carrie's tree blocks my view, so all I get to look at are the empty lots across the circle from me and nothing happens over there." She attempted a smile at her joke but it went unnoticed by both men.

Detective Cunningham finished filling his last jar, and she wiped the rims and put on the lids and rings. He didn't sit down, but simply moved aside and leaned against the counter.

"And you were here, inside, at the window all morning?" Detective Madsen pressed.

"Yes," Sadie said, her annoyance rising. "All morning."

"Making applesauce?" the disbelief in his voice was obvious and she couldn't understand why it was so hard for him to believe her. The evidence was right in front of him.

Sadie opened her mouth to tell him so, but Detective Cunningham didn't give her a chance, reentering the game after his self-imposed time-out.

"And there is no other access to the cul-de-sac?" Detective Cunningham asked. It may have been Sadie's imagination but she felt sure his tone was softened on purpose in order to make Detective Madsen's seem even harder. He still had on the apron, and his crossed arms covered everything but "give her chocolate!"

"Our little cul-de-sac was considered the outskirts of town when it was built more than twenty-five years ago, and despite recent developments, we're still surrounded by fields. It's certainly not convenient to get in from that direction, but there is an old farm road that provides access to the barbed wire fence that runs a few yards past the property line behind Anne's house and Mr. Henry's. The neighbor kids ride their bikes and build forts in the trees on the south side." Her own kids had loved playing in the field when they were young. Then she remembered that Anne had died there. She swallowed. She'd never feel the same about that field.

Detective Madsen spoke again. "And did you have reason to go to Ms. Lemmon's home this morning?"

"No," Sadie said. She finished preparing the remaining jars and set them aside so they could wait their turn for the water bath. She took off her apron and indicated for Detective Cunningham to do the same. Laying both aprons over a kitchen chair, she invited the two men back into the living room. They all took their original places as Sadie continued.

"Anne usually stays up late—sometimes until two or three in the morning. And then she sleeps in. I've told her that she's going to have to get a better schedule for Trevor. He'll go to school in a few years and she'll regret not . . ." She stopped and swallowed. Anne would never regret anything again. Sadie looked at the floor and took a deep breath, trying to hold back another round of tears.

"So maybe you went over there," Detective Madsen began. She lifted her head and looked at him—he couldn't mean . . .

"You said yourself that everyone else in the circle had gone for the day and based on the timer on Ms. Lemmon's oven that left just you and—"

"Well, Mrs. Hoffmiller, you've been very helpful," Detective Cunningham cut in. "We may need to ask you a few more questions later. Will that be okay?"

"Sure," she said, stunned by the accusation Detective Madsen had thrown at her but still wanting to be helpful. She looked at Detective Cunningham. "Thank you for your help with the applesauce. You saved me a lot of time."

"You're welcome," he said. As soon as he shut his mouth Detective Madsen was talking again.

"You'll be staying in town?"

Her heart sank again. That's what the TV cops said to people who were considered "people of interest" in a case. Was she a person of interest? Could she really be a suspect?

"My friend's daughter is getting married in Colorado Springs next weekend—I can still go to that, can't I?"

"Hopefully we'll have this all wrapped up by then," Detective Cunningham said.

Detective Madsen stared at his partner before adding, "But you will need to check with us first." He seemed to be trying to make Detective Cunningham understand it as much as Sadie.

"I didn't kill Anne," Sadie said, her voice shaking. How could they think such a thing?

"No one said you did," Detective Madsen said, turning to face her, his expression blank. Detective Cunningham's jaw flexed and he shook his head slightly while Detective Madsen continued. "Why are you jumping to that assumption on our part?"

Sadie looked at the floor and tried to think of an explanation that wouldn't make her seem even more guilty. She was about to speak when the front door flew open. Both men were on their feet in mere moments.

CHAPTER 4

Sadie was hardly rattled—apparently her nerves were sufficiently numbed from the day's events.

"Ron," she said with a sigh, getting up from the chair and walking to him. He pulled her into a tight hug. It had never felt so good to be held. She hoped he'd never let go and everything would just disappear in his embrace. She was surprised, however, to feel how tense he was.

"I just heard," Ron said into her hair. "Do you know what happened?"

"I thought you weren't married," Detective Madsen said, interrupting the moment.

Sadie pulled out of the embrace, but Ron kept a protective arm around her shoulders that, for some reason, made her feel uncomfortable, as if his reasons were not solely to comfort her. "Ron Bradley, this is Detective Madsen and Detective Cunningham. Ron and I have been dating for about a year and a half."

"We're engaged," Ron said, pulling her a little closer.

Sadie's cheeks reddened, embarrassed that she hadn't said it first and yet not liking the way it made her sound like some silly girl. "Well, yes, we're engaged." She caught Detective Madsen's eyes as they darted to her ring-free left hand and she felt the need to explain. "We haven't gotten around to rings yet."

"She's not answering any more questions without a lawyer," Ron announced bluntly.

Sadie snapped her head to look at him. "What?" she asked.

"Is that the case?" Detective Cunningham asked in his smooth voice. "Are you requesting legal representation?"

"No," Sadie said, shaking her head. She didn't want to give them any reason to feel suspicious of her; she had nothing to hide. What was Ron doing?

"Yes," Ron said almost as quickly. "You can leave now."

Sadie's mouth hung open as she looked between Detective Madsen and Detective Cunningham not knowing what to say. Detective Madsen opened his notebook and wrote something down. When he looked up at her, his face was hard—more than it had been. Detective Cunningham didn't write anything down, he simply looked at her, then at Ron and back to her again. She felt he held her eyes a little too long and it made her feel small somehow. Then the detectives nodded in tandem and headed toward the door.

"We'll let ourselves out," Detective Cunningham said, his voice tight and yet perfectly professional, contrasting the help he'd been with the applesauce. He reached in his jacket pocket and pulled out a card. "Please have your attorney contact us.

I'm sure we'll have a lot more questions for you." As Detective Cunningham spoke, Detective Madsen fumbled in his pocket and quickly found a card of his own, shoving it into Sadie's hands.

Sadie was in shock. Earlier, the detectives said they *might* have a *few* more questions for her, now they were *sure* they would have *a lot?*

She waited for the door to shut before she pulled away from Ron.

"What are you doing?" she asked, her voice shrill. "Now they suspect me more than ever!"

"What did you tell them?" Ron replied, panic in his eyes. "What did you see?"

Sadie paused, confused. "What?" she asked slowly, trying to absorb what was happening.

Ron took a step toward her and grabbed her arms. His fingers pressed into her skin and she felt a whole new emotion—fear. Ron was taller than six feet, and she was forced to look up into his face as he seemed to glare down at her. "Tell me everything you told them. Everything."

She swallowed, wishing she dared scream for help. How did he even know about Anne's murder in the first place? He was supposed to be in Denver. His grip tightened and she hurried to get the words out. "I told them when Anne moved here, what I knew of her past, what I saw from the window."

"What did you see?"

"I . . . I saw what I always see. Mr. Henry went to work, the Baileys went to school and work, and Carrie headed to the gym. Then I saw two police cars go by." His hands on her arms relaxed and his face softened. His relief scared her more than his anxiety had. She pulled her arms out of his grip and stepped back, putting distance between them and watching him with trepidation. "Why are you asking me this?"

Ron took a deep breath and rubbed his left hand over his thinning hair, cut close to the scalp. He turned away from her and looked out the front window, staring at nothing. Ron was five years younger than Sadie, something that bothered her at first but she'd grown accustomed to. He had soft features, a stocky build, and a rounded middle, but they suited him just fine, as did the neatly trimmed beard and mustache he'd worn for as long as she'd known him. She wasn't sure when the initial feelings of friendship had transitioned into their recent discussions about weddings and merging households. She wasn't ready to set a date—she wanted to get used to the idea before they began making plans—but she'd looked forward to the prospect of sharing her life with him.

When Ron spoke again she could barely hear him. "She was alive when I left last night, I swear she was."

CHAPTER 5

Sadie's blood ran cold and she stared at this man, the only man she had really cared about since Neil's death. He'd been at Anne's house last night? Why?

Part of her wanted to run out of the room and never find out.

She took an instinctive step backward, and the movement caught Ron's attention. He turned from the window to look at her, his eyes pleading. "I swear I didn't hurt her, Sadie," he said, his tone begging. "You know I couldn't do anything like that."

"Why would you even be there?" she asked, forcing herself to remain calm.

"I went because . . . someone asked me to. I needed to settle something for him."

"Who? Settle what?" she asked. This made no sense. It was as if she'd woken up to a whole different world this morning. She wanted her old, boring, rather predictable life back. She wanted to look forward to her kids coming home one weekend every month, pull some weeds, and make more applesauce—

with ginger this time. She had a hair appointment on Friday and was planning on getting blonde highlights. She wanted to think about those things, not this. Not any of this.

Ron groaned out loud. "I can't tell you that, at least not yet. I need to find out what happened after I left." He shook his head. "She was so mad."

"Mad about what?" Sadie said, her voice rising.

"I can't tell you yet."

Sadie blinked and felt anger raise her defenses. "You just told the police I wanted a lawyer, now you're telling me you were with Anne last night and you won't explain it to me? Do you really expect me to shrug this off?"

"I wasn't *with* Anne," he said as if just now realizing the obvious implication. "I was just talking to her, for a friend. I didn't do anything inappropriate."

"Are you kidding me?" she said, taking another step backward, wanting—needing—distance from him right now. "She's dead—you went to see her at night without telling me, you won't even tell me your reasons now, and . . ." She paused, her mind clearing and allowing more thoughts inside. "You're supposed to be in Denver." Did she even know this man at all? Looking at him now, at the emotions playing across his face, was almost like looking at a stranger. She'd read things like this in books before, but she'd never lived it. She worried she was being overdramatic while at the same time wondering how else she could regard him after hearing what he'd said during the last few minutes.

Ron hurried toward her and though she tried to get out of his way, she was walking backward and wasn't fast enough. He grabbed her arms again but surprised her by pulling her into another embrace, as if that would somehow change the way she was feeling.

She stood stiff and unmoving, her arms at her side as she stared at the window behind him. The warmth she usually felt when he held her had disappeared. Everything was different.

After a few seconds, he pulled back and looked at her with such sorrow and regret that she felt tears overflowing in her eyes as tears formed in his. "Give me an hour to get some answers," he said in a quiet voice, his tone begging for her to understand. "Then I'll come back and tell you everything I know."

Sadie blinked at him. *Was he serious?* "You think you can come in here, drop these kinds of bombs on me, and expect me to do nothing about them? A woman is dead, Ron, a person, a mother—my friend. The police are considering me a suspect—me! You obviously know something. Do you really expect me to do nothing about that?"

"No," he said sadly, shaking his head as if accepting a reality he'd hoped to avoid. "I don't expect you to do nothing. I only ask that you wait an hour, so I can give you answers."

"Give them to me now," she demanded, wiping her eyes and wishing she could stop the tears completely.

"I don't have them, or at least, not enough." He looked at her a long time, and she held his gaze. She thought she loved this man and yet right now she was afraid of him and wondering how she could have misjudged him so badly. What friend would need Ron to act as some kind of go-between for Anne? Anne didn't even know Ron's friends—except Jack. Ron and Jack worked together, but if Jack needed to talk to Anne, he'd do it himself. And what would Jack need to talk to Anne for anyway? He'd moved out just weeks after Anne had moved in. To Sadie's knowledge, they had never met other than the brief introduction she had given them one evening. There were so many missing pieces of this puzzle that Sadie didn't even know where to start.

"Please give me an hour," Ron asked again. "Please."

Sadie just shook her head, as much to say no to his request as to communicate how unbelievable this all was.

"Can't you trust me?" he asked. "Just a little."

"Trust you?" Sadie repeated.

"I know it sounds crazy, but please. I love you, Sadie. I would never do anything to hurt you. I promise to tell you everything I know—just let me get a few answers first. Please." He paused, looking at her, and she could feel her resolve crumbling. They had shared so much, been so important to each other. Didn't that earn him an hour?

She nodded before realizing she'd made the decision. He pulled her into another embrace, and this time she found herself clinging tightly to him, pushing away the defenses that had risen a few minutes ago, and choosing to believe he meant what he said—that he wasn't responsible for Anne's death and that through him, she'd get some answers. He pulled back and she let him kiss her, but it was flat.

"I'll be back in an hour," he said as he hurried for the door.

The timer for the applesauce started beeping. She ignored it, shutting the door behind him and resting her back against the door. She looked at the clock—10:48. For little more than an hour she'd known that Anne was dead and Trevor was missing. She felt as if her entire world had been turned upside down.

CHAPTER 6

After removing the hot jars from the canner, Sadie put another batch of jars into the boiling water, wishing she'd been able to add ginger. Carrie's car drove back out of the cul-de-sac ten minutes after Ron had left—reminding Sadie that she hadn't talked to her sister-in-law yet. A year ago Carrie would have been one of the first people Sadie sought out. Jack's leaving had changed everything. When he'd been here, they'd all felt like one big family—at least to Sadie.

After Neil died, having Jack close had been such a blessing. Neil had lost his own father when he was young, so he'd made sure that his family would be cared for, should something happen to him. Jack had not only helped manage and invest Neil's insurance policy to ensure Sadie would have financial security for the rest of her life, but he'd also been a shoulder for her to cry on and strong arms to lift her children when she couldn't do it herself. Though ten years younger than Sadie, Jack had come to her rescue better than any big brother ever could.

The ringing phone brought to mind how silent the house was. The caller ID read Garrison Hospital. She picked up the phone and said a breathless "Hello?"

"Sadie? It's Mindy."

Her neighbor, Mindy Bailey, worked part-time at a dermatologist's office located in the medical complex connected to the hospital; Sadie would have assumed the doctor's name would have come up on the caller ID, not the hospital.

"Mindy," Sadie said, "how are you?"

"I'm just fine except for what I heard about Anne—is it true?" Mindy was one of those hyperactive women who talked and moved faster than everyone else around her. The fact that she had a horrible Dr. Pepper addiction didn't help. In a word, the woman was exhausting. Before Sadie could answer the question, Mindy continued.

"I just got off the phone with Steve who said he heard about Anne on the police scanner they always have on in the back office. Can you believe it? Do you know what happened? Steve just left to go talk to the police, and I'm just sick about the news—and that poor boy! I sure hope the police find out who did it—that's why I'm calling you. I told Dr. Paxton and he said he could call his wife to cover for me so that I could go home but I don't want to go home with a psycho on the loose and his wife always makes such a mess of my files and then I remembered that the kids will be coming home from school and I don't get off until five so I asked if I could leave at three and Dr. Paxton said I could. So I'm leaving at three and he won't have to call his wife in—his nurse can cover for me, thank goodness—but I have a fifteen-minute drive and the kids will beat me home and so I wondered if I could call their schools and tell them to go to your house and then pick them up when I get off work so that they aren't home alone. Would that be okay?"

Sadie couldn't process what was being said as fast as Mindy could say it. It was one reason why she and Mindy weren't particularly close—and why Sadie assumed Steve Bailey liked to work overtime. *What did she ask me?* Sadie repeated in her mind as she tried to pluck out the question from all the other stuff. Kids—my house—after school.

"Sure the kids can come over, I'll be here. They get home about a quarter to three, right?"

She heard Mindy take a breath—ammunition for the next round. "Yes, the bus drops them off at 2:47. They're the first drop—well, Caleb and Gina that is. Brandon, Sheri, and Chris are on the elementary bus and they don't get home until 3:04. Oh, thank you, I can't tell you what a relief it is to know you're there. I hope they don't hear about Anne at school. I know it will be so disturbing and it makes me wonder if Carrie doesn't have the right idea—I heard she was going on vacation, you know. I wish Steve could get time off and we could all disappear for awhile until things get worked out. So do you know what happened? I mean, it's just incredible that something like this could happen in Garrison, let alone in our neighborhood, ya know? Do the police know who might have done it? Have they come and talked to you? I wonder if Carrie saw anything."

Sadie had opened her mouth to answer Mindy's questions a few different times, but finally just closed it and waited for her to finish. As soon as Mindy paused for air, Sadie broke in, talking as fast as Mindy had to ensure she got all the words out. "They're still investigating; I'm not sure what direction they're going." She kept her own suspect status to herself. "I'll look for the kids after school."

"Thanks, that would be wonderful. Tell them I'll be right there—but if they don't know about Anne, don't tell them, okay? I don't want them to be scared or anything not having me there. Hopefully they haven't heard already—would they tell the school? I don't think so, since Anne didn't have any kids there. Oh, I'm just sick about this. Maybe I should come home? But I'd hate to be alone too—I guess I could come to your place but—"

"No," Sadie quickly interjected. She couldn't imagine having Mindy at her ear all day. Things were bad enough already. "At a time like this it's better to have something to keep you busy. I'll watch for the kids."

"Oh, thank you, Sadie. I knew I could count on you. I'll call the schools and tell them to tell the kids to—"

"Okay," Sadie broke in again, "that sounds great. I've got to go, Mindy."

"All right, thanks again. I just don't know what I'd have—"

Sadie hung up the phone. It was out of character for her to be so impatient, but she didn't have the energy to keep up with Mindy today.

Sadie went back to her applesauce, arranging the cooling jars on the dish towel. Trevor's painting kept catching her eye over and over, causing a pang in her gut each time she saw it. She walked to the fridge and turned it over, but after another minute, she flipped it back, the bright blues and reds crisscrossing the paper. Tears filled her eyes once again before she hurried to get out the vacuum. She had to stay busy! She thought of calling her kids, but they had class and work. Not to mention she didn't know what to say or how much to tell them. She'd wait just a little while—until she had more answers.

When the floors were vacuumed, the counters scrubbed, and the second batch of applesauce finished, Sadie took a deep breath and looked at the clock—something she'd determined not to do once Ron had shut the door behind him.

It was 11:53. Ron's hour was up.

"What do I do now?" she said out loud. Then she took a deep breath to get extra oxygen to her brain. She needed to think—something she'd been trying to avoid. In order to better facilitate her concentration, she went into the living room and sat in her favorite chair—an armchair she'd given to Neil on their last Father's Day. Three months later, when she'd come back from the hospital alone, she'd curled up in that chair and just smelled him. Later that night, after getting the kids to sleep, she'd gone back to the chair, crying, sobbing, letting her heart break into a million pieces. Sometimes she felt like her heart was still in this chair, still connected to Neil in some weird, metaphysical way. But whatever her romantic notions, the chair was the furniture version of comfort food.

She needed anything she could get, so she curled into the soft, brown suede-type material—rubbed smooth on the seat and the arms—closed her eyes and just thought.

Ron and Anne—what possible reason would he have to go see her? Sadie knew the obvious suspicion but the thought made her sick. Anne was young and beautiful. Ron wasn't either one, but he had a certain appeal; Sadie had certainly fallen for him. She shook her head. Surely there were perfectly reasonable explanations for Ron to be at Anne's house . . . late at night . . . without Sadie's knowledge.

She'd introduced Anne and Ron a couple weeks after Anne had moved in, and they'd run into each other at Sadie's house often enough to be considered acquaintances. She'd never noticed anything between them. Had she been so lovesick over Ron that she'd missed something? She shook her head again. It wasn't possible. She'd have known. She might be a romantic, but she wasn't an idiot.

Wouldn't she have known?

Growling out loud, she lost patience with her pondering, got up and went to the phone, dialing Ron's cell-phone number by memory. She'd given him his hour and now she needed answers before she made herself crazy. The phone rang four times before his chipper voice asked her to leave a message. She slammed down the phone and stared out the front window. It would be foolish to withhold information from the police—that would only put her at risk of further suspicion. And yet as she grabbed her jacket from the back of the couch, the heaviness in her heart slowed her hands. Tears came to her eyes and she took a deep breath, willing herself to do what she knew had to be done.

"You're stronger than this, Sadie Hoffmiller," she said to herself, the whisper sounding loud in the silent house. "And you know what the right thing to do is."

With that, she put on her jacket, said a little prayer, and headed out the front door.

CHAPTER 7

When Sadie and Neil bought their corner lot, Old Man Tilly owned all the land. He'd lived there for years and grown alfalfa until he reached his seventies, at which time subdivisions made more money than hay. Spurred by one of his sons, he'd developed the cul-de-sac, putting his house on a paved road for the very first time. The land around the cul-de-sac was divided into eight lots and the remaining acreage was left for future development that never happened. Tilly lost interest in developing a subdivision once he had sold the second lot to Jack and Carrie, leaving two empty lots to the west of them, and three empty lots east of his house as well.

The lots remained vacant as incentive for his children to move closer to him. The incentive became an inheritance once Forrest Tilly died eleven years ago. Now and then, one of the lots would go up for sale—which is how Mr. Henry and the Baileys had come to join the neighborhood—but the Tilly kids wanted a premium for the land and there were cheaper, more modern subdivisions on the other side of town that were more attractive to potential buyers. No one had knocked on Sadie's door to ask about the remaining empty lots directly across from her for more than a year. That suited Sadie just fine; she loved the neighborhood just the way it was and although everyone in the circle had their eccentricities, they all got along well enough.

From the sidewalk, once she'd cleared the tree, Sadie looked toward Anne's house. There were a few vehicles in front of the house and she wondered if the detectives had discovered anything new. The low hum of an approaching car caught her attention and she looked left, hoping it was Ron. It wasn't. It was just Carrie coming home again.

Some of the people huddled in front of Anne's house looked up when Carrie pulled into her driveway, including Detective Madsen, who immediately headed toward her.

Sadie stood where she was, not knowing what to do. She'd been planning to talk to Detective Cunningham and explain what Ron had told her, but now faced with that decision, she couldn't make herself do it.

Then she remembered the tart.

Her eyebrows came together as the inconsistencies seemed to jump out at her. Ron had said he'd been at Anne's last night. But the tart had been put in at . . . 9:00 this morning if the timer had been set for forty minutes. So, if Anne was baking, then she had to have been alive after Ron left, just like he said.

Sadie felt her heart lifting like a balloon at the discovery. But then it sunk again. There was still the issue of Ron being there at all. Sadie hadn't gone to bed until after eleven—there had been a *Grey's Anatomy* marathon on TLC—she'd have seen Ron in the circle if he'd come while she was still up. Her TV was situated so that she could see it and the window at the same time. Anne would have been up earlier than usual, which seemed strange after a late night, not to mention that she seemed to have put the tart in at *exactly* 9:00. Not 9:07 or 9:13. That was odd.

"Mrs. Hoffmiller?"

She jumped, her frazzled nerves too much on edge to show any restraint. Detective Cunningham blinked at her and she wrapped her arms around herself as if she were cold. However, it was nearly noon and the morning had warmed considerably, the air scented with burning corn stalks and the last of the summer weeds. She usually loved the smell of smoke in the air, the reminder that the stride of life was moving forward in the most basic of ways, but today it seemed suffocating.

"Detective," she said evenly as she felt her cheeks color. He must think she was some kind of nut job to be standing on her front walk in her sticky flip-flops doing nothing. And she'd forgotten to check her hair on her way out the door—how embarrassing. She glanced toward Carrie and watched her take a few bags of groceries out of her car. It seemed like a betrayal to Anne's memory that Carrie would do something so mundane as grocery shopping on a day like this. And yet, hadn't Sadie made applesauce? She felt so guilty all of a sudden.

Detective Madsen stood at Carrie's elbow and the two women shared a brief look before Carrie said something to Detective Madsen and then headed inside, alone. Detective

Madsen finished scribbling some notes, looked over at Sadie and Detective Cunningham, and then walked back to Anne's house. She wasn't sure, but Sadie thought she'd caught a scowl in their direction before he turned.

Detective Cunningham cleared his throat. "I'd like to confirm whether or not you have requested legal representation or if I can still talk with you?"

Sadie shook her head, embarrassed at the man's formality and wanting to return to the casual exchanges they had shared that morning over applesauce. "Ron said that, not me," she said sadly, hating to relive those moments again.

"So you are comfortable with continued questions?"

Sadie just shrugged and looked at a crack in the sidewalk at her feet.

"Is that a yes?" Detective Cunningham asked. "It would be very helpful if you would continue answering questions for us. You knew Ms. Lemmon and so far you're the only person with any intimate knowledge of her life. We would appreciate your assistance."

Sadie had always been a sucker for people needing her help—it's why she served on half a dozen volunteer committees and was the first person everyone called when someone was in need of a casserole. She just had a genetic disposition to help, and people knew it.

"Any word on Trevor?" she asked.

Detective Cunningham shook his head. "We've issued an Amber Alert and there is a separate team working on his disappearance. What we need from you is help figuring out who Anne Lemmon is and who could have done this."

Sadie nodded. "I'll do anything I can to help."

"Did Anne have a phone? We haven't found one in the house."

"Yes," Sadie said. "But only a cell phone. I told her she should get a landline, but she didn't seem to understand how important it is to be listed in the phone book and she didn't want to pay two phone bills." She shrugged. "Her cell was small and silver. She took it everywhere with her. Why?"

"We'd like to check it for personal numbers and things," Detective Cunningham said.

"Oh," Sadie said. That made sense.

He looked back at his notebook, then met her eyes again. He had hazel eyes with dark lashes—the kind of lashes women would kill for. "Do you know where Anne kept her personal papers, bills, documents?" he asked. "We're still waiting for the crime scene unit to arrive but upon our initial inspection we've found almost nothing of that sort in the house."

"Well, she kept almost everything in the filing cabinet next to her bed. I've been there when she's opened her mail and she puts it all right into the appropriate files. She mentioned that she used to work as a receptionist and she liked organizing things like the office—everything in its place."

"By the bed," he muttered, writing it down.

"I was wondering," Sadie said. Cunningham looked up from his notes. "About the purse in the field. Trevor's shoes were in the house, and Anne was in quite a state of . . . disarray, and yet it looks as if she'd taken her purse outside with her."

"And this strikes you as odd?"

Sadie nodded. "Yes, it does. I wonder if perhaps someone took Trevor and she was going after them. It's the only scenario I can think of that would excuse her forgetting his shoes."

"It is something to consider," Cunningham said. "But that would mean someone attacked her after she left the house and then killed her in the field."

"Well, of course," Sadie said, nodding, but her thoughts were still spinning. "But that would be rather risky, wouldn't it? Killing her outside when she has neighbors."

Cunningham nodded, still watching her carefully.

"You think someone moved the body?" Sadie asked, her heart racing again. For some reason the possibility made it all the more sinister. "And then . . . the purse would be there as a decoy." The thought gave her chills. "So calculated," she said under her breath.

He held her eyes for another moment and then wrote some more before closing his notebook. "It's not typical for us to bring people into a crime scene, but if you don't mind, I'd like you to come inside and verify some things I believe have been altered inside Ms. Lemmon's house."

Sadie hesitated. She didn't want to appear too eager, but she wanted to help in any way she could and *she* knew she had nothing to hide. The trick was to convince the detective of that. Helping him would not only make her feel better, but it would also show him she was not an enemy. She wished he wouldn't talk so cryptically though.

After a few moments, Sadie nodded, hoping the hesitation would keep her from looking too anxious. All through school she'd been accused of being a teacher's pet, a people pleaser who was always trying to get into her superiors' good graces. She hadn't done that at all; she just liked to do well at things and if it made people happy in the process, well, that wasn't such a bad thing.

Detective Cunningham smiled and it made her feel better.

"Aren't there supposed to be a lot more people here?" she asked as they approached the house. On TV there were always all kinds of cars, bystanders, people running around, women crying.

"We're not a large jurisdiction," Detective Cunningham said as he nodded at the two officers by the front steps. Sadie was half a step behind him. "We have a couple crime scene officers on their way and the coroner has been called, but they're all coming from Fort Collins so it will be a while. When we enter the house, please clasp your hands behind your back and don't touch anything."

Sadie nodded and did as she was told, holding her hands tightly together and hoping she didn't touch anything on accident. Entering the house, she thought it looked the same as it had this morning. Sadie took a deep breath; she could still smell the lemon tart.

"I'd like to start downstairs," he said without looking at her.

She followed Detective Cunningham to the top of the stairs just off the kitchen that led to the basement. Sadie's skin bristled as she thought of Anne being killed in this house, and then someone moving her dead body outside. Sadie blinked back more tears and tried to keep her emotions in check.

When they reached the basement, Detective Cunningham motioned for Sadie to stand next to him in the doorway of the family room. She stepped closer to him, their shoulders nearly touching. The room was long and narrow, with a TV and a couch at one end, and a washer and dryer at the other. The area around the washer and dryer had been tiled, whereas the rest of the room was carpeted. On the wall across from the doorway where they stood was a large window, allowing the room to be fairly light, despite it being a basement.

"The curtains aren't right," Sadie said immediately, scanning the panels of fabric while searching her mind for what was wrong. When she realized what it was, she felt a rush of excitement. "She always tied the curtain panels to one side, making a big swag." But now, instead of the swag, the panels were separated and pulled to their respective sides. It looked perfectly ordinary, but it wasn't the way Anne had kept them. Sadie wondered what the implications of such a detail might mean.

"When was the last time you saw the curtains tied that way?"

Sadie searched her memory. "About two weeks ago," she said, her eyes scanning the room and resting on a framed print above the TV. Her hands slipped apart and she quickly clasped them behind her back again, fearful she would mess something up. "I gave Anne that print." She nodded toward it, afraid to point. "I found it at a discount store and thought the colors would be good for this room. I helped her hang it up."

"Would she have changed it between then and now—the curtains I mean?"

"Possibly. I always made certain she didn't feel some obligation to do things my way, but she had seemed to like the curtains with the one swag. I even sewed the tieback for her because she couldn't find one in the stores that matched." She couldn't believe that just hours after Anne had turned up dead, she was discussing curtain arrangements with a detective.

"Describe the tieback," he said, pulling out his notebook.

"Well, it was about three feet long, made out of a floral-patterned, cotton-poly blend. It was just a long rectangle—like the belt of a bathrobe—with buttonholes on either end. The pattern was big flowers, peony types, mostly pink, but with smaller purple flowers—like hyacinths or something small but puffy like that. And there was also some yellow and—"

"How was the tieback secured to the wall?" Detective Cunningham asked, interrupting a description Sadie thought could be very important. But he was the detective. He walked into the room, leaving her in the doorway. With a pen, he pulled back the left curtain pane. The gold hook that she had helped Anne install was no longer there. Instead two nail holes stared back at them like eyes.

"A small gold hook," Sadie said softly, staring at the holes. "Do you know . . . how Anne died?" she asked, not wanting to jump to conclusions.

Detective Cunningham looked at her for a moment before he answered. "That's not available to the public and needs to be confirmed by the coroner."

Sadie nodded her understanding, but couldn't help picturing Anne being strangled with the tieback. She forced the image out of her mind before she lost control of her emotions.

"Is there anything else that doesn't look right?" Detective Cunningham asked.

Sadie looked around the floor, wondering if the hook had rolled under the couch but the room looked in order—perfect order in fact. Sadie's eyes narrowed and she took a longer scan of the room.

"What?" Detective Cunningham asked, and she looked up at him, not realizing he was watching her.

"It's just that everything is so clean."

"How do you mean?"

"Well, Anne's a working single mother—that means certain tasks are prioritized. Anne worked hard to keep the upstairs tidy, but when she came down here, it was to do laundry. She'd turn on the TV and let Trevor play while she worked, then she went back upstairs. This room is usually covered with toys. You know, out of sight, out of mind." As she spoke, her eyes scanned the clean floors, not a toy in sight, and the laundry basket in the corner that served as Trevor's toy box was near overflowing. There was a basket of clothes on top of the washer, and some miscellaneous bundles of fabric on the dryer. Other than that, the room was pristine.

"Huh," Detective Cunningham grunted. He looked past her shoulder and Sadie turned, surprised to see Officer Malloy behind her. She hadn't heard him and he seemed intent on ignoring her completely. "Have the crime scene techs check all the toys in this room for prints," Cunningham said. "Tell them to be very thorough here."

Malloy nodded and headed back upstairs.

"Let's continue the walk-through," Detective Cunningham said. "Tell me if anything else looks out of place."

The downstairs bathroom was a mess—just as it always was. The storage room was only roughly organized. Anne had shown up with nothing and hadn't accrued much in the nine months of living here. Back upstairs everything looked as Sadie would expect, somewhat orderly but not as detailed and clean as the family room downstairs. They reached Anne's bedroom and Detective Cunningham turned to her. "You said she kept a filing cabinet in here?"

Sadie nodded as she stared at the bed pushed against the wall—no filing cabinet in sight.

"It was one of those two-drawer cabinets. It was between the bed and the wall so she could use it like a nightstand. The bed wasn't against the wall like that." She scanned the carpet and could just make out the indentations from the wheels of the bed frame a couple feet closer to them. She released her hands long enough to point to the floor. "That's where the bed used to be."

Detective Cunningham stepped into the room and surveyed the area she'd pointed to. The indentation was faint—it would be hard to see if someone didn't know it was there.

He walked around the bed, looking at the one-inch gap between the bed and the wall. "Malloy," he called out. As if by magic Malloy was suddenly in the doorway. "Is CSU here yet?"

"Not yet," he said. "But I expect them any minute."

Detective Cunningham shook his head. "Will you get working on photos and measurements of the bed until they get here? We need to move the bed out from the wall about three feet—I'm looking for evidence of a filing cabinet being there." Then he turned his attention back to the almost imperceptible mark in the carpet. It would have been made by the lower leg of the bed and Sadie followed his eyes toward where the head of the bed would have been. There was a similar mark about two feet out from the edge of the bed. Malloy left the room.

"Would she have moved the bed?" he asked.

"I suppose," Sadie said. "But where would she have put the filing cabinet? I haven't seen it in any of the other rooms."

"Yeah, me neither," the detective said. "But I would expect a bed to make a deeper impression in the carpet if it had been moved just hours ago."

"Is it wet?" Sadie asked, taking a step closer just as Malloy returned with a measuring tape.

Detective Cunningham looked up at her with a questioning expression. He did have very nice eyebrows. "Wet?"

"This is a thick plush carpet. If you put an ice cube in the indented area and let it melt, it fluffs the carpet back up."

"This well?"

"On a high-quality carpet like this—maybe. With mine I have to use my hand or the vacuum hose to fluff it up when it's mostly dried, but my carpet isn't this nice. This carpet was new when Anne moved in." She stepped back so Malloy could measure the distance of the carpet marks with the wall at the head of the bed.

"How long would it take for the carpet to spring back up?"

"However long it takes to melt an ice cube and have the moisture begin to evaporate, restoring the air into the carpet fibers and therefore expanding its overall shape—I would guess two or three hours."

Detective Cunningham looked at her in surprise. "Really?" he asked. "My daughter would love to know that." Then his expression turned serious. He stepped forward and put his hand on the carpet. Sadie held her breath, thrilled at his positive reaction and hoping she'd been right. He looked up at her. "It's damp," he said, looking pleased. "But just barely."

Sadie tried to contain her excitement about having helped, even in a small way. She wondered if he was no longer regarding her with suspicion. She hoped so.

Just then two men entered the room. They were in street clothes, but each carried a bag and wore latex gloves. The lost CSU people, Sadie suspected. Malloy handed over the measurements he'd already made on a pad of paper and left the room. Detective Cunningham gave them some instructions on what he wanted them to do and then he and Sadie got out of their way. The men immediately went to work.

"Is there anything else different in there?" he asked Sadie once they were in the hallway looking back into the bedroom.

Sadie searched her memory and frowned. "I really don't know. I'm not very familiar with her bedroom. We're usually in the kitchen, or on the back porch." At least, they used to be in those places. Not anymore.

"When did you last see the cabinet?"

"Maybe last month," Sadie said without confidence.

They were silent for a moment, watching the techs. It gave Sadie the creeps—people going through Anne's house trying to figure out how her life ended. As much as she wanted to help, she was feeling the heaviness of the day press upon her. And Trevor was still out there. "Can I go now?" she asked, her voice sounding timid.

He nodded. "I'll show you out."

She backed into the hallway in order for him to pass—her hands still tightly clenched behind her back. They had reached the kitchen when Sadie remembered her earlier ponderings about the lemon tart. She quickly looked around the kitchen, her eyes resting on the stove. It was off and she felt a little thrill of discovery rush through her.

"Detective Cunningham?" Sadie asked quickly. The other heads in the room turned toward her as well and she swallowed, not wanting to make a scene. She had the distinct impression that she was now slowing the detective down.

"I wonder if anyone turned off the oven," she said, shifting her weight uneasily from one foot to another. Every head in the room turned to look at the oven, which showed no lighted display or indication it was still on. Then, as if watching a tennis match in slow motion, they all turned back to look at her.

"Why do you ask?"

She felt as if she were on stage and straightened her spine just a little. Her shoulders were beginning to ache from holding her hands behind her back. "Well, I was thinking about my lemon tart recipe, which was the first thing I ever taught Anne to cook." She looked at the people watching her and smiled. "It was my mother's recipe—and Anne wanted it to become her signature dessert," she explained, not wanting to sound arrogant but feeling it necessary to explain why she believed it was hers. She looked at Detective Cunningham. "Anyway, the timer went off at exactly 9:40, which means Anne must have set it at exactly 9:00. But Anne's rarely awake before ten."

No one said anything, which she took to mean they had no idea where she was going with this. "So I wondered if maybe she had the oven on time cook."

"Time cook?" Cunningham asked.

"Yeah, you put something in a cold oven and then set the oven to turn on at a certain time. I showed Anne how to do it months ago so that she could put a frozen dinner in the oven before she went to work and come home to a hot meal. She was eating a lot of fast food before then."

"Isn't it dangerous to leave the oven on when you're not home?" Malloy broke in. "Suppose she didn't come home on time."

Sadie smiled at him as if he were a student and she was teaching him something of great importance. "Well, see, that's the thing. You can do a stop time as well, so the oven shuts off after a certain period of time. And the food stays warm as the oven cools off. If no one turned off the oven this morning, maybe it was set to start at 9:00 AM with a stop time exactly forty minutes later. Normally you cook the filling for about thirty minutes, but she could have added ten minutes to account for the crust not being hot and to preheat the oven. But anyway, if she got up at her usual time of ten or eleven the tart would be done. Although I'd never do that with a tart." She looked at the detective. "Tarts require more supervision than a frozen lasagna." She paused for a moment. "And I'm not sure why she'd go to the trouble. I mean, what did she need the tart for at ten in the morning?"

The room was silent, seeming to consider the question.

"So time cook sets the timer as well?" Detective Cunningham asked as he stepped over to the oven and looked at the digital display.

The lemon tart was still on the stove top, and Sadie wondered for a moment what would happen to it. It needed to be dusted with powdered sugar soon, and it would be a shame for it to go to waste but it didn't seem appropriate to ask for it. "Mine does—and *someone* set the timer for the tart. It's the fact that it was set at exactly 9:00 that seems odd."

"Hmmm," Detective Cunningham said, then he looked at Malloy. "Find out if anyone turned off the stove." He turned to Sadie again while Malloy went out through the back door, leaving two other officers still in the kitchen. "So she could have put it in the oven at any time?"

"I think there's a limit—mine is ten hours. But the tart has eggs in it so it would be irresponsible for her to leave it sitting in the oven for too long. You know, salmonella and all that." They were all watching her, nonplussed. "Once, at a family reunion, my cousin Pam—she's named after our maternal great-grandmother—she drove all the way from Durango to Boulder with a potato salad and no air conditioning. It was in July, mind you, and every person who ate that salad was throwing up for the next two days. Pam felt horrible about it, of course, but it just goes to show that eggs are to be respected, and since mayonnaise is made from—"

"Cunningham," Detective Madsen suddenly said from the back door, causing all the heads to turn in his direction this time. "What is she doing in here?" he asked, cocking his head to the side and narrowing his gaze.

"Doing a walk-through," Detective Cunningham answered, his voice controlled but laced with irritation now that Madsen had appeared. He turned toward Sadie and opened his mouth to say something, but Detective Madsen didn't let him.

"That's completely against procedure," Detective Madsen said. "If this goes to trial, the defense will have a heyday!"

"Shut up, Madsen," Cunningham said calmly, but his eyes were on fire.

Sadie swallowed and shrunk back a little at the same time Detective Cunningham took what could have been interpreted as a protective step forward, putting Sadie further behind him. She was glad to have someone on her side, but she was in no mood to be in the middle of their tension again. However, she

70

was as curious as the proverbial cat as to why things were the way they were between the two men.

"She's given us some excellent information," Detective Cunningham continued.

"She's a suspect!" Madsen shot back, causing Sadie's heart to jump in her chest. He turned to glare at her. "By her own admission she was the only person in the area when the murder was committed!"

CHAPTER 8

S he's a neighbor!" Detective Cunningham's voice was on
 the verge of yelling and it sounded like thunder in the
house. "And until the official time of death is properly estab-
lished, we don't know *when* it happened." Detective Madsen
was struck by the power of the older man's words and shut his
mouth—but not for long.

"Well, while you've been strolling around and discussing
details of the case, the coroner's been looking for you. He's got
some questions." He glanced briefly at Sadie and scowled at
her, making her shrink back even more until she was officially
in the hallway rather than the kitchen. As Madsen headed
back outside, she heard Detective Cunningham mutter "Imper-
tinent snit" under his breath.

"Excuse me?" Sadie said, wondering if she'd misheard him.
Maybe he meant to say "important bit" or something like that.

"Nothing," he growled and started leading her to the front
door. As she passed the fridge, her shoulder brushed against it,
sending a hamburger-shaped magnet and a piece of paper to

the floor. The sound of the magnet bouncing across the lino-leum sounded as loud as a rocket ship.

Sadie froze, holding her hands so tight she worried that she'd cut off the circulation. "I'm so sorry," she said, not know-ing what to do. She'd been told not to touch anything and so she simply stood there and looked at the paper on the floor. It was nothing more than the Garrison community newsletter that arrived with everyone's water bill.

She blinked and looked back at Detective Cunningham. "I'm so sorry," she said again. "That partner of yours has me a bit frazzled."

"It's okay," he said, but she knew it wasn't. At least Madsen hadn't witnessed it. "We'll take care of it." He turned toward the door again and she glanced back at the paper.

It would be so easy to pick it up and put it back on the fridge. Couldn't it be considered a hazard to have the magnet and paper on the floor like that? Suppose someone slipped. She looked to the space it had left on the fridge and her eyes were drawn to another note held in place by an Oreo magnet: "Library books due FRIDAY the 21st!" It was another reminder of how normal life had been yesterday. Anne had gone to work, come home, taken care of her son—and then everything changed.

Sadie saw the books on the kitchen table and she had an idea. She cleared her throat. "There is a note on the fridge about Anne's library books being due," Sadie said, keeping to herself that they weren't due for another week. "I was planning to head over there later—could I possibly return them for her?"

Josi S. Kilpack

"Absolutely not."

She and Detective Cunningham both turned at the sound of Detective Madsen's voice again. He was back in the kitchen, his hands on his hips and his jaw tight. "It is completely inappropriate for her to be in here and she will not remove any items from the premises."

Detective Cunningham turned on his partner in an instant. "Get out of here, Madsen," he said like a frustrated parent. "I asked Mrs. Hoffmiller to come here and she's been a great deal of help. You, on the other hand, are being a royal pain in the butt. Shut up and let me do my job."

Sadie nodded sharply in agreement. Cunningham didn't notice, but Madsen did. His neck turned red, and he took two huge steps forward, suddenly inches away from Detective Cunningham. The younger man may have been taller, but Detective Cunningham's presence was much more imposing. Sadie took a step away from the confrontation and looked at the front door—should she make a run for it? Would Detective Madsen shoot her if she tried?

"If you'd just do your job, I wouldn't have to babysit you," Detective Madsen said.

Detective Cunningham gave a rueful laugh, but in the next instant his hand shot out, grabbing and twisting Madsen's tie as he pulled him closer. Madsen tried hard to hide his fear, but his Adam's apple bobbed as he swallowed and his tuft of chin hair trembled.

"I've been doing my job since you were in diapers, Madsen. The silver spoon in your mouth might give you the feeling of superiority, but that is nothing compared to instinct and gut reactions. Mrs. Hoffmiller isn't going to return the library books—nothing is being removed from the crime scene. However, I *am* going to escort her home and thank her for the help she's been, and you're going to go outside and work very hard to stay out of my way until you have to leave for that hearing."

He let go of Madsen, who stumbled backward until his back hit the kitchen counter, knocking Sadie's smiley-face key ring from the counter to the floor in the process. It skittered across the linoleum, coming to a stop as everyone in the room went silent again. Sadie stared at the keys—her keys—and nearly leaned down to pick them up while every set of eyes watched Madsen straighten up and try to smooth the wrinkles out of his shirt. Sadie noticed that many of the people in the room seemed to be trying hard to conceal a smile at witnessing Madsen's comeuppance. Clearly, most people felt toward Detective Madsen the same way Detective Cunningham did. She looked back at the keys on the floor.

"I'm calling the captain," Madsen said loudly, turning on his heel and storming toward the back door.

"And your daddy, I suppose," Detective Cunningham said back, his tone lowered to a normal range which made Madsen's echoes seem even louder and more out of place.

Daddy? Sadie wondered. She'd give her entire *Seinfeld* DVD collection to know what *that* meant.

Detective Madsen scowled over his shoulder, and saw the key ring. He bent and picked it up—shoving it deep in his pocket while Detective Cunningham turned to look at Sadie, a polite smile on his face and an odd light in his eyes, as if his moment with Madsen was terribly fulfilling to him. "I'll walk you home," he said, indicating for her to lead the way.

"Uh, could I get my keys back from Detective Madsen first?" she asked, feigning meekness. She was pretty sure they had no grounds to keep her keys and the truth was she wanted to get her own dig in while she had the chance.

"What?" Detective Madsen yelled, turning sharply, his hand on the back door.

"My keys," she said. "The key ring you've got in your pocket belongs to me."

He shook his head as if annoyed and pulled the door open. "It's part of the investigation," he said in his demeaning tone.

"I've been entrusted with the keys to the homes of my neighbors," she said, emboldened by his pompous attitude. She'd have put her hands on her hips if not for the magnet incident. "You can't just take them away from me." She kept her voice calm and looked at Cunningham. "He can't keep the keys to other homes, can he? I mean, what do I tell the neighbors? They'll never trust me again, and the only reason I gave them to the police in the first place was because I was trying to do anything I could to help out." She turned back to glare at Madsen with her best angry-teacher expression. "If I'd have known that—"

"Fine, but we keep the key to this house," Detective Madsen said as he stomped over to her and pulled out the ring, fumbling through the keys as if he knew which was which.

"Of course," Sadie said as if she'd never considered otherwise. "Anne's is the one with the red heart sticker on it," she offered helpfully, even though that particular key fit the lock to Jack and Carrie's house. She refused to analyze herself enough to figure out why she was lying to an officer of the law. But she knew why. Suppose she needed to get in Anne's house, suppose they continued to treat her like a suspect and she had to prove her own innocence. Plus, Detective Madsen hadn't been very nice and tricking him made her feel better. All was not chocolate sprinkles with Sadie Hoffmiller, but they didn't need to know that.

It took several seconds for Detective Madsen to extract the key, which he promptly pocketed before handing Sadie the supposedly Anne-free key ring and storming toward the door again. All of which he did with plenty of dramatic flair, though it fell completely flat.

Sadie nodded at Detective Cunningham, indicating she was ready to leave. He kept his expression blank but his eyes danced. He'd liked her little game with Detective Madsen. They didn't say anything until they reached the sidewalk. Two police cars were parked by the entrance to the cul-de-sac, presumably to monitor the people driving in.

"Can you tell me about your neighbors as we walk?" Detective Cunningham asked. He started walking, and Sadie fell in step next to him. Instead of cutting across the cul-de-sac like she usually did, he seemed intent on taking the sidewalk.

"Sure," Sadie said with a chipper smile. She loved that she could help him, and without a doubt she was the right woman for the job of talking about her neighbors. She indicated Mr. Henry's house as they crossed his driveway. "Mr. Henry is in his early sixties. He's from Canada, with two ex-wives and four children, but I've never met any of them. He's an engineer and works at the GM plant. He works a lot, likes to travel when he can, but keeps to himself." She leaned in to the detective a little bit. "He's got a girlfriend," she whispered. "And he goes to her house every Friday for dinner. A woman in my yoga class lives just down the road from her. She and I both think it would be a good match. He's lonely."

Cunningham smiled, though she couldn't tell if it was polite or sincere, but no matter. She really did hope Mr. Henry married again. It would be wonderful to have another woman in the neighborhood. She paused until they passed Mr. Henry's property and entered the stretch of sidewalk in front of the Baileys' house. "The Baileys have five children ages seven to sixteen. Steve manages a sporting goods store and Mindy's a medical assistant in a dermatologist's office. Steve's from California, but Mindy is from here. They met in college and lived in Sacramento for a few years before she demanded he find a job where she could be closer to her family. The irony is that her parents moved to Scottsdale a few years back." She shrugged. "But they seem happy here anyway. She has three sisters who live within an hour or so."

Detective Cunningham removed his notebook from his back pocket and finally began taking notes. They crossed in front of Jack and Carrie's driveway. "This is Jack and Carrie

Wright's house," she began, hesitant this time. "Jack's my brother."

"He is?" Detective Cunningham asked, looking up. "You didn't mention that before."

"Is it important?"

Cunningham shrugged. "You said before that he left his wife some time ago."

"Yeah," Sadie said sadly. "They'd been married twenty-seven years and he left about eight months ago—in March."

"Why?"

Sadie looked at the house and let out a breath. "I honestly don't know. Jack and I have always been close, but our relationship has changed the last year or so—especially after Dad died last December. When Jack left, he sort of pulled away from everyone. We've talked a few times but I'm afraid we have one of those proverbial elephants in the room whenever we do. He wants to believe it's not any of my business and I want to pretend nothing has changed." She smiled at how silly that sounded and shook her head.

"What would be your guess as to why he left? Surely you have your suspicions."

That she did, and she wrestled with the definition of gossip for a moment. Was it gossip if she told it to a police officer? She decided it wasn't. "Carrie's always taken her mothering very seriously and she had a hard time when her girls started leaving home." It was something Sadie had never understood about her sister-in-law. On the one hand, she and Neil had tried to have children for several years before adopting Breanna and then Shawn—those empty years had been so hard and Sadie had had to fight the temptation to completely lose herself in her children once she had them in her arms. And yet, she and Neil were a team and she'd have given anything to have had Neil by her side to help raise their children. That he'd died when they had only just begun to realize the joy of their family was a horrible twist of fate.

Sadie sighed and looked at the house. "In some ways, Carrie and Jack stopped being a couple the day they became parents. She's a doting, if not overly-protective mother, and her girls have always come first. Their youngest, Trina, graduated from high school the same year as my son Shawn. Jack wanted her to go to college, like their other girls had, but Carrie and Trina were best friends—they did everything together and Trina wouldn't leave. Jack put up with it for two years, and then one day he kinda snapped. Last winter, he enrolled Trina at Colorado State, got her an apartment in Fort Collins, drove her there one day, dropped her off, and came home—didn't even let her take her car for fear she'd just drive back. Carrie nearly lost her mind." Sadie paused and pushed her hands into her pockets. "Jack told Carrie if she went and got her, he'd leave. Apparently the fear of truly being on her own was greater than her fear of losing her last hold on motherhood. But she was so mad. Then Dad died. I think once Jack knew he wouldn't disappoint Dad, he tried for a few more months and then left anyway, even though Trina was doing pretty well at college, thanks to his insistence. It's been really hard."

They stopped walking when they reached the black walnut tree. Sadie scanned Jack and Carrie's yard, noticing that none of the perennials had been cut back and the roses needed pruning. She shook her head. Jack had always taken such pride in their yard. Its lack of care seemed a kind of mourning for his absence.

"It seems odd he never gave any reason," Detective Cunningham said, looking over the yard as well.

"I'm a widow, Detective," Sadie said, an air of authority in her voice this time. "I've mourned Neil for twenty years. I think Jack's embarrassed to admit he couldn't make his marriage work—whereas I'd have given anything for the chance to have mine back."

Detective Cunningham said nothing, just nodded his understanding and smiled sympathetically, holding her eyes a long time before looking down at his notebook again.

"You mentioned Carrie does temp work?"

Sadie nodded, and her sympathy for her sister-in-law returned. "I think she's pretty intimidated to be back in the workforce after so many years of being at home. So far it seems to be working out pretty well. I think Jack's still paying all the bills. He's that kind of man."

"And what does Jack do for a living?"

Sadie wondered why he wanted so much information on Jack and Carrie. He hadn't asked this many questions about Mr. Henry or the Baileys, but then she'd offered all these same facts without being prodded. "He's jumped between several careers, but has been an agent for Riggs and Barker for the last nine years—you know the real estate company?" She decided not to tell him that's where Ron worked; she preferred not to say anything about Ron at all, even though that's the reason she'd come outside earlier.

"Were the two of you raised here?" Detective Cunningham asked. Sadie shook her head and shifted her weight from one foot to the other. Having thought of Ron, she felt guilty for not telling the detective that Ron had been at Anne's house. She also wondered if he'd called since she'd been out. She should have brought her cell phone, but then imagined getting a call from him while she was standing with the detective. That would be uncomfortable. She remembered that Cunningham had asked her a question.

"We grew up in Boulder and have one more sister between us—she lives in New Hampshire. Neil and I moved here about twenty-seven years ago—Neil got a vice principal position at the high school—and Jack and Carrie moved out here a few years later because we raved about it so much."

"And what do you do for a living?" Detective Cunningham asked, moving on.

Sadie nodded. "I'm a teacher—well, I was a teacher. I taught for several years before I met Neil, quit when we adopted our children, then went back to work after he died and the kids were in school all day. I took early retirement so I could care for my dad when he got sick. I substitute now; the flexibility is nice and I've always been a homebody at heart."

"You do a lot of volunteer work," he said rather than asked. "I seem to remember your name popping up in the community section a fair amount."

Sadie blushed. "I was thirty-seven years old when my husband died—my kids became my life. I volunteered for anything they were involved in, and things spiraled from there."

"If only everyone was so generous with their time," he said, smiling at her. This time she knew he meant it and his sincerity made her strangely uncomfortable.

Detective Cunningham finished writing and closed his notebook. "I really appreciate all the information you've given me; it's helpful for us to get the background. I might need to talk with you again," he said. "Will that be okay?"

"Sure," she said. She turned and let herself back into her house, disappointed that she hadn't told him about Ron, but unable to find the words. She looked at the clock. It was 12:35. Ron was now an hour late. The empty house made her stir-crazy and she wondered what on earth she was going to do until the Bailey kids got home from school. She needed a few groceries, but the idea of doing something so ordinary on a day like this seemed horribly wrong—not to mention she'd already judged Carrie for doing the same thing. The ringing phone saved her from having to make a decision.

"Sadie?"

"Carrie," Sadie replied, recognizing her sister-in-law's voice. "Are you okay?" Sadie asked. "This is just so awful."

"Yeah, quite the shock to wake up to. I noticed they let you in her house," Carrie continued. "What did they tell you?"

Grateful to have someone to talk to, Sadie told her what they'd found. After a few minutes of Carrie listening, she concluded. "So I think she was strangled, but I don't know for sure and they wouldn't tell me."

"Wow," Carrie said, her voice soft and obviously over-whelmed. "I guess it just goes to show you can't run away from your past."

Sadie thought about that. "We don't know that it was her past," she said. "We don't know anything, really." Except that Anne was dead. The thought caused another pang of regret and Sadie wondered what could have been done differently to prevent this. Could it have been prevented?

"Right," Carrie said. "But she was certainly no shiny penny—no one can run away from their mistakes forever."

"I suppose not," Sadie said, but she didn't like the tone of Carrie's observations—as if Anne somehow deserved what had happened to her. "But you'd hope for a chance at a better life once you changed your choices."

"I guess that depends on how many people get hurt before you change those choices. Or if you really change at all."

Was everyone determined to think the worst of Anne? Even with Ron's shocking admission of being with Anne last night, Sadie felt sorry for the girl. She didn't deserve this, no matter what she might have done.

The doorbell rang and spared Sadie from having to explain her perspective or lecture her sister-in-law on being compas-sionate. "I've got to get the door, Carrie. I'll talk to you later."

A few moments later she opened the door. "Officer Malloy."

He nodded in greeting and stretched out a hand holding all three of the library books she'd seen at Anne's house earlier. Sadie looked at them without making any move to take them from him, forcing Malloy to explain himself. "CSI cleared them and the detective asked me to bring them over and ask if you'd return them."

"Oh," Sadie said in surprise. "Really?" She met his eyes and he shrugged. She pictured Cunningham giving the books to Malloy to give to her. She'd have to make him cookies when all this was over. Was he an oatmeal-raisin or a chocolate-chip man? She took the books from Malloy and smiled. "Tell him thank you."

Malloy nodded again and headed down the steps.

She shut the door and spent five minutes eagerly poring over the books before determining there was nothing of significance in their pages other than a blank Post-it note that seemed to have been used as a bookmark. With a sigh, she stacked them on the table and wondered what she'd thought she would discover. But at least she had something to do.

She changed into her favorite pair of Gap jeans and white Skechers. After considering the sweaters in her closet, she decided to stay in the CSU hoodie. She spent a few minutes on her hair, trying to coax some style out of it without having to do it completely. Then she rubbed some moisturizer over her face and applied her makeup, hoping she wouldn't cry it all off before the end of the day. She hadn't showered and hated the grimy feel of her skin, but she wasn't going to take time to clean up now. Later.

CHAPTER 9

"Yes, hi," Sadie whispered when it was her turn in line to check books in at the library. The young librarian with green-rimmed glasses smiled and took the books. She had only worked at the library for a few months and Sadie didn't know her. "Can you tell me if there are any fines on these books?" Sadie asked, even though she knew they were being returned early. She just wanted . . . something.

"Sure," the woman said, running each bar code under her scanner. Once she'd finished, she looked at the screen and then at Sadie. "No fines—they're all early in fact."

"Any other fees on the account?" Sadie asked, hopeful that perhaps there would be so she could prolong the conversation.

"Nope," the woman said, though her expression seemed to have fallen a little bit. The woman behind Sadie made a grunt and the librarian's eyes looked past Sadie and gave the woman a sympathetic smile.

"Oh," Sadie said, having run out of questions. She stepped out of line and looked around the aisles and aisles of books.

Anne was a faithful library patron, preferring romance novels over anything else, whereas Sadie was a more eclectic reader, enjoying nearly every genre—except horror and Harlequin. But as she looked at the rows of books, Sadie found herself wandering to the racks full of gaudy covers in the romance section. The images of half-naked women and action-figure men draped over one another made her roll her eyes.

She turned a rack, smirking at titles like *Gloria's Awakening* and *The Devil in Blue Dress Boots*. There had been a time in Sadie's life when she'd read these same books, but she liked to think that was before she matured into a real woman. These days she couldn't imagine reading them anywhere but in a closet with a flashlight, just so no one would know. It wasn't that Sadie was a prude, it was just tacky.

Obviously the books didn't embarrass Anne, though. Sadie looked up at the other women in the section and tried to imagine Anne among them. She recognized a woman who worked at the high school and instinctively tried to hide behind one of the racks before realizing that only made her look guilty of something.

"Excuse me."

Sadie jumped, and turned to see a library worker with a cart full of books waiting to move past her.

"So sorry," Sadie stammered, then looked up and recognized the face behind the cart.

"Oh, hi, Sadie," the young woman whispered with a smile.

"How are you, Jean?" Sadie whispered back. Jean's mother was on the Red Cross committee and Sadie always helped with the biannual blood drive at the Presbyterian church on Oak Street.

"I'm good," Jean said with a smile as she slid a paperback into a space on the rack. They chatted for a minute about Jean's mother, and Jean's recent college graduation with her English literature degree. She had a job lined up as an editor for a publishing house in Los Angeles come January, but she was still working at the library until the end of the year. They ran out of small talk about the same time a large woman scowled at them nearby. Sadie hadn't noticed that their voices were louder than they should be.

"Tell your mom hi from me," Sadie whispered as Jean pushed the cart away.

"I will," Jean replied with a smile. Sadie watched her push the cart to the next rack, then she looked at the newly replaced book. It was the title Sadie had just returned—the last romance novel Anne had ever read. Once Jean had moved on, Sadie pulled it out of the rack and looked at it. The cover was like all the others—tawdry and certainly trite. And yet . . . Anne had seen something of merit in it.

Chalking it up to nostalgia she couldn't even begin to understand, Sadie walked up to the check-out counter. The counter was actually a big circle of countertops in the middle of the room with several check-out stations to keep people from having to stand in line. The new library had been built just a few years ago—Sadie had helped with the fund-raising— and it might very well be the most modern building in all of Garrison.

"Didn't you just return this?" the librarian in green-rimmed glasses asked as she took the book. Apparently she wore many hats—checking in and checking out.

"Oh, yes, I did," Sadie said as she handed over her library card. "I was returning it for a friend."

"And now it's your turn," the librarian said with a smile, running the bar code on the book under the scanner. "Next time we can check it in and check it right back out to you if you want."

"Oh, well, I'll keep that in mind," Sadie said with a nod. "My friend died this morning," she heard herself say. Then she looked up and felt her cheeks flush. The librarian froze, her mouth slightly open.

"I—I guess I'm looking for a connection," Sadie added, now anxious to get the book back and run away.

A few moments of silence hung between them while Sadie wiped her eyes and scolded herself. What was she doing?

"I'm so sorry," the librarian said as she tore off a receipt and put it inside the book. Sadie put her library card back in her wallet before taking the book and removing the white slip of paper. It had the title of the book she'd just checked out— *Enrapture at Sea*—and today's date along with the date it was due back. It also had her name, library card number, and a list of the other books she'd checked out last week and hadn't returned yet. She should have brought them with her.

"Is there . . ." She paused, quickly hid the book in her purse, and looked up. She had certainly embarrassed herself well enough already, she may as well finish the job. "Is there any way to get records of what books someone has checked out?" she asked.

"Your record?"

"No," Sadie said, allowing her eyes to fill with tears specifically for manipulation value. "My friend, the one who had checked this book out. I—I might want to read some of the other books she'd liked so much."

Much to Sadie's relief, the woman's face softened. "Sure," she said. "What's her name?"

"Anne Lemmon—with two M's," Sadie said, hoping her voice didn't sound too eager. The librarian's fingers clicked across the keyboard, then paused, and then she hit one final button and the tape began to print . . . and print . . . and print.

"She liked to read," the librarian said, then her own cheeks turned pink and she looked away. Sadie just smiled as if she didn't catch the slip into past tense. The librarian looked back at the tape, now curling around itself. "Anne Lemmon," she said almost under her breath. "Why does that sound so familiar?"

"Well," Sadie said as the tape stopped, "she did like to read and she came in every week for story time with her son." Sadie's stomach clenched like a fist. What was she doing at the library checking out romance novels when Trevor was still out there?

"Yes," the librarian said, distracted, "I remember a Lemmon on the story time list. But there's something else." She turned and scanned the check-out area behind her where two other librarians were busy helping other patrons.

"Jean," the librarian said as the other library worker entered the round counter and walked within whispering range. "Why is the name Anne Lemmon ringing a bell for me?"

"Anne Lemmon?" Jean repeated, smiling at Sadie again, then furrowing her brow in concentration. Sadie held her breath, hoping she would remember. If not, Sadie would wonder all day why Anne's name had held recognition. Jean's face lit up after a few seconds and Sadie could breathe again. "She's that one who always has papers in her books—remember? If I'm not mistaken we forgot to give them back to her last time she was in," she said, moving to the left and pulling open a drawer. "She's the Southie," she added.

"Southie?" Sadie repeated.

Jean nodded but continued fumbling in the drawer. "In my final semester I took a class on North American language. It's fascinating how speech is influenced by different regions and climes of our country."

"And Anne?"

"Was a Southie—from the south side of Boston. She'd tried to refine her speech patterns, which made it even more exciting when I pegged it. She was surprised I'd noticed." Jean looked up and was about to hand over the papers she'd recovered from the drawer when she paused. "Oh, wait, I need to give these to Anne. Sorry, Sadie."

"Anne died this morning," the green-rimmed librarian commented as discreetly as possible. "This woman is her friend; she returned her books for her."

Jean was stunned. "Oh," she said after a few shocked seconds. "I'm so sorry."

"Me too," Sadie said, looking at the counter and thinking fast. She had to get those papers. "I'm trying to get her house ready for family. I could take the papers with me and put them with her other things."

Jean's face softened with sympathy and she didn't hesitate to hand the papers over.

"Thank you so much," Sadie said, looking between both women. "Anne loved coming here. She said she'd never had such great customer service." Both librarians smiled and nodded. Sadie smiled back, put the long printout of Anne's former reading into her purse, and headed toward the front doors. She went through the first set of glass doors and stepped to the side in an alcove before pushing through the exterior doors. She couldn't wait another second to look at the papers Anne had used for bookmarks in her last round of steamy reads. Maybe she'd used a letter from Trevor's father, or a postcard from her parents.

The first paper was a grocery list:

Peanut butter
Vegetable oil
Tampons
Peaches
Pizza

Sadie moved to the second one—a past receipt for books Anne had checked out three weeks ago. The third bookmark slowed her breathing. It was a business card from an attorney here in Garrison. Sadie's heart rate increased and she read the information slowly.

ATTORNEY SUSAN M. GIMES

Specializing in all matters of family law

Sadie flipped it over, not believing her luck when she found a handwritten note on the back:

Wednesday 9:00—bring papers.

"I'll take those, Mrs. Hoffmiller."

Sadie startled and looked up into the eyes of Detective Madsen. She pulled the card to her chest and took a step backward. "What—what are you doing?"

"Conducting a police investigation," he said through tight lips. "Something you just can't seem to stay out of—which only makes it more and more obvious to me that you have far too much unwarranted interest in this case."

CHAPTER 10

Sadie straightened and clenched her jaw. "You followed me?"

"And for good reason," he said. "Now give me the papers."

Sadie hesitated a moment and then held the items in question even closer. "I don't think so," she said, lifting her chin. "They were given to me to put with her other things."

"Her *other things* are all part of a crime scene—those papers are hereby part of the investigation too."

Sadie pursed her lips and said nothing as she tried to figure a way out of this.

"You don't want to push me," Madsen said, leaning so close to her that she could smell the coffee on his breath. Library patrons continued to walk in and out of the building, looking at them. "I've taken as much interference from you as I'm going to."

"And I've helped you out a great deal as well," Sadie fired back—not bothering to whisper at all. An older woman stopped to stare at them openly. Sadie couldn't tell if she was simply watching for entertainment or truly concerned for Sadie's safety. "Yet you continue to suspect me, and now you're even following me after Detective Cunningham told me I could return Anne's books."

"Detective Cunningham?" he asked, raising an eyebrow, a look of amused arrogance on his face.

Sadie reviewed what Officer Malloy had said when he handed over the books. He'd simply said the detective asked him to bring them over. She'd assumed it had been Cunningham. Apparently she'd assumed wrong. "Why go through all the trouble of having me do this?"

"Because I wanted proof that you're a troublemaker, that's why. I'm on my way to a hearing and thought I'd give it a shot. And sure enough, you found something and you want it for yourself."

Sadie rolled her eyes. "You have all the logic of a fourteen-year-old," she said. "I haven't even left the library—I didn't have time to call you."

The old woman was still standing there, glancing between Sadie and the check-out counter as if trying to decide whether or not to call for help. Sadie looked at her imploringly, until another woman several feet ahead of her turned and said, "Julia, are you coming?" The old woman gave Sadie a shrug, as if to say she'd help her if she didn't need to get inside. Sadie was not impressed. Was there no such thing as a good citizen anymore?

"Come with me," Detective Madsen said through clenched teeth. He took her arm, none too gently, and led her out of the building. Sadie tried not to show her own panic, though she realized what she ought to do was scream for help. She stumbled to keep up with him until they reached the same blue sedan she'd seen in front of Anne's house earlier. He opened the back door.

"I'm not getting into that car with—" The next thing she knew she felt his hand on the top of her head and within mere moments she was in the car. How'd he do that? The next second he was in the car too, right beside to her.

"Look," he said in a voice thick with frustration as he slammed the door shut. "I'm trying to solve a murder here."

"That you think I committed."

"You are not helping yourself by being so difficult."

She scooted as far away from him as possible—it wasn't decent to be squished up against him in a parked car, even if she was a decade or two older than he was. What if someone saw them? She tried to open the door to get out, but it was locked.

"I'm not being difficult," she said. "I'm only trying to help. I don't believe it is within your authority to detain me against my will."

"I think you happen to know an awful lot about things you shouldn't know and it's most certainly within my authority to investigate that."

Sadie furrowed her eyebrows. "What do I know that I shouldn't know?"

"Where she was killed. Where all her important papers were kept—"

"You people asked me those things!" she yelled.

"And you knew the answers!" he yelled back.

"I'm trying to be helpful!"

"You're making a mess of it. This is real life, lady, not some game. You're not going to beat us to the punch and solve the crime, so if that's what you're trying to do, it's time to give it up."

"I'm only trying to help," Sadie said again and folded her arms over her chest.

"If you wanted to help, you'd keep your nose out of things."

Sadie pursed her lips to keep from saying that she had no choice but to put her nose into things. This wasn't just about Anne. Ron was involved, and Trevor was still gone. She considered the enormity of the answers she still needed to find, and felt tears rise up; she quickly blinked them away. "Fine," she said, handing over the papers. "But I want it on the record that I think you are treating me very unfairly and that I have cooperated at every turn. Whatever issues you have with Detective Cunningham are your problem. Trying to one-up him by badgering me is a pretty lousy substitution for whatever you're trying to get."

Madsen's neck turned a dark pink and his jaw flexed. She'd hit a nerve. He let out a grunt and shook his head. "Just back off and let the professionals do their job," he said as he took the papers from her.

She bit back the sarcastic comment on the tip of her tongue about just how professional *he* was being. He looked through the papers and lifted his eyes to meet hers. "I need the other one too," he said with exasperation.

"Look, I gave you what I was given, if—"

"The business card," Madsen said in sharp tones. "Give it to me or I'll arrest you for interfering with a police investigation. I'm already late for the hearing so just give me the card and let me do my job."

Sadie let out a sigh and pulled the card from the sleeve of her hoodie where she'd managed to hide it. She told herself she would have given it to him later, but he brought out the worst in her and made her act like the Sadie who once hid her dad's golf clubs because he wouldn't let her go to a party after a high school football game. He never did find out she was the one who put them behind the water heater and made him miss his tee time. Passive-aggressive was likely the technical term, but Sadie thought of it as quiet justice. Madsen took the card and then held her eyes. She didn't flinch.

"Can I expect you to stay out of this now?" he asked in what she supposed was a *professional* tone but was actually a ten on the offensive scale.

"Does Detective Cunningham know you're here, pulling me into an unmarked car and threatening me?"

The pink on Madsen's neck inched its way up. He said nothing.

Sadie nodded sharply. "That's what I thought. Will you please let me out, or should I start screaming for help?"

He let out a long breath and finally opened his door. He slid out and she stepped out a moment later, not looking at him or allowing him any parting comments. Her car was only a few spaces away, and once inside, she waited until Madsen had pulled out of the parking lot. Then she reached under her seat to retrieve her local phone book. She always kept last year's edition in her car for reference while running errands.

It took less than a minute to find Attorney Gimes's address. She smiled to herself and shifted into drive.

CHAPTER 11

Sadie pushed through the glass doors and approached the reception desk. She cleared her throat. "Hi," she said to the twenty-something blonde behind the desk. The desk groaned under the weight of papers and files piled everywhere and the receptionist was sufficiently frazzled. "I wondered if I could speak with Susan Gimes," Sadie asked.

"Do you have an appointment?" the young woman asked without looking up from the files in her hands.

Sadie shook her head. "No."

The receptionist looked at her for the first time. "Are you a client?" she asked and Sadie could have wrung the condescension from her voice like water from a dishrag.

"No, but a friend of mine was."

The woman's face hardened even more—apparently being the friend of a client and having no appointment didn't count for much. "I just wanted to talk with Susan Gimes for a minute. I guess I should have called first."

"A call would have been nice," the receptionist said almost too quiet to hear. Louder, but with no more enthusiasm, she added, "Have a seat. I'll see if she has a minute."

"Thank you," Sadie said. She backed up and sat in one of the red upholstered chairs in the waiting area. She'd no sooner sat down when her cell phone rang, causing her to jump.

Is it Ron? she wondered, her insides knotting up. She wasn't ready to talk to him, but a look at the caller ID showed a number she didn't recognize. Deciding not to take the chance, she hit the end button and waited until she heard the chime indicating a voice message had been left. After dialing her mailbox, she listened to the message.

"Mrs. Hoffmiller? This is Jean from the library. After you left I remembered something else Anne Lemmon left at the library at story time on Friday. She'd been on the computer and had printed some pages. But her son started throwing a tantrum and she left without paying for her copies. We put them aside for her to pick up next time. If you wanted to put them with her other things, you're welcome to pick them up— but you'll need to pay the fees for them. It's fifteen cents a page. I'm so sorry for your loss—let us know if there's anything we can do. Thanks."

Sadie saved the message before closing her voice mail. She remembered that day because Anne had asked Sadie to watch Trevor while she went to her job interview that afternoon. Anne had still been frustrated about Trevor's tantrum when she dropped him off but Sadie told her she'd done the right thing, taking him home and putting him immediately in time-out.

Sadie wondered what Anne had printed and was eager to get back to the library. But first things first. She looked around the office, feeling antsy. It wasn't large or fancy, but it was very cozy and Sadie made a note to compliment Ms. Gimes on that if she had the chance.

Sadie had never been very good at waiting. When she went to the doctor's office she always took a book. But she'd not anticipated waiting in the office of an attorney she'd never heard of and the minutes felt like hours. She tapped her fingers on her purse and tried not to watch the second hand of the large clock hanging above the reception area, but it was hard not to. After four minutes she considered making an appointment and coming back, but that was silly. She was a grown woman, surely she could wait a few more minutes.

She scanned the waiting room again and saw copies of *Time* and *Working Woman* on an end table. Neither one held any interest for her. She did have the library book in her purse, but there was no way she was going to read that in public. It had been a lot of years since she'd read a romance novel and she wasn't sure she was prepared for other people to see her with it. Then she remembered the book list the library had printed for her. That was something she was planning to go over anyway. With anxious relief to have found something to do, she reached into her purse and dug out the list.

After scanning half the list, one title stood out to her: *My Father's Eyes*. Sadie fumbled in her purse for a pen and underlined it, even though she was unsure why it had caught her attention. She read through the rest of the tape and found at the bottom, where fines or unreturned items were listed, that *My Father's Eyes* had never been returned—Anne had paid for it before it was even overdue. Sadie stared at the title again. There was something familiar about it but she couldn't think what it was. Had Sadie read the book? Not likely.

After reading through the list again and determining there was nothing else that stood out, she folded the list and returned it to her purse, ignoring the hidden romance novel for a second time. However, her nerves tightened with every second, and she finally gave in. The waiting area was empty anyway. She unzipped her purse and opened the book hiding inside, careful to keep the cover in her purse. She had barely gotten through the flowery description of the buxom main character, when the receptionist interrupted her, bringing her back to the present.

"Mrs. Gimes will see you now," the receptionist said in a tone of forced politeness as Sadie quickly zipped her purse back up.

Susan Gimes was on her feet when Sadie entered the office. She was very tall, at least six feet, Sadie guessed, with black hair cut short and trendy, and large brown eyes. Her very presence was quite imposing, something Sadie felt sure was an asset in her line of work. The two women met halfway across the room and Sadie shook the proffered hand before taking the seat offered to her.

"My apologies for my receptionist—we're in the middle of updating our files and computer system and we ended up shorthanded today. Because of that I'm afraid I only have a couple minutes to meet with you," Susan Gimes said with a very professional smile as she sat behind the large mahogany desk.

"That's okay," Sadie said with a nod. "I'm sorry to have interrupted you, Ms. Gimes, but—"

"Call me Susan."

"Okay, thank you. My name is Sadie Hoffmiller—you can call me Sadie." She cleared her throat and opened her mouth to continue.

"You headed up the Youth in Action program a few years ago, right?"

Sadie blinked and allowed her thoughts to shift. "I did," Sadie said with a smile. "Did we meet then?" It would be nice if they had, though Sadie would be embarrassed not to remember.

Susan shook her head. "No, we didn't. But you worked with my daughter, Laura Johanson—I remarried after her father and I split up and I took my new husband's name." She gave Sadie a soft smile. "She was really struggling. In fact she was arrested for shoplifting and the judge offered her the option of working with Youth in Action instead of putting it on her record. She had a wonderful experience working with you, Mrs. Hoffmiller." She looked down, seemingly embarrassed. "I always meant to send you a thank you card, and I didn't get around to it."

"Oh, it was my pleasure," Sadie said, invigorated by something positive, by the reminder that she had done good things in the lives of other people. "Laura was a sweet girl. Did she ever make those cinnamon-ginger cookies I taught her to make?"

Susan nodded. "She did and they were wonderful. She makes them every Christmas now. I have to admit I was surprised she took to cooking so well. I grew up watching my mother slave away in the kitchen and swore I'd never do it. I've been good to my word, so it's been surprising to me to see how much Laura enjoys it."

"Well, Laura was a good girl and a quick study in the kitchen. It was my philosophy, especially with those young girls, that directing them back to the basics of cooking, cleaning, and taking care of themselves allowed them to build self-confidence from the inside out instead of basing so much of their self-image on social labels. If they know what they are capable of at home, then they can enter the world with that same confidence and help themselves and the people they love." She suddenly realized she might be offending this woman who had just told her she personally hated kitchen work; she felt her cheeks heat up. "Um, I mean, it works for some girls, and then others are, uh, directed elsewhere for those same—"

Susan's smile got even bigger as Sadie attempted to save herself and she finally laughed out loud, cutting Sadie off. "Laura's in culinary school in New York right now. You were a wonderful influence for her at a difficult time in her life and set her on a good path—I'm not the least bit ungrateful for that. In fact she taught me how to make a few things and cooking's not as bad as I thought."

"I'm so glad to hear it," Sadie said. "Tell her hi from me; I'm excited for her success."

They both smiled at one another, but the silence became awkward.

"I'm sorry," Susan finally said. "I got off the subject. What can I do for you today?"

A pall fell over the room. "Well, I'm here because . . ." She paused, not sure where to start. "My friend, Anne Lemmon, passed away this morning—actually, she was murdered." Susan Gimes' eyes went wide and her back straightened. "I found your card in her papers and I'm trying to . . ." She paused. What was she trying to do? Detective Madsen thought she was trying to solve the case. But she wasn't. Was she? Sadie felt her shoulders slump. "Well, I guess I don't know what I'm trying to do. I just . . . well, I never asked much about Anne's past— she was trying to make a fresh start. And now that all this has happened, I'm hoping to find something that will help me find her son and I—"

"Her son?" Susan leaned forward slightly. "What happened to her son?"

"He's gone," Sadie said. "Sometime this morning or last night Anne was killed, and we haven't found her son."

Susan leaned back, her fingertips together. "And so you came to me to try to find out more about her?"

"She kept all her papers and things in a filing cabinet and it was stolen. Both the police and myself know very little of where to start."

"Do the police know about me?"

Sadie nodded, trying to keep the sour expression off her face as she thought about Madsen taking the card. "Yes, I'm sure they will be contacting you."

Susan fixed her with a pointed look. "Do they know you're here?"

Sadie squirmed. "Uh, not really." Though she wouldn't be surprised if Madsen showed up as soon as his hearing was over. "Anne was a good friend of mine, and I helped her with her son. I can't do nothing. I'm hoping to get some answers—something to help things move forward. I know she was from Boston, but I don't know who her parents are, and with the filing cabinet gone, I have nowhere to start."

The room was silent for several seconds. "I'm afraid I can't give out any information about Anne. It's protected by client privilege."

"Oh," Sadie said. "I hadn't thought of that." She looked at her hands and let out a breath. She looked up and smiled apologetically. "I'm very sorry to have taken your time today—though it was wonderful to hear how Laura's doing. I should have thought things through better before I came." She stood up, embarrassed to have wasted the time of this woman, but grateful that Susan was as kind as she'd been.

"Why don't you give me your name and number," Susan suggested. "There might be something I can give you, but I'll need to review the file first."

"That would be wonderful," Sadie said. She started fumbling in her purse, looking for a pen. Susan handed her one along with a pad of paper. Sadie thanked her and began scribbling down her information.

A buzzer from the desk startled her and she jumped slightly as the receptionist's voice came over the intercom. "Susan, Garrison PD is here. They need to speak with you."

Sadie felt her face fall and her hand freeze, but she tried to contain her panic and finish writing her phone number. Her mouth was suddenly dry as she anticipated how she would explain her being here. Would they believe it was just a coincidence?

"You don't want them to know you were here?" Susan asked, correctly reading the look on Sadie's face.

"I wouldn't ask you to lie about it," Sadie replied, forcing a smile. She handed the pad of paper to Susan and was relieved when the other woman quickly put it in her desk. "But, well, no, I'd rather they didn't know."

"Why don't you wait here," Susan said as she stood. "I can talk with them in the waiting area and then show you out when I'm finished." She was dressed in heeled boots and a long skirt that she smoothed in anticipation of leaving the room.

"I don't want to get you in trouble," Sadie said.

"Not at all," Susan said with a smile. "Just sit tight, this will only take a few minutes. You might want to sit over there." Susan indicated a chair next to the door that was out of view from anyone looking in from the waiting area.

Sadie nodded and sat in the chair, taking a deep breath while Susan took long strides to the door. When the door opened and she heard Madsen's voice, she felt her stomach tighten and she pressed herself against the back of the chair. Hadn't he said he had a hearing to go to? She'd expected that to buy her some time. Susan closed the door and the voices became muted. Sadie was forced to wait again. Even with the adrenaline rush of knowing Madsen was out there, Sadie was bored and fidgety within thirty seconds.

After a full minute, she began wondering if she could shimmy down a drainpipe. The fantasy became even more tempting when the voices in the waiting area increased in both volume and speed. Sadie couldn't make out exactly what was being said, but the overall gist of the conversation came through perfectly clear. She swallowed. If Madsen found out she was in here. . . . She shuddered at the probable scene that would follow. The door opened and she looked up. Susan's face was tight as she headed for a bank of long filing cabinets along one wall. She didn't acknowledge Sadie was there and left the door open.

"Of course it's up to you," Madsen's voice called through the door. "But you know the drill. If I come back with a warrant, I can look through whatever I think might be helpful."

"And make as big a mess as possible," Susan said hotly over her shoulder.

Madsen said nothing, and Sadie remained frozen, pressed against the chair with the open door just a few feet away. Susan looked up for just a moment, shooting Sadie the quickest *don't-move* look Sadie had ever seen. Sadie was quiet as a mouse and still as a statue while Susan retrieved a file and left the room, closing the door behind her again and allowing Sadie to breathe once more. She assumed Susan would be right back, but the moments stretched into minutes again. Sadie tried to resist, but kept thinking about the romance novel still in her purse. She gave up after a few more seconds and discreetly cracked it open.

Sadie was on page twelve when the door opened and then shut behind Susan Gimes. The book disappeared into her purse again and Sadie's cheeks flushed hot. Sadie would have never guessed the captain's quarters on a merchant ship could be so . . . exciting. She'd nearly forgotten where she was.

She looked at Susan expectantly as she zipped up her purse and held it on her lap. Susan went around her desk and sat back in her chair.

"Detective Madsen and I have a short but unsavory history," Susan said with a tight smile. "I hate taking on other people's problem children." She took a deep breath.

"Problem children?" Sadie questioned.

Susan looked up with an incredulous look. "Yeah, don't you know?"

Sadie shook her head, not having the slightest idea what Susan was referring to but wanting very much to learn. Especially if it went to further discredit Madsen.

"The name Madsen—doesn't it ring a bell?"

Sadie thought hard. Madsen—Marlene Madsen had been a girl in Sadie's graduating class, but Sadie didn't think that's what Susan meant.

"Think upper levels of the Colorado state judicial system," Susan prodded, a half smile showing her amusement.

Sadie's eyebrows went up. "Madsen as in Barney Madsen, attorney general of Colorado?"

"Bingo," Susan said, leaning forward across the desk with a glint in her eye that Sadie knew too well—gossip was on its way. "Barney Madsen has one son—Sterling." She said "Sterling" as if she were a serpent, elongating the S and letting the rest of the name seep out from between her teeth. "He was a second-year cop in downtown Denver, maybe you remember how our distinguished AG made a big deal about his son finding the criminals and Barney prosecuting them."

Sadie nodded. She had a vague recollection of that very sentiment being part of Barney Madsen's reelection campaign a couple years ago. The good ole boy who'd raised a son who would fight on the front lines of their own community.

"What you probably didn't hear about, because it was quickly buried," Susan continued, "was that Sterling was also part of the street racing scene, assisting in setting up races where he knew there were no officers on patrol. Any other cop would have lost his badge. But our little Sterling disappeared for a year and then shows up in Garrison about ten months ago with a stamp on his forehead and a promotion to detective."

Sadie gasped. "That's awful."

"I agree. In fact it makes me, and every other professional in the justice department, a little sick to our stomachs." She leaned back in her chair and threw her hands up. "But what do you do about it? He came with a clean record and nothing but gossip and supposition to discredit him."

"He sure isn't making any friends in Garrison," Sadie said, remembering the power struggle between him and Detective Cunningham. "He's been an absolute bear to deal with so far and I just met him this morning."

Susan grunted and nodded. "I've dealt with him on two other occasions and let me tell you, he's a piece of work; one of those men who love lording their power over everyone else." She straightened in her chair. "But back to the topic of Anne— I've decided I can tell you a few things." Sadie got the impression that Susan's newfound cooperation was her way of rebelling against Detective Madsen. Since it meant Sadie would get answers she otherwise wouldn't, she wasn't about to argue. "Anne wasn't actually my client," she said just as Sadie's cell phone began to ring.

"Oh, I'm sorry," Sadie said, unzipping her purse and fumbling through the contents until she found her phone. She quickly hit the end button, sending the caller to her voice mail without seeing who it was. "Sorry," she said again.

Susan smiled. "As I was saying, Anne wasn't my client, something the detective out there made a big deal about— demanding my file since it wasn't privileged."

"She wasn't your client?"

"Well, not officially," Susan said with a nod. "Anne came in about three weeks ago for a free consultation. No money exchanged hands and she didn't show up for her second appointment, hence I wasn't officially retained as counsel."

"Oh," Sadie said dumbly. She had no idea how these things worked.

"Anyway, she came in with some questions about filing a—"

Sadie's phone rang again. This time Sadie looked to see who it was and swallowed when she saw Ron's cell phone number on the display. She made a split-second decision and turned the entire phone off, accidentally pushing her purse off her lap in the process. She couldn't risk being interrupted again, and she wasn't up to talking to Ron right now. "I'm so sorry," she said as she shoved the phone into the pocket of her hoodie and replaced the purse on her lap. "I turned it off this time—sorry."

Susan smiled a bit tighter than before and nodded almost imperceptibly. Sadie hoped she wasn't regretting her decision to help.

"You were saying that Anne came to ask some questions about filing something?"

"Yes, a paternity suit against the father of her son."

"Paternity," Sadie repeated as everything seemed to make sense. "She needed more child support. Of course."

"Well, actually, she was already receiving support—quite a bit. She brought in bank statements to prove that he had acknowledged his fatherhood through the financial responsibility he'd taken, but he wasn't on the birth certificate and she wanted legal institution of the paternity."

"She wanted her son to have a father," Sadie summed up, her heart softening at the understanding that what Anne wanted was a good thing, the right thing. And she wanted it for Trevor.

"Right," Susan said, her voice a bit softer as well. "We discussed her options and she was going to return and get the ball rolling as soon as she had all the documentation."

Sadie blinked and tried to take in all the new information. Why didn't Anne ever tell her about this? It was almost . . . offensive that Anne hadn't confided in Sadie. But since discovering Ron's involvement, she knew Anne and she weren't as close as Sadie had thought they were. And yet it still hurt that Anne hadn't trusted her.

Susan looked in the file and let out a breath. "I keep meticulous notes of every meeting and we made copies of the bank statements as well as of the child's birth certificate she'd brought in with her, but I can't find her file." She looked up. "We've spent the last week and a half scanning all our documents into the computer so we have a copy of everything on the server. This one should have been done already, so my receptionist is looking to see if we have an electronic copy somewhere."

As if on cue, the speakerphone on Susan's desk came to life. "I'm sorry, Susan, it doesn't look like that file got scanned in."

"Great," Susan grumbled. Then she raised her voice and spoke toward the phone. "Wasn't it K through M that was supposed to be done just yesterday?"

"Yes," the receptionist said. "I'm sure they got mixed up somehow—like the Anderson stuff. I'll keep looking for the hard copy."

"Thank you," Susan said and the line clicked off. She looked at Sadie. "I can't wait to call Detective Madsen and tell him that," she said dryly before shaking her head. "Anyway, until I find the contents of the file I'm afraid I'm not much use to either of you. I remember that the birth certificate said the little boy was born in Boston."

Jean at the library had said enough that Sadie had all but figured that out.

"But it didn't have the father's name on it?" Sadie asked.

"No, that's why she was here—to fill in that blank."

Oh, right. "And she didn't say who the father was?" Sadie asked. "I've wondered if he could have . . . well, taken Trevor."

"I'm afraid she never told me the name. In fact she was pretty secretive about it. She wanted to know exactly how the process of establishing paternity worked before she gave me any information." She paused for a moment, pursing her lips slightly as if she were concentrating. "There was, however, a cosigner on the bank accounts. One was for her use and one was a college fund set aside for her son, but the same cosigner was on both accounts so she couldn't just clean them out; all withdrawals had to be approved."

"Do you remember the name of the cosigner?" Sadie asked.

Susan closed her eyes in concentration. "His first name was Ronald—I remember because that's my brother's name. The last name was Bronson or Bradshaw or—"

"Bradley?" Sadie offered as her stomach lurched off a cliff.

Susan opened her eyes, smiling widely. She nodded her head. "That's it. Ronald Bradley—but I think she called him Ron."

Cinnamon-Ginger Cookies

1 cup butter
1 ½ cups white sugar
3 tablespoons light corn syrup
2 eggs
3 cups all-purpose flour
1 cup quick oats
1/2 teaspoon salt
1 teaspoon cinnamon
1 teaspoon ground ginger
1/4 teaspoon ground cloves

Cream butter and sugar. Add corn syrup and eggs. Mix well. Add dry ingredients to the butter mixture, and mix well. Roll into teaspoon-sized balls (refrigerate if dough is too soft) and bake at 350 degrees for about 6 minutes or until bottom edges are barely browned.

Remove cookies from oven and press flat with a glass dipped in sugar. (Spray bottom of glass with cooking spray for first "press" and then dip back into sugar between each cookie thereafter.) Let cookies cool 1 minute on baking sheet before removing to cooling rack.

To make sandwich cookies, spread a layer of cream cheese frosting between cookies.

Cream-Cheese Frosting

1/4 cup butter or margarine
8 oz. cream cheese (Neufchatel or fat-free works fine)
1/2 teaspoon vanilla
1 ½ cups powdered sugar

Cream butter and cream cheese. Add vanilla and mix until smooth. Add powdered sugar until desired consistency is reached;

you want a thick frosting to hold the cookies together. If frosting is too thick, thin with evaporated milk. If frosting is too thin, thicken by adding more powdered sugar. Spread between cookies when cookies are cool.

Makes about 2 dozen sandwich cookies (or 4 dozen single cookies).

CHAPTER 12

Sadie managed to thank Susan for her help without falling apart. Once outside the building she headed for her car where she sat for almost ten minutes, absorbing what she'd just learned. Ron had been at Anne's house and he was a cosigner on her bank accounts. There was no way around it—Ron had to be Trevor's father.

The betrayal ran deep. What a fool she was. "He moved her here," she said out loud as she put details together. "He moved her to the same neighborhood I lived in?"

And Anne pretended to be Sadie's friend, acting as if she were so needy. It was bad enough to be played by Ron, but Anne too? That cut twice as deep. And yet Sadie couldn't even cry. She felt so spent of all emotion that to cry seemed like a waste of water at this point.

She shoved the keys into the ignition and started the car as a barrage of questions engulfed her. Why had she come here at all? Why hadn't she listened to Detective Madsen when she had the chance and kept her nose out of it? And yet, would she rather not know any of this? *Not really,* she admitted. She just didn't know what to do with the information now.

She threw the gearshift into drive and headed for home. It was almost two o'clock and she was ready to climb into bed and pull the covers over her head. Maybe she'd make her famous German chocolate cheesecake. It had taken second place at the state fair two years ago and had the perfect chocolate content to calm her nerves.

It wasn't until she was driving past the library that she remembered the papers Jean had called about. "Forget it," she said out loud. She wanted to put her hands over her ears and sing "La, la, la, la" like a six-year-old child. But as she came up on the last entrance into the library parking lot, she cranked the wheel to the right and pulled in. She didn't even allow herself to think about her motives as she parked the car and went inside. She'd never been a quitter and even though she wanted to forget all of this, she had started something and after years of habitual follow-through she couldn't stop now.

It only took a minute to pay the sixty-cent fee, claim the manila folder, and thank Jean. Sadie knew at the very least what Jean had done for her was a gray area—at the most she may have broken all kinds of federal library patron privacy regulations. Sadie made a mental note to bake her some sugar knots as a thank you gift.

As soon as she got back in the car, Sadie took a breath and opened the folder. The first few papers were regarding establishing paternity in Colorado and looked to be printed off some official Web site. Sadie felt her stomach tighten and she quickly put them behind the other papers. The next paper was an e-mail Anne had printed out.

> On Oct 19, at 4:54 pm, Marla Boyd wrote:
>
> Anne—
>
> We're very excited to have you join our team as well. The Boston office had nothing but positive things to say about you. They miss you. I think you'll find our office and staff a lot like Boston, just on a much smaller scale. We've been very successful on the local level here—unprecedented for such a small town. As for training, since you're a previous employee for the company, we don't need to do the full regime. We'd like you to come in next Wednesday, just to brush up and get familiar with the Garrison office. You can start the following Monday. Let me know if there's a problem; otherwise, I'll see you Wednesday.
>
> Sincerely,
>
> Marla Boyd
>
> Director of Human Resources, Garrison office
>
> Riggs and Barker Realty

It wasn't until the company identification at the bottom of the e-mail that Sadie caught her breath.

Riggs and Barker Realty.

It was the national real estate brokerage Ron had worked at for almost twenty years. He'd recently been promoted to senior sales manager of Northern Colorado.

And Anne had worked in the Boston office?

The main office?

The office that hosted the quarterly training conferences?

Sadie swallowed, but the lump in her throat didn't go away. It was all laid out for her like a road map. Ron had met Anne in Boston. He'd fathered her child, left her in Boston, then brought her here two years later, and now he was getting her a job.

Sadie wanted to throw up. A million questions swirled in her head, but the big question was what purpose did Sadie serve? Ron had a young, beautiful mother of his child. Why date Sadie—a fifty-six-year-old widow who, though remarkably well-kept for her age, if she did say so herself, wasn't exactly in her prime?

Why move Anne just down the street? That part didn't make sense and she wasn't sure she wanted it to. She thought back to what Anne had told her about Trevor's father, that he had another family. Was Sadie the other family? Did somehow, for some depraved reason, he want both of them? She was going to be sick.

She started the car and was shifting it into gear when a young mother and her children walked in front of her car. There was a little girl who looked to be four or five, and a little boy close to Trevor's age.

Trevor.

He was out there somewhere, alone and scared, missing his mother who he may or may not know was dead. Sadie refused to consider that he could also have been killed. The police had enough to do with investigating Anne's murder; could they truly give Trevor the attention he needed? The attention she could give him?

New resolve rushed through her and she mentally put Anne and Ron and whatever may have existed between them on the back burner. She couldn't give up. She'd come this far, learned so much, and she would tell Detective Cunningham everything as soon as she could. But facts were facts—Trevor was Ron's son, Anne was his mistress, and he'd been at Anne's house last night. That meant that Trevor must be with Ron. The whys and the how-comes were irrelevant in contrast to the need to find Trevor. She drove past the turn that would take her home.

She'd made her decision—it was time to talk to Ron.

CHAPTER 13

It was 2:16 when Sadie pulled into the parking lot of Ron's condominium complex and she reminded herself she had to be home in time for when the Bailey kids would get off the bus. With the constraint on her time she knew she should really save this for later—but she couldn't. Trevor might be in Ron's condo right now! She couldn't put that off.

Ron's car was gone from his parking space, something that both disappointed and relieved her. If he wasn't here, then Trevor wasn't either. But the scared and shaking part of her was relieved that she wouldn't have to confront him. She had no idea what she would say when that moment arrived. However, she had no intention of not making the most of her trip out here.

She parked far away from his condo. It seemed prudent to use stealth in case he came home. The condominiums were of a San Francisco design, tall and narrow with shuttered windows and bright facades. They were built in sets of eight, stacked and scrunched together as if space was as big a concern in Garrison as it was in the Bay area of California. There were ten blocks of condos arranged to offer a narrow strip of grass in front and a small fenced-in yard with covered parking in back. Ron's block was almost in the middle of the complex.

She approached the outer gate and jiggled the latch that led from the parking area to the small backyard. The gate was unlocked and she opened it slowly, stepped in, and carefully shut it while scanning the area to see if any neighbors were watching—not that she'd have done anything other than wave if any of them were. But she was in luck, the coast was clear. She approached the back door and found that unlike the gate, it was locked up tight. She reached into her pocket and removed her smiley-face key ring, glad that she'd slipped Detective Madsen Carrie's key instead of Ron's—though she hoped the detective still believed it was Anne's. The key to Ron's house was right next to Anne's on the ring. How appropriate. The key turned smoothly in the lock and she opened the door, hating how her heart hammered in her chest and wishing she were the type of person who enjoyed the adrenaline rush of rebellious behavior.

Even as a little girl Sadie would get sick with anxiety when she played hide-and-seek. One time she had actually started crying when the child who was "it" kept walking around and around the shed where she was hiding. The fear was too much for her—and she'd been ten. She'd rarely bothered to play the game after that. This felt the same. What if Ron came home? What if he found her? And what was she hoping to find anyway?

Toys, she told herself, *diapers, cookies, dirty toddler clothes—that's what I'm looking for. I'm doing this for Trevor.* She looked around, slowly at first, her ears pricked to every sound. A car drove by outside and she froze, then tiptoed to the back door—relieved that Ron's parking spot was still empty. She let out a breath and locked the door for good measure.

The first thing that caught her attention in the kitchen was a box of graham crackers on the counter. Trevor loved graham crackers. But so did Ron. It wasn't conclusive evidence by any stretch, but it was a start. She searched each room on the main floor one by one—kitchen, living room, master bedroom, bathroom, and laundry area—looking in corners and closets, under beds and in drawers, anywhere he might have hidden evidence.

The condo was very clean, more so than most single men's homes she was sure. Ron always said his mother didn't tolerate much of a mess, and it had stuck. She began thinking about how things would change when they got married—she'd have to do better at picking up around the house so he didn't end up cleaning up after her—then she stopped herself. Everything was different now and she knew there would be no wedding. The thought brought tears to her eyes and she tried not to think about it.

She'd finished the first floor and found nothing except the knowledge that Ron wore briefs. She'd have guessed him to be a boxer man. She made her way upstairs, proud of herself for feeling more relaxed. *This isn't like hide-and-seek at all,* she told herself. No one knew she was here and she'd leave nothing behind to indicate she ever had been. It was an expedition, not a stakeout. Nothing to it.

The second level consisted of a loft-type den, a guest room for when his kids and grandkids came to visit, and another bathroom. She was sure the guest room would be her best bet, and she took a breath to prepare herself as she opened the door. And yet, preparation aside, she was shocked at what she saw.

Strewn across the bed and floor were the contents of the toy box Ron kept for his grandkids. Even though she'd prepared herself to find exactly this, she was shocked to be proven right so quickly and she just stared as the acceptance seeped into her heart. Ron's grandkids hadn't visited for weeks which meant Trevor *had* been here. Why did being right feel so horrible?

But then, where was Trevor now? Where was Ron? Had Trevor been in the car when Ron had stopped by her house this morning? For nearly a minute she thought about these questions but had no idea what the answers could be. She remembered seeing some receipts on Ron's dresser—maybe there would be another clue there. And there was also the basement—a workshop of sorts. She'd nearly forgotten about that.

After hurrying down the stairs, she was in the doorway of the master bedroom when she heard a key in the lock.

CHAPTER 14

No! She screamed in her head as her heart rate doubled. Her eyes darted around in search of escape and she realized she was trapped. It had turned into hide-and-seek after all. She hurried toward the walk-in closet, the only obvious place to hide, but there were no doors on it, just an archway that led into a space almost as big as the room itself. It was the kind of closet meant for a woman with a shopping addiction. Ron had it less than half full—nothing to hide behind. She heard the back door open, the rubber weather strip scraping against the tiled floor, and thought she might pass out.

Her eyes scanned the room again, her heart pounding. She focused on the antique wrought-iron bed set against the middle of the opposite wall. There was no other option. Flattening herself on the floor, she army-crawled underneath the bed using muscles she didn't know existed anymore. Were it not for her yoga class she'd surely have broken something. As it was, they had never done this in class.

Only when her head struck a box did she realize she should have checked to see if there was anything under the bed. Then again, she hadn't had much time. She reached forward and carefully pushed the box toward the head of the bed, causing a pile-up of other boxes. She paused and then pushed more slowly, trying to keep quiet and making sure none of the boxes popped out of either side of the bed—the whole time she pictured Ron in the doorway watching her. The boxes moved a few feet, but then stopped—sufficiently crammed against the wall.

It would have to do. She curled around herself and pulled the rest of her body under the bed. The bed was old, something Ron had inherited from his mother, and didn't have the traditional box springs to support the mattress. Instead it had a metal lattice—bedsprings—like fencing stretched across the metal frame. The bed wasn't high off the ground either. She could barely lie on her side and did the best she could in order to get her feet in. She pulled her knees up as high as she could and clenched her teeth when a box corner poked into her back. How long would she have to stay here? Her knees were already aching.

The sound of footsteps in the kitchen took her mind off the stabbing pain in her back. She tried to hold her breath, though after ten seconds or so she realized that was a bad idea and let the air she'd been holding out as quietly as possible— her lungs lobbying heavily for a fresh breath. Her heartbeat pulsed in her ears and she was sure Ron could hear it. If it was Ron. She didn't think anyone else had a key to his place, but a lot of things she had believed to be true yesterday had been proven false today. She didn't dare not be suspicious of everything.

She heard footsteps coming from the kitchen and into the bedroom. Whoever it was fumbled with something on the dresser. If a person could die from fear, Sadie knew she'd have no need for the pesky breathing anymore. She'd never been so scared in her life.

"Sadie," she heard Ron's voice say.

She held her breath again and began to panic. He knew she was here! How?

"I really wish you would have answered the phone. We need to talk," he continued, and she realized he was talking to her voice mail. "I'm late, I know that, but I had to do some things. I stopped by your house a little bit ago but I'm hoping you're home by now. If you are, please call me as soon as you get this message."

She started breathing again, as slow and quiet as possible, terrified she would sneeze or do something else that would alert him to her presence. She heard him sigh.

"Sadie, I'm so sorry, but let me explain this and please don't tell the police—not yet. I had a hard time finding the information I needed in an hour, but it's not what you think. I'll try your cell phone again. When you get this message, call me, please."

She heard a nearly silent beep—him ending the call—then he dialed another number. Several seconds passed before he spoke.

"I just left another message at the house. Please call me back—we really need to talk." He hung up the phone with another quiet beep and Sadie heard him sigh. He walked to the side of the bed; she watched him step out of his shoes before he sat on the bed. She willed him to remember something he needed to do on the other side of town. Instead, he lay down. The mattress and bedsprings sank a couple of inches, pinning Sadie's shoulders between the bed and the floor. She closed her eyes and bit her lip.

He's going to take a nap? she screamed in her mind. *With all this going on he can sleep?* Her opinion of him, though dismal at the moment, sank even lower. Then again, he'd been back and forth to Denver *and* at Anne's house last night—no wonder he was tired.

After what she assumed was five minutes, her shoulder was throbbing, her knees ached, and the box corner in her back had surely drawn blood. The sound of Ron's soft breathing was the only noise in the house. If he snored, and she weren't pinned beneath his weight, maybe she could sneak out, but he *didn't* snore and she *was* pinned. The situation was hopeless. What was she going to do?

That's when she remembered her phone. She'd put it in her hoodie pocket after shutting it off at Susan Gimes's office. But could she reach it, all crunched up in a ball the way she was? And if she could reach it, then what? She couldn't call him, he'd wonder why her voice was in stereo.

Text message.

Bless you, Breanna, for insisting I learn how to text message, she thought as she tried slowly and carefully to adjust her position enough so she could retrieve her phone. It took at least an hour, she was sure of it, well, more like another ten minutes of slow, painful contortions—first to free her arms, then to find the pocket, and eventually the phone. She was nearly in tears, due to the physical pain of certain movements she had no right to be performing at her age, and the sheer frustration that everything was so difficult. All the while she had to be sure she didn't move so much that the bed moved with her.

Finally, she managed to hold the phone in her hands. She took a breath and stared at the black-and-silver phone that seemed the size of a fun-size candy bar. *I've got to think this through,* she thought, forcing herself to be slow and calculated. *What does the phone do when I turn it on?* She searched her memory banks and groaned inwardly. Her phone sang a little welcome jingle when she turned it on. She couldn't very well risk that. Ron rolled over in bed, freeing her shoulders a bit, and she scowled up at the mattress springs. *You couldn't have done that five minutes ago?* she thought. Finding the phone would have been much easier with her newly restored, though still limited, range of motion.

She refocused her attention on the phone. *Can I muffle the music?* she wondered. After several seconds, and no one answering her question, she decided it was her only option. She pulled up as much of the thick sweatshirt fabric of her hoodie as she could, causing the box to shift from poking into her back through the sweatshirt to poking directly into her skin—nice. She tried to ignore it, sent a little prayer heavenward, flipped the phone open, and pushed the button before quickly wrapping the phone as best she could in the folds of her hoodie.

As soon as she heard the first muffled note, she knew it was too loud. She pushed her legs away and down from her chest and rolled over on top of the phone. Her hair got caught in the bedsprings and she winced, lifting her head to relieve the pulling. The sound from the phone disappeared except for the faintest of melodies, one she was sure Ron couldn't hear through the mattress. But she'd moved too fast. She felt the bed shift, heard Ron's breathing stop for a moment, and was sure she'd been caught.

She clenched her eyes shut like a child who thinks you can't see her if she can't see you and prayed until his breathing returned to normal. Opening her eyes, she realized he'd readjusted to a position that was even better for her. But having her face so close to the neglected carpet proved too much for her thus far stalwart sinuses and she sneezed silently— causing her sinuses to ache. Good thing she'd mastered all-but-silent sneezes when she waitressed in college. Her feet were poking out from under the bed, but she was at the eleventh hour now.

The music stopped and she slowly pulled her arms out from under her, sliding them up until they held her phone just a few inches in front of her face. She couldn't see anything that close up—she hadn't thought to bring her glasses—not to mention it was pretty dark under the bed. She tried to extend her arms, but, thanks to the boxes in front of her, that necessitated wriggling backwards. And in order to move backwards, she had to untangle her hair from the springs—only half of the clump was sacrificed. Her legs were now almost completely exposed—thank goodness Ron was asleep—but at least she was in position and the bluish light of the cell phone illuminated the darkness.

After toggling into "Settings," she cringed at the quiet beep the phone made and paused to see if Ron reacted to it. It wasn't anything like the welcome jingle, but to her it sounded like a gong. Ron didn't move and she wondered how long her luck could hold out. She turned the sound off on her phone and felt much relieved when the screen flashed "Silent Mode." It took a minute for her to toggle into the text message menu, where she painstakingly typed in a message. Breanna and Shawn used all kinds of abbreviations, but Sadie was always worried she'd do them wrong and say something completely different than what she intended, so she always spelled things out.

Meet at Baxter's now

She asked herself if this was the best idea. Baxter's was their favorite restaurant, but she had no desire to meet him there. Unfortunately, she couldn't think of anything else that would get him to leave. She took one last breath, said one last prayer, and hit send.

It wasn't until his phone started ringing that she remembered her feet were still sticking out. She rolled back to her side and pulled her knees up again, her heart racing as the panic returned. *Please let this work,* she chanted in her mind.

By the second ring, Ron's breathing had stopped. In the next instant he was off the bed and across the room. She couldn't hear what he was doing but after a minute her phone began to vibrate. Ron didn't know how to text message, and curled up like she was, she couldn't bring the phone to her face anyway, though she pulled it close to muffle the hum of the vibrations. She breathed slow and deep, willing Ron to leave. Her left hip was going numb. Moments after her phone stopped vibrating she heard Ron cuss under his breath. Then his footsteps retreated, the back door opened again, and when it shut, Sadie was alone in the uncomfortable silence.

She waited at least two or three minutes before she slowly pulled herself out from under the bed. Her whole body ached. She peeked through the kitchen window to be sure his car was gone and for the first time in thirty minutes, she could breathe normally. Without wasting another minute she ran out the door, not bothering to lock it since Ron hadn't taken the time to do so. By the time she reached her car she felt like crying with relief. She took a deep breath, willing her blood pressure to lower, reminding herself that she hadn't been caught. Then she had to ask herself if she was going to meet Ron at Baxter's. If she didn't, he'd keep looking for her and who knew when he'd catch up. At least Baxter's was a public place.

She blamed her parents for the good upbringing that made it feel so wrong to stand him up. Even if he was a depraved murderer.

CHAPTER 15

Ron's black Jetta was parked in the front of the restaurant. He wasn't in it. Sadie pulled into a parking space a few slots down from his car, took a deep breath, and finger-combed her hair before stepping out of the car, embarrassed to be so underdressed. She wasn't even wearing lipstick. Baxter's wasn't a hoodie-and-jeans kind of establishment. Still, the hostess smiled politely when Sadie came in.

"I know I'm underdressed, it was last minute, I'm sorry," Sadie said, knowing it was too much information but wanting to be sure the girl knew Sadie wasn't an informal person and that she knew what the expectations were. The girl gave her an odd look and said it was okay.

"I'm meeting someone," Sadie continued nervously. "A man."

"Oh, yes," the plump blonde said. "Mr. Bradley. He's over here, follow me."

Ron met her eye when she rounded the corner booth and he stood, his face a mask of relief and anxiety. When she reached the table he stepped forward as if to hug her but she slid into the booth before he could touch her and she kept her hands clasped and rigid in her lap. He paused, then slid back into his seat. The tension between them was unlike anything Sadie had felt before. She looked at the high-gloss tabletop and wished she'd ignored her manners and let him sweat it out.

"I know about you and Anne," Sadie finally said, glancing up quickly.

"Anne and me?" Ron asked, his tone was careful, cautious.

"I know about the bank account, about the Boston office—everything."

Ron's eyes went wide. "How do you know that?" he said, then he shook his head and spoke again before she could. "It doesn't matter." He took a breath. "It was a mistake for me to do it, I know that now, but I was only trying to help—to ensure that Trevor was taken care of and that lives weren't disrupted more than they already had been."

"Really," Sadie said, shocked that he'd admitted it all so easily. "Forgive me if that isn't a big comfort to me, Ron." Their waitress approached, smiling as if there weren't a missing child and a dead mother in town.

"What can I get for you two?" she asked sweetly.

Sadie glanced at the unopened menu in front of her. Baxter's had an amazing honey-glazed salmon with spinach orzo pasta—a recipe she had not successfully reproduced at home—and her stomach growled at the idea of food, but Sadie didn't think she was up to eating. Especially with Ron as her lunch companion. "I'm not staying," she said, suddenly anxious to get out of there.

Ron offered the waitress a pained smile. "Can you come back in a minute?" He reached over and grabbed Sadie's hand as she tried to stand, preventing her from leaving. The waitress looked a bit concerned but she finally nodded and hurried away.

Sadie stared at Ron's hand holding hers. Twenty-four hours ago it would have sent a thrill through her entire body to be touched by him. Now it left her cold and seemed to mock her own foolishness for trusting her heart to this man. She looked up and met his eyes.

"I can't imagine how I gave any indication that I would be okay with this, Ron," she said with as much calmness as she could muster despite the panic inside her. "We obviously don't know each other nearly as well as I thought we did."

"It was a mistake," he repeated.

"A mistake?" Sadie said, shaking her head. He made it sound like he'd lied about his weight to the DMV. "A woman is dead, Ron. Her life is over, and her son's life has been unalterably changed." She paused, wanting to leave but realizing she had an opportunity to make herself clear and possibly even put an end to her concern for Trevor. "If you'll tell me where he is, I'll go with you when you turn yourself in."

"Turn myself in?" Ron said. "Cosigning a bank account isn't against the law, Sadie. And why would I know where Trevor is?"

Sadie pulled her hand away. "You were there last night, Ron, you told me that. Trevor hasn't been seen since."

Ron stared at her and blinked, then he sat back, a look of incredulity on his face. He was very good at this whole pretending innocence thing—it made her crazy. "You think I killed her," he said. "You really believe that?"

"Is it so far-fetched? You father her child, set up accounts for both of them, and then move her out to Garrison. You knew she was trying to establish legal paternity and you lost it and killed her. What I can't figure out is why you bothered keeping me around. What was my role supposed to be in this? Was I the trainer? Bringing Anne up to par." The words burned her tongue on the way out, searing the flavor of his deception into her brain.

"Your role," he repeated, though he managed to continue to appear stunned. He was silent for several seconds. Then he leaned forward with his elbows on the table, and when he spoke his words were crisp and louder than she thought they ought to be. How could he be angry with her for discovering the truth? "I am not the father of Anne's baby, Sadie. I set up the account, I talked to her now and then, but that's all I did. *She* moved out here, after promising to leave him alone. I've been the middleman, I admit that, but only because—"

"You went to see her last night," Sadie spat back, hating being lied to, hating that he thought her such a fool. She'd talked to the attorney, she'd read the e-mail. She was not the idiot he had taken her for. "You were supposed to be in Denver but you weren't, you were with her. And now she's dead and your son is gone."

"I didn't kill her and I'm not the father of her kid!" he nearly shouted. "If you'd just shut up long enough to hear what I have to say, I could explain."

Sadie was flabbergasted. She couldn't remember the last time someone had told her to shut up.

"Sir!"

Sadie and Ron looked up to meet the eyes a very tall, very black, man. The tag on his vest said Jerome—Manager, and his black licorice eyes bored into Ron's. To Sadie he was Superman, Spider-man, and her personal favorite, Captain America, all wrapped up into one. "Is everything okay?"

"No," Sadie said at the same time Ron said, "Everything's fine."

Ron took a breath and spoke again, his eyes on Sadie. "Please leave us alone," he said through clenched teeth.

"I think it would be better if *you* left *her* alone," the manager said as he grasped Ron's arm in what looked like a pretty strong grip. Sadie took advantage of the distraction to slip out of the booth and run for the door. She heard Ron call for her to stop.

"I think it best to let the lady leave," she heard the manager say behind her. Sadie wished she dared pause long enough to thank her superhero for stepping in. Ron said something, but her heart was pounding in her ears too loudly for her to hear it. She was almost to the door when she heard the sound of a fist hitting flesh. She turned to see the manager reel backward, knocking over a table, sending a vase and four sets of silverware to the floor. Sadie gasped, a waitress screamed, and someone else yelled for someone to call the police. Sadie didn't waste a single second. She ran for her car, jumped in, and squealed out of the parking lot without even putting her seat belt on.

A few blocks from the restaurant she stopped at a red light, her hands still shaking and tears on her cheeks. She hoped they did call the police, she hoped Ron was arrested. Maybe they could get him to confess to Anne's murder once he was in custody. And yet, it still broke her heart to feel this way. She took deep breaths and then noticed the papers from the library on the passenger seat. Detective Cunningham had left his card with her; where had she put it?

Before she reached the next red light—when she could search her purse—she looked at the clock on the dashboard. It was 3:09—why did she feel like she was late for something?

CHAPTER 16

The Bailey kids!

Sadie's heart sank. Baxter's was on the opposite side of town and she was still ten minutes from home. She imagined the kids waiting on her front porch, alone, scared. And Mindy would be home any minute. She pulled out her phone and dialed Carrie's number.

"Carrie, I'm so glad you're home," she said when her sister-in-law answered.

"Sadie?" Carrie asked.

"Yes, I need a favor. Can you go outside and have the Bailey kids come over to your house? I'll be right there."

"You're too late," Carrie said. "Mindy showed up just a couple minutes ago and flipped her lid to find the kids sitting on your porch."

"Oh, no," Sadie breathed.

"She came over here wanting to know if I knew where you were. She was mad as a hornet and said you'd promised to watch her kids for her. Is that true?"

"They were supposed to come over to my house after school—she couldn't get home in time and didn't want them home alone." Sadie felt horrible and couldn't help but put herself in Mindy's position. If her children were still small and all this had happened, she'd be irate too.

"Can you blame her?" Carrie asked with a determined lack of sympathy.

"It's been a very hard day," Sadie said. "I got . . . held up . . . with some things and—"

"It's been a hard day for all of us, Sadie," Carrie said, her words patronizing whether she intended them to be or not. "But the kids are safe now—Mindy took them home."

Safe—since Sadie had made them unsafe. "Okay," Sadie said, suddenly eager to get off the phone. Carrie had no idea how awful this day had been for her and Sadie wasn't about to explain it—but was a little sympathy too much to ask? Carrie knew that Sadie and Anne had been friends. Surely she could imagine this would be difficult. "I'll call her when I get back," Sadie said, more thinking out loud than anything else.

Hanging up without saying good-bye, Sadie started thinking of what she could whip up as an apology for Mindy. Baked goods were her best bet for mending fences.

A few minutes later, the vibration of the phone still in her hand caught her attention. She looked at the caller ID. It was from her house. She answered it, wondering who it would be.

"Hello?" she asked.

"Mom?"

"Breanna," she said in surprise. "What are you doing at the house?"

"Trina called me," Breanna said, referring to Jack and Carrie's youngest daughter. The cousins both attended Colorado State University in Fort Collins; Breanna was a senior, but Trina hadn't yet gotten enough credits to be officially called a sophomore. "She told me what happened," Breanna said. "She wondered if I could drive her home—she was really upset. What happened?"

"It's just horrible," Sadie said, anxious to get home. "But you missed your afternoon classes."

"Mom," Breanna said, "come on. Anne's dead! There's some freak on the loose and you're worried about my classes?"

"I'm still your mother," Sadie said weakly.

"Well, forget about that stuff for a minute—where have you been? I tried calling before I left school and you didn't answer here or on your cell. Then I get home and you're not here at all—I about had a heart attack! I thought something happened to you."

"I'm sorry to have worried you, and I'm sorry I didn't answer, I had my phone off."

"Your friend gets murdered and you turn off your phone?" Breanna asked, obviously unimpressed.

Sadie wasn't ready to try to explain that she suspected her fiancé, the man she'd told her kids would be their stepfather, had murdered Anne and she didn't want to take his calls. "It's been a trying day on many levels," Sadie said, wishing Breanna had arrived just twenty minutes earlier—then she could have covered for her with the Baileys.

"I'll bet. Are you coming home now?"

"Yeah," Sadie said, making a left-hand turn. "I'll be there in about two minutes."

"I'll start the fettuccine," Breanna said resolutely. "You need comfort food."

"That I do," Sadie said with a laugh, remembering all the times she'd made her daughter's favorite meal to help her through hard moments. No matter that fettuccine was Breanna's favorite dinner, not Sadie's; having her daughter come to her aid was a priceless commodity. "Did Trina go to Carrie's?" she asked.

"Yeah, we just got here. Trina's really upset about this, you know how emotional she gets. See you soon," Breanna said before hanging up.

Sadie pulled onto her street a few minutes later and couldn't take her eyes off the yellow tape surrounding Anne's house. It gave her the creeps, casting a pall over the entire circle. There was one police cruiser still in the driveway but Sadie couldn't see anyone else around. Mr. Henry wouldn't be home from work yet since he worked twelve-hour shifts. She had little doubt the Baileys' doors were locked and her stomach knotted up again at how she had failed her friend. Mindy was a chocolate lover—maybe Sadie had time to whip up some apology brownies.

"Oh, I'm glad you're here," Sadie said when she entered the house a minute later. She locked the door behind her, wanting very much to feel safe and secure in her cozy little home. She put the papers from the library on the kitchen counter.

Breanna looked up from the amassed Alfredo sauce ingredients next to the stove and smiled. Her long brown hair was darker, straighter, and thicker than Sadie's had ever been and Breanna had pulled it into a ponytail at the base of her neck. As usual, she didn't have any makeup on; she was a zoology major and didn't bother with much fanfare when it came to looks. It helped that she was a natural beauty, having inherited all the most beautiful features of her birth mother's Polynesian heritage.

"So tell me what happened," Breanna said as Sadie pulled a head of broccoli out of the fridge and started chopping. They never had fettuccine without broccoli.

Sadie took a breath and told her the whole story—sans Ron's part in it. She wasn't ready to put that information out there yet. She did, however, mentally commit to call Detective Cunningham as soon as she had a free minute. She couldn't keep what she knew to herself any longer—but that didn't mean Breanna should be the person to hear the details.

"So then I was late getting home and now Mindy's mad at me and I'm sick to my stomach over Trevor."

The big pot of water on the stove had come to a boil and Breanna put the dry noodles into the pot, pushing them down into the water as they softened while the Alfredo simmered on another burner. "Have you told Shawn?"

"Not yet—I better call him right now," Sadie said, thinking of her twenty-year-old baby boy. He was studying to be a professional sports trainer at the University of Michigan. Why he chose Michigan, Sadie would never know. They spoke on the phone once a week or so but he was pretty caught up in college life. She put the broccoli in the microwave and headed for the phone. He didn't answer so she left a message for him to call as soon as possible.

"Should I set the table?" she asked when she hung up the phone.

Within a few minutes, Breanna had finished the noodles and Alfredo, and Sadie had successfully sautéed the steamed broccoli in brown butter and topped it with grated Mizithra cheese. They had a nice meal, despite the fact that it wasn't yet five o'clock in the afternoon.

Sadie was grateful to have someone with her—especially Breanna. She'd always been solid, such a great support. Though she didn't know how she'd been so lucky, Sadie was eternally grateful that her kids didn't seem to suffer the bouts of rebellion and anger that she saw in so many other children of single mothers. *So many children, period*, she thought, amending her judgment. Jack and Carrie's girls had put them through the trenches many times and they had two parents who loved them. Sadie knew she was greatly blessed.

After dinner they did the dishes together and Breanna finally asked if Sadie had talked to Ron. Sadie paused, but she couldn't hold it back any longer and wasn't willing to lie about it. She took a breath and told Breanna everything she'd learned about Ron today—down to her flight from the restaurant.

"Are you going to turn him in?" Breanna asked, level-headed until the end. Through Sadie's explanation, she'd only made noises of surprise with an "oh my gosh" now and then.

"I'm going to tell the detective what happened. They'll take it from there." The knot in her stomach had returned and she blinked back the threatening tears.

"Wow," Breanna said as she closed the dishwasher door. She turned and looked sympathetically at her mom. "I'm so sorry. What a day you've had."

Sadie nodded. What a day indeed.

"So what's next?" Breanna asked.

Sadie lifted her eyebrows in a gesture of innocence. "What do you mean?"

Breanna rolled her eyes. "I'm sure you're not giving up now."

Sadie smiled. Breanna knew her so well it made trying to hide her plans a waste of time. "I need to figure out where Anne came from—I mean I know she lived in Boston." She paused, picturing for a moment a pregnant Anne opening her apartment door and smiling at Ron, the father of the child she was carrying. It brought bile to Sadie's throat and she pushed the image away. "I'd like to find her parents, friends—something."

"Aren't the cops already doing that stuff?"

"Probably," Sadie said with a shrug. "But I doubt very much they'll tell me anything, and I think I've already proven that I can get an awful lot accomplished by being sweet and naïve."

She flashed her daughter an innocent smile and batted her eyelashes. Breanna laughed. "Right now, however, I need to make some brownies for Mindy. I feel so bad about not following through."

"It's probably the first time in your whole life you've not done exactly what you said you'd do," Breanna said by way of justification. "And if you ask me, the circle relies on you too much already. If she had any idea what this day has been like for you then I'm sure she'd understand."

"I don't think I'm ready to tell her everything I've learned," Sadie said, moving to the drawer next to the stove and opening her little black book—a rather ordinary journal she'd used to record her favorite recipes over the years. Most people used recipe boxes, but Sadie liked something more portable. No recipe went into the little black book without having been tried three or four times so she knew it was worthy of the honor. She ran her finger down the nonalphabetical contents, hovering over Sadie's Better Brownies—a recipe she'd perfected several years ago. "Sometimes baked goods say it all." She paused. "Do you think brownies are the right thing for a death in the neighborhood?"

"Well, chocolate has calming properties," Breanna said.

"Oh, that's right, it does," she said, bending the book open to the right page, an easy thing to do since the journal had been so well used over the years. She began pulling ingredients out of the cupboard. Then she remembered the e-mail from

Riggs and Barker. She felt her determination, which had been slowing down, speed back up again.

"Will you do the brownies?" she asked Breanna as she crossed to the counter where she'd deposited the papers she'd brought in from the car. She found the e-mail and scanned it, reorienting herself with the information. Then she sat at the computer, did a Google search for Riggs and Barker, found the home page, and within seconds of the idea forming in her mind, she had the contact information for the Boston office. She copied the e-mail address for the human resources person, a woman by the name of Marianne Humphry, and pasted it into a new e-mail message.

"What are you doing?" Breanna asked from the kitchen, twenty feet away from the computer station. She was measuring out the salt.

"E-mailing the Boston office of Riggs and Barker," Sadie said as if it were obvious. "I wonder if they can give me any more information." She knew what she was doing wasn't exactly right, but she didn't know what else to do. It took her a few minutes to figure out the best lie to tell, though she preferred to think of it as investigative work.

Ms. Humphry,

I'm contacting you in regards to a mortgage I'm processing. Anne Lemmon is attempting to buy a home and claims she worked for your company a couple of years ago and was recently rehired. In light of the new federal bankruptcy laws, and because of the volatile market, we are attempting to determine whether her employment with your company is secure, where she worked before coming to your office, and under what conditions her employment with you was terminated. Any information you can give us would be helpful. The cosigner for the mortgage is one Ronald Bradley, who also works for your company. I need to verify his employment status as well. Thank you for your assistance.

"Mom!"

Sadie jumped and looked over her shoulder where Breanna was reading her message. "I just need a little information," she explained.

"By lying about her buying a house?" Breanna said. "Can't you get in trouble for that?"

Sadie shrugged, and then changed the Sadie Hoffmiller in her signature line to S. Hoffmiller. "I'm just covering my bases," she said. "I like to think that's why the information came to me in the first place—a kind of fated happenstance that will lead me to find justice for Anne and find Trevor before it's too late."

Breanna shook her head and returned to the kitchen. "You'd kill me if I ever did something like that. Remember the time you dragged me to the principal's office because you found out I'd spent some of the money I was supposed to donate to the fund-raiser on buying a pop?"

"That was different," Sadie said, hitting send. "You have to understand why the rules are made in the first place before you can break them."

"I'll keep that in mind the next time I'm tempted to *break the law*," Breanna said, shooting her mother a look that showed she wasn't impressed. "You're going to get in trouble," she added.

Sadie shrugged and let out a sigh as the message disappeared from her outbox. The sun was setting, and true to the sunsets of northern Colorado, the sky was lit up in a hundred shades of pink and orange, filling the house with colored light. It seemed strange that such beauty should be cast when a day such as this was coming to an end.

"So what if I do get in trouble?" she said. "Can it matter that much in the grand scheme of things? Anne was murdered, Trevor was kidnapped, Ron's been lying to me the whole time we've been together—what's a little mixed up e-mail in relation to all that?"

Homemade Alfredo Sauce

1 cup heavy cream*
1 cup butter
1 cup Parmesan cheese, shredded (Shawn likes more cheese)
Salt and pepper, to taste

Combine all ingredients in small saucepan (not Teflon-coated) and simmer on low until melted and mixed, stirring continually (about 20 minutes). Whisk until smooth before serving over pasta. Can be refrigerated and used again if reheated on low heat. (Remember to whisk again!)

Makes 4 servings.

*Half-and-half or evaporated milk can be used for some or all of cream to reduce fat but the consistency won't be as rich or as thick.

CHAPTER 17

Breanna didn't say anything but she was stirring the brownies at a contemplative speed. "You haven't even told the police about Ron. You're so dead set on getting this solved but you don't give the information to those who can do something about it."

Sadie hated that her daughter was right. She let out a breath. "Okay, I'll call Detective Cunningham," she said. "I'm just not sure what to tell him."

"The truth, for starters," Breanna said, glopping the dark brown batter into the 9x13 pan and obscuring the word *Hoffmiller* that had been etched into the glass; Sadie had taken a workshop at the high school with a friend last year and had put her name on all her glass dishes.

Sadie almost smiled at the role reversal between her daughter and herself, but it wasn't that funny. "This will sound horrible," she said, coming over to help scrape the remaining batter from the bowl. "But it seems like I should get something for giving them the information—doesn't it?"

"You should be rewarded for doing the right thing?" Breanna goaded her. "Wow, you've left all ethics in the dust today, Mom."

"Not like that," Sadie said. "But Detective Madsen seems determined to connect me to this—he even set me up specifically to get me in trouble. No one has called to tell me what they've found, and they only have one cop protecting Anne's house even though there could be some madman out there. And here I have this bombshell information that I technically shouldn't have anyway. Who's to say telling them won't get me in more trouble—assuming they even believe me. It just seems there ought to be some kind of benefit in my helping them, that's all."

"Maybe the benefit will be catching Anne's killer and finding Trevor."

Dang, Breanna was good at this. Sadie felt sufficiently guilty. "Okay," she sighed, taking the scraped-out bowl and putting it in the sink. "I'll call him."

Breanna nodded sharply, a satisfied smile on her face. "Good," she said. After sliding the brownies into the oven she washed her hands. "In the meantime, I think we ought to look for Anne on findpeople.com."

"What's that?"

"It's a web site that helps you find information about specific people. You enter whatever information you know and it helps track them down."

"But I know where Anne is," Sadie said, saddened to think of her neighbor in the morgue. Even though Sadie now doubted the friendship they'd had, she was still sad Anne was dead. She also couldn't help but think that if Anne had told her the truth, she'd still be alive today.

"Yeah, but you can find out other stuff like old addresses and police records. It's really amazing."

Sadie turned to look at her daughter. "You sound like you know this firsthand."

Breanna's cheeks went pink and she opened the freezer, taking her time to give an answer. "I may have used it," she said casually.

"May have?" Sadie repeated, laughing at her daughter's embarrassment.

Breanna took out the pineapple sherbet, a staple in their home, and put it on the counter. "Well, there's this . . . guy."

Sadie's eyebrows rose. Breanna wasn't one to pursue the opposite sex, at least not at this point in her life. She dated a little, but her real focus had always been her career. She'd take an afternoon with a Siberian lynx over most men any day of the week.

"You were looking for some guy online?" Sadie said, forgetting about the promised call to Detective Cunningham. "And you didn't tell me?"

Breanna's cheeks got brighter and she finally met her mom's eyes. "It's no big deal," she said.

"Who is he?" Sadie asked. "Why did you have to look for him online?"

Breanna sat down at the kitchen table with the sherbet and some bowls. "Calm down, Mother." She only called Sadie

"Mother" when she was trying to rein her in. "Remember that first internship I did at the San Francisco Zoo right after high school?"

"Of course," Sadie said, nodding. It had been a great way for Breanna to get hands-on experience before choosing her major. She'd roomed with five other girls doing the same thing. Sadie had been scared to death letting her baby girl go so far away at the age of 18, but it was impossible to say no. Since then, Breanna had spent every summer at a different zoo around the country. After she graduated, she hoped to return to the Brevard Zoo in Melbourne, Florida—it had been her favorite. She was especially fond of big cats such as tigers, jaguars, and lions.

"Well, there was this guy that worked with the interns, his name was Liam. We didn't date or anything." Her cheeks refused to return to their normal hue.

"You must have done something for you to go to all the trouble to find him again."

"Mom!" Breanna said.

Sadie laughed but didn't say anything, inviting Breanna to continue by staying silent. "We got along really well—but he was twenty-four and I was only eighteen. We were just friends, I swear, but he gave me his number when I finished the program. When I got to CSU I started seeing Brandon and by the time things were sufficiently fizzled with him, I'd lost Liam's number."

"But he was still in your heart," Sadie said with a romantic sigh, playing it up for all she was worth. Who knew when she'd get this chance again.

"Mo-om," Breanna said, shaking her head and pushing the bowl of sherbet she'd dished up across the table. "He was especially fascinated with bats."

Sadie grimaced. "Bats?" she repeated, automatically suspicious. What kind of man had a fascination with bats?

"I know that probably sounds creepy, but it wasn't. He just loved bats. They are quite a unique animal, ya know. A mammal that flies with limited vision and has such a wide variety of species. Their echolocation is incredible, and did you know you can find bats anywhere, in every region, because they are so adaptable? In fact—"

"Okay, I'm convinced they're amazing. So what do bats have to do with your romantic interest in this guy? Does he have his own Batmobile?"

"Who says I'm interested in him romantically?"

"Uh, your red cheeks, the fact you never mentioned him before, and of course, your assurance he's *not* a romantic interest. But let's get back to the story."

Breanna paused, but she had a light in her eyes that well communicated how eager she was to discuss this. "So in my Climate Ecology class we have to do a research paper and I chose to do it on the ecological qualities of the small tube-nosed bat in relation to the quantitative research in woodland demographics and the relation to Aves anatomy."

"Huh?"

"Basically, in what ways woodland bats are like birds."

"Oh, I can tell you that," Sadie said, taking a bite of her sherbet and swallowing quickly. "They fly."

"Ha-ha," Breanna replied dryly. "They also fly in flight patterns, they have similar diets, and certain roosting and hunting similarities suggest that bats might be the missing link in bird evolution rather than the more commonly held theory that they evolved *from* birds."

"Fascinating," Sadie said, simulating a yawn. Breanna scowled and smacked her spoon on Sadie's bowl. Sadie put another spoonful of sherbet on her tongue and let it melt.

"So I thought I'd track down Liam to see if he was aware of any lesser-known research on the subject."

"And you found him?"

Breanna smiled wide and full, showing her beautiful teeth, the result of four years in braces. "I did."

"And did he have this amazing and unique knowledge of resources you were hoping for?"

"He did."

"And when do I get to meet him?" Sadie was no fool. There was something special about this guy.

"Maybe at Thanksgiving. If you're good."

Sadie laughed. "I'll be good," she said, making an X over her heart. "I promise. Where does he live now?"

Breanna scowled. "Portland. He's part of the Oregon Zoo bat exhibit," she said. "And before you ask, no, I haven't seen him yet. It's only been a few months and it's not like we're dating or anything, we just e-mail and talk on the phone a lot."

Sadie smiled, loving the sparkle in her daughter's eyes.

"Anyway," Breanna said, "I looked him up on findpeople.com, and there he was in Portland. I know I could have just looked him up in the phone book or something, but for $50 you can get a whole background check, and, well"—she shrugged her shoulders as if still trying to justify herself—"we had kinda, ya know, hit it off and so just in case he had a past I thought I ought to find out as much about him as I could." She scraped the bowl with the edge of her spoon, capturing the last of the sherbet, then ate the final bite, smiling with the spoon still halfway in her mouth. "You can't be too careful these days."

"And no red flags?"

"Nope," Breanna said. "I mean, other than the drug charges he's an upstanding citizen in every way."

Sadie raised her eyebrows.

"Kidding," Breanna quickly added. "But I got his current info as well as former addresses, school history, and criminal record."

"And he's not an ex-con?" Sadie wasn't always thrilled with her daughter's teasing nature.

"No," Breanna said. "But he was once part-owner of a mall kiosk that sold "Save the Wildlife" T-shirts—he had to get a business license. The point is that if I found Liam, I bet we could find Anne."

"Well, a search like that sounds perfect," Sadie said, finishing off her sherbet as well. Breanna seemed to have forgotten all about calling Detective Cunningham, which was fine by Sadie now that she had a lead on getting more information about Anne. "If I could find a family member, maybe I could call and talk to someone. Or an old landlord."

"Or a probation officer," Breanna added as they put their bowls in the sink and headed to the computer again.

"Funny," Sadie said as Breanna slid into the office chair. Sadie grabbed a chair from the kitchen and returned to find Breanna already logged into her Yahoo e-mail account and clicking through the web site that promised to put the World Wide Web at your fingertips.

It took Breanna only a minute to get logged on to findpeople.com. She entered Anne's name and they waited almost a minute before the site brought up a screen full of Anne Lemmons, and Annette Lemmons, and Andreas, Antonias, and Annabelles. There were 167 names. To the side of some of the names were an age, and on the left were lists of possible relatives.

"How do we know which one is the Anne we want?" Sadie asked, feeling a little overwhelmed.

"Well, we know she's in her mid-twenties, so this one that says she's 67 isn't someone we need to worry about."

"Okay, so that rules out half the list," Sadie said, leaning against the back of her chair.

"Hang on," Breanna said. She started clicking in little boxes. "I can eliminate a lot of them." She kept clicking and after a few minutes the possibilities were down to sixty-four. Still daunting.

"Was Anne her full name?" Breanna asked. "Or was it short for something else?"

"I don't know," Sadie said. "But we know she came from Boston."

"Right." She started clicking again and narrowed the list down to twenty-one names. Sixteen of them had no cities listed as addresses, two had addresses in Massachusetts, and three showed Boston. Breanna clicked on "Advance Search" and a pop-up window appeared full of empty fields for additional information.

"So you don't know anything else? What city she was born in? The street she lived on in Boston? Date of birth? If we have a little more it will narrow the search for us. Of course we'll still have to pay for the final report, but we can be more sure it's the Anne Lemmon we're looking for."

"No," Sadie said. "But," she paused, "she was turning twenty-six in January."

"Do you know the exact day?"

"No," Sadie answered. "Let's try putting in just the year of her birth."

A pop-up appeared with the warning that they needed more information to get the correct record.

"So you knew Liam's birthday?" Sadie asked. "How else did you find him?"

"His full name is William Harrison Martin the third—all us interns used to tease him about that. And his birthday happens to be on July 4, so he brought cupcakes for those of us working that day. Apparently there are a lot of Anne-related Lemmons, though."

Sadie stared at the screen, thinking about the calendar on the fridge at Anne's house. She got up casually and went to the front window, only then remembering she couldn't see Anne's house from there. Stupid tree. Heavy clouds had moved in during the last hour, making the day seem more spent than it really was; it was barely 5:30.

"Huh, well I still need to call Detective Cunningham," Sadie said, feeling defeated as she eyed the clouds and wondered if they were holding rain or snow. She'd spent this whole day trying to figure things out, and all she'd succeeded in doing was uncovering Ron and Anne's relationship and making Detective Madsen extremely mad. "Maybe he's figured out her date of birth."

"I don't think he'll tell you, Mom, *he's* the detective."

"And I'm Anne's friend," Sadie said, turning from the window. She smoothed a lock of hair off her face, only then remembering what a mess she was. Her hair was sticky and for a moment it confused her, but then she caught sight of the jars of applesauce on the counter. She was always a sticky mess when she put up fruit. She attempted to reshape her hair and hoped it didn't look too awful. "You know, they won't even tell me what's going on. Outside of harassing me, they give no consideration at all to my stake in this. Trevor's still gone and they won't tell me anything."

"It's not their job to tell you anything," Breanna said, turning in her chair to face her mom. "I know you cared about Anne—though if I were you, I'd be a heck of a lot more upset about what she was doing with Ron—but the police can't just hand information out left and right. They don't *know* you."

Sadie snorted. "They won't even try to get to know me. If they did they would know that I am only trying to help, not to mention that all the nonprofit work I do ought to speak for itself."

Breanna started laughing and gave her mom an *are-you-kidding?* look. "Mo-om," she said as she shook her head. "The world doesn't work that way. They are trying to solve a murder."

So am I, she thought to herself, but she knew better than to say it out loud. Breanna seemed primed to lecture her and Sadie braced herself for it, just as a little bell dinged. Breanna quickly turned around and began typing into a pop-up window that had appeared on the screen. Sadie moved close enough to look over her shoulder.

"Liam?" she asked after reading the user name of Batman-Brit.

"Yeah," Breanna said with a nod, suddenly distracted. She typed some more and then looked up at her mom. "A little privacy?" she asked. "And don't you need to call Detective Cunningham?"

Sadie smiled and took her cell phone and Detective Cunningham's business card to the back bedroom. Once the door was closed, however, her smile fell. She did not relish this at all, but she picked up the card and punched the number into her phone.

As she listened to the phone ring, she realized she still didn't know what she was going to say or just how much she was going to tell him. By the time the phone had rung three times everything she'd done seemed stupid since she really hadn't figured anything out. All she had were more questions. After the fourth ring, the call went to voice mail. She was relieved.

"Detective Cunningham, this is Sadie Hoffmiller. Could you please call me at your earliest convenience? I have some information I need to tell you." She hung up the phone and stared at it. "So not fair," she said, throwing the phone on the bed. She was working as hard as he was.

When she returned to the kitchen Breanna was still instant messaging on the computer and the rich chocolate scent of baking brownies was beginning to fill the room. Sadie took a deep breath of the heavenly aroma, rolled up her sleeves, and set about doing the dishes. After that, she retrieved her phone and went through the messages—two from Breanna and half a dozen from Ron—she deleted them without listening. She stared out her window, the color of the setting sun had turned to a more appropriate shade of gray and the already darkened sky seemed to isolate her from the world on the other side of the glass. She thought about everything she'd learned today. She officially admitted to herself that she'd been wrong; Trevor wasn't with Ron. At least not anymore.

The cold outside the window was seeping inside, surrounding her, making her joints ache and her head throb. *Trevor's alive,* she told herself. She refused to believe he was dead—it was impossible. Ron must have taken him somewhere, but where? Trevor was two years old, he couldn't be left alone. But who would Ron have asked to take his son? One of his other kids? It seemed unlikely he'd do that when he'd been working so hard to keep his secret a secret.

It was a hopeless circle of questions without answers and she turned away from the window as the police car that had been stationed at Anne's house left the cul-de-sac. It would be dark soon, and Trevor was still out there somewhere. It was going to be a long night.

The timer on the stove startled her and she removed the brownies from the oven while Breanna continued typing. Sadie folded some laundry, and paid a couple bills that had come in the mail. Finally, at nearly 6:15—the brownies sufficiently cooled enough for travel—and Breanna still online, she told Breanna she was taking the brownies to Mindy and she'd be back soon. She pulled her green oven mitts over her hands, then had to take them off in order to put on her jacket. A couple minutes later, she let the screen door shut behind her, took a deep breath of the crisp air, and began her journey down the front steps. Amid everything else, Sadie absolutely hated knowing Mindy was unhappy with her, and with so much heartbreak and despair, she very much wanted to repair things if she could. There was so much she couldn't fix that she was glad there was something she could make better.

Sadie's Better Brownies

3 cups semi-sweet chocolate chips (using ½ mint chocolate chips is delicious!)

1 cup (2 sticks) unsalted butter

5 large eggs

2 cups granulated sugar

1 tablespoon vanilla

1 ½ cups all-purpose flour

1 teaspoon baking powder

¼ teaspoon salt

1 cup walnuts (pecans are better than walnuts though Shawn hates both)

Preheat oven to 350 degrees and melt chocolate chips and butter in a double boiler. (Or melt in microwave in 30-second increments, stirring between each heating until smooth.) Remove from heat and set aside to cool slightly. In a separate bowl, mix together the eggs and sugar. Mix in the melted chocolate and the vanilla. Add the flour, baking powder, and salt to the chocolate mixture and mix well. Pour into a 9 x 13 greased pan and bake for about 35 to 45 minutes, or until a toothpick comes out with just a few moist crumbs. Remove from oven and let cool before cutting into 2-inch squares.

Makes 24 brownies.

CHAPTER 18

Sadie headed down the walk, glancing into the windows of Jack and Carrie's home as she approached. It was a ranch-style home, almost a perfect square, with a carport on the side furthest from Sadie's house. Jack had talked for years about buying some land and building their dream house, but Carrie had wanted the kids to finish their schooling in the same district, then she'd wanted them to come back to a home they'd always known, so the dream was put off over and over again. But they had a nice house, and Jack had already paid it off. The white aluminum siding seemed to glow in the darkening evening, the windows shining just a little bit brighter behind the closed blinds.

Sadie really was glad Trina had come home tonight. Otherwise, despite Carrie's earlier lack of sympathy, Sadie would still have been trying to find a way to comfort her. It was nice to have one less person to worry about—though Trina wasn't necessarily gifted in thinking about other people. Carrie had held on tighter to her youngest child, Trina, than to any of the other girls. If Jack hadn't forced her to go to college, Trina would probably have lived at home forever.

Sadie was crossing Jack and Carrie's driveway when she heard the squeal of tires around the corner. Her first thought was that it was Ron tracking her down, demanding they talk about this again. She immediately planned her self-defense—she'd throw the still-hot pan of brownies in his face and run for home, screaming if necessary. She looked over her shoulder long enough to see a truck, not a black Jetta. It was coming right for her though and she turned toward Jack and Carrie's porch, her heart hammering as she tried to get out of the way.

She was halfway up the front steps when the truck came to a screeching halt in the driveway. It was all she could do to hold on to the brownies while she ran. The driver's door opened and she imagined herself being gunned down. She was a risk to Ron, since she'd told him she knew everything. Would he try to silence her? For good? Would Breanna be able to find a decent picture for the obituary?

"Sadie?" said a voice she knew all too well. She stopped and turned, letting out a breath as she recognized Jack's truck that had been only a blur of headlights a moment before. She would not die today. Thank goodness.

"Jack," she said with relief. It had been more than a month since she'd seen him last and she wanted so much for him to give her a little-brother hug and assure her that everything was fine. He'd been there to do just that during every other trial of her life, every other loss. But things were different now. She could feel it. Jack looked past her to the front door, and then back at her. She sensed he was eager to get inside.

"I heard about Anne," he said, his voice low. He cleared his throat and seemed to be uncomfortable. Then she wondered if he knew Anne too. He'd been to the Boston office many times, though not as often as Ron. Her stomach sank lower. Had Jack known all along? Had he been hiding this from her as well? Were all the people she believed to be above reproach liars? Really good liars? Suddenly a hundred questions flooded her head. Jack continued, "I . . . uh, came to see how Carrie's doing with all this."

Sadie shrugged since she really didn't know. She held out the pan of brownies. "I was bringing this over," she said on impulse, wondering if she could weasel a few answers from him. "It's hot so I'll just take it into the kitchen." She had to find the right way of asking him about Anne and Ron. And she was curious to see him and Carrie together. That he was here for her was a good sign, Sadie thought. Maybe all was not lost between them. And then she wondered if Carrie also knew about Anne and Ron. Was Sadie the *only* person who didn't know the truth?

"Oh, um, I'll just take it in for you," he said, but when he grabbed the pan it was too hot and Sadie hurried to get it back from him.

"Just let me bring it in," she said with irritation. Did everyone have to be so difficult today?

But Jack had already shoved his hands into his sleeves and reached them out to take the pan—just as she had when she removed the lemon tart from Anne's oven that morning. "You're sweet to think of us," he said, taking the pan from her while she tried to think of another protest. Preferably one that would work.

He quickly walked past her and kicked the door a few times, as if knocking with his loafers. Trina opened the door. Her blonde hair was down, but looked unkempt, and her eyes were red as she ushered him into the house.

"Thanks, Aunt Sadie," she said, trying to manage a smile. Then as fast as she'd opened the door, she shut it again.

Always a dramatic one, Sadie thought after standing there a moment. She didn't remember if Trina had even met Anne, but she reminded herself that sometimes young people were deeply affected by such tragedies. Slowly descending the steps, she shook her head at having wasted the pan of brownies. They hadn't garnered her any answers at all and now she had nothing to take to the Baileys.

She turned toward home, trying to decide whether to make another batch or put the apology off until tomorrow, when a police cruiser drove into the circle. It slowed as it passed Anne's house, shining a spotlight across the property. Sadie headed toward home, slow enough to listen to the car, but not making herself too obvious by looking over her shoulder. Less than thirty seconds after the car entered the circle, the engine revved up again and the car drove right back out. It seemed an inadequate inspection to her and she wondered if all the talk she'd heard about budget cuts affecting the Garrison police department was something she should pay more attention to.

When she reached the top of her porch steps, she looked back at Anne's house and wondered if they were going to keep driving by all night.

"Is Mindy okay?" Breanna asked, still at the computer.

"I ended up giving them to Jack," Sadie grumbled, shaking her head at the waste of time and effort.

"Uncle Jack's home?" Breanna turned in her chair and looked at Sadie. "That's good."

Sadie reflected on the encounter and shrugged—there simply was no accounting for the way people acted when something like this happened. Jack finally came home, overwhelmed with concern for his estranged wife, and Trina acted as if the perpetrator would dive through their front door if she opened it more than a foot. "Yeah," Sadie answered. "It's good. But now I don't have anything for Mindy."

Breanna scrunched up her face as if in deep thought. "Why don't you take the leftover fettuccini?" she suggested. "We made plenty and you'd be right in time for dinner."

Sadie considered that and looked in the fridge to assess just how much leftover fettuccini she had. It wasn't enough for a family of seven, that was for sure. But maybe she could make some more. It took only a minute to realize she had enough cream and Parmesan for the Alfredo sauce. And she always had plenty of pasta on hand since it was an easy meal to whip up, either for herself or for her and . . . Ron if he happened to stop by after work. *Ron,* she thought, allowing herself a moment to fantasize about the man she had thought he was, the life she had thought they would have together. Then she shoved those thoughts away and reprimanded herself sharply. It was masochistic for her to dwell on what could have been. Instead, she thought about the edible apology she needed to offer Mindy. If she worked fast it would take only fifteen minutes to make another batch of noodles and sauce, compared to forty if she made a new pan of brownies. It wouldn't be chocolate, but cheese and cream was the next best thing.

"You're a genius," she said, smiling over her shoulder at her daughter. But Breanna was back to her typing.

It ended up taking twenty-one minutes to cook it all up, but when she finished, she had a large steaming pot of pasta tossed with enough Alfredo sauce to clog even the hardiest of arteries. Not exactly baked goods but a sackcloth-and-ashes offering all the same.

"I'll be back soon," she said for the second time in thirty minutes.

"Have fun," Breanna said in a distracted voice. Behind the box containing Breanna's instant messaging conversation was the home page of findpeople.com.

If only Sadie could get Anne's birth date. As she let herself out she glanced at the calendar hanging on the wall near the phone but tried to talk herself out of the idea forming in her head.

This time she hardly glanced at Jack and Carrie's house. When she reached the Baileys' house she took a deep breath and rang the doorbell.

Gina, the fourteen-year-old Bailey, answered the door. "Hi, Mrs. Hoffmiller," she said with an uncomfortable smile that assured Sadie she had been the topic of some less than friendly conversations.

Sadie forced a smile. "Is your mom here?"

Mindy Bailey came around the corner just then, her face drawn and her eyes narrowed. "Gina, go finish your homework," she said. Sadie thought it might be the shortest sentence she had ever heard the other woman utter.

Gina did as she was told but Sadie doubted very much that she had gone far enough that she wouldn't hear the exchange. Sadie swallowed her pride and dropped the smile in order to look properly penitent.

"I'm so sorry, Mindy," she said. "I know that's no excuse, but I feel just horrible about what happened."

"My children were left alone, Sadie, alone with a psycho on the loose! Do you have any idea what it felt like when I realized they'd been sitting on your porch in broad daylight for fifteen minutes? They may as well have had bull's-eyes on their backs! To think that I . . ." She went on for a full two minutes, with Sadie nodding and apologizing each time Mindy stopped for breath. Sadie tried really hard to shed a tear or two, but her annoyance was too great. Yes, she'd let her friend down, but it hadn't been on purpose and the kids had been fine. She was sorely tempted to tell Mindy that Ron had no reason to hurt her children, but she kept that to herself and looked at the ground so as to avoid Mindy's eyes.

"I've always trusted you, Sadie," Mindy continued. "I always thought you were the type of woman that—"

Sadie couldn't take it anymore. She lifted her chin. "I *am* that type of woman, Mindy. And I have always helped you in any way that I can. I am so very sorry for what happened today and I don't blame you for being angry—but it wasn't on purpose and if I could change things I would."

"Oh, well, that's easy to say now, isn't it? And since they weren't your kids I'm sure you had a hundred more important things to do than—"

"Ron was at Anne's last night," Sadie cut in. Mindy stopped in the middle of a word and blinked. "Did you know that?"

"Um, no," Mindy said and Sadie could see she was drawing the same conclusion Sadie had.

"Yeah, I didn't either until he told me. And I've spent the whole day trying to make sense of it. I met him at a restaurant to talk about things—it didn't go very well. That's why I was late."

"I . . . I don't know what to say."

That was certainly a first for Mindy Bailey. Sadie just nodded. "I am really sorry though," she said, handing over the pot. "I made some dinner for your family; I figured you could use it tonight."

Mindy took the pot and nodded. "Thank you," she said softly, surprising Sadie with how fast her mood had changed. Amazing what a little gossip could get a person sometimes.

"You're welcome," Sadie said. She managed a small smile and turned around. She was at the end of the walk when she heard Mindy call her name. Mindy met her halfway down the sidewalk, no pot in her hands, and no shoes on her feet.

"I didn't see him there last night," Mindy said in a whisper. "But," she paused and took a breath, wrapping her arms around herself. Sadie steeled herself for what she feared was coming. "A few months ago Gina had the flu and I was up with her really late. We finally crashed on the couch and sometime during the night a set of headlights passed in front of the window. It woke Gina up and I went to get her some water. When I came back into the living room I decided to shut the blinds, but I noticed a black car parked in front of Anne's house."

"Ron's Jetta?" Sadie asked.

"I'm not sure," Mindy said. "But that's what I thought that night. I told Steve and asked if he thought I should tell you but he didn't think it was a good idea—I mean, I didn't even know for sure it was a Jetta, let alone that it belonged to Ron. It's just that Ron's is the only black car that's in the circle regularly."

Sadie nodded and looked at her shoes. He'd been there before. It was further evidence that the affair had been ongoing. The one man she'd dared consider spending the rest of her life with. How could she be so stupid?

"Thank you for telling me," Sadie said, putting a reassuring hand on Mindy's arm. Mindy offered an apologetic smile. "It's important that I know this."

"Do you think he killed Anne?" Mindy whispered, leaning in as if afraid of being overheard.

"I don't know," Sadie said. "The Ron I knew and loved never would have, but I've been learning today that there is very little I really know about him. Thanks again for telling me."

Mindy nodded and started toward home again. When she was halfway to her own house, the police cruiser entered the circle again. This time the car pulled up alongside Sadie.

"Can we help you, ma'am?" the officer asked after rolling down the passenger window. "This is the second time we've seen you out here."

"I'm Sadie Hoffmiller," she said, pointing to her house while watching to see if her name was familiar to the officer. She wondered if the police were talking about her, if she was really a suspect in anyone but Detective Madsen's mind. He didn't react with anything other than an intense stare. "I live on the corner and I've been taking things to my neighbors." As an afterthought she added, "To make sure everyone's all right."

"We'd appreciate it if you would return home," he said, smiling to belay any offense in what he'd said. "We've got this circle under surveillance and would certainly hate to have anything happen to you."

"Sure thing," she said with a nod, just now realizing the risk she was taking being outside at all. It was full dark and Ron was still out there somewhere. The officer thanked her and continued on his inspection as she continued toward her house. But when he left the cul-de-sac, Sadie stopped underneath the black walnut tree. With everything that had happened that day, with all she'd learned, it just didn't sit well with her to go home, lock her door, and twiddle her thumbs.

After a few moments of thought, she casually crossed the street. When she reached the other side, she stopped and looked around again. There were no unfamiliar cars parked anywhere in the circle and a quick look over her shoulder showed her there were no cars in the field either. The Bailey and Henry houses were both lit up but their blinds were drawn as if that would offer them some protection from the unknown attacker they all feared. Jack and Carrie's house was mostly blocked by the blasted tree, but she didn't think anyone could see her.

The area behind where she stood was filled with weeds and wild trees, all dead and skeletal with the onset of winter. She scanned the area carefully, then as casually as possible, she walked to a particularly thick tangle of branches and ducked beneath its cover. Her knees, already feeling picked on for her under-the-bed adventure, groaned as she squatted there—waiting, watching the cul-de-sac. She tried not to think about spiders and mice, but each time the leaves rustled she bit her lip a little harder.

Jack's truck left a few minutes into her stakeout. But by her watch it was almost exactly ten minutes before the police cruiser entered the cul-de-sac again. It drove slowly, and when it had followed the loop around to Anne's house, it stopped and shone its spotlight into the windows and along the front of the house. After less than a minute, the spotlight went off and the car left the cul-de-sac as smoothly as it had entered. Sadie waited only long enough for the taillights to disappear before she hurried out of her hiding place, looked around to be sure all the blinds in the neighborhood were still pulled tight, and then hurried up the front steps of Anne's house.

CHAPTER 19

Sadie knew the back door would give her better cover, but she couldn't make herself walk that close to the field where Anne's body had been found. It was dark back there. She wondered if the police had figured out she'd given them the wrong key yet. Certainly Detective Madsen would have read her the riot act if he'd discovered her deception. She hadn't had any idea she'd be doing this when she'd switched keys—but she was glad she'd thought ahead.

Putting the key in the lock, turning it, pushing the door open and then pushing it closed took her less than ten seconds. Once inside, she took a deep breath and caught herself before she leaned against the closed door. She looked around the darkened house; its eerie emptiness gave her the creeps. She felt the familiar anxiety of being where she knew she shouldn't be. *But I'm not hurting anything,* she told herself, clasping her hands behind her back as Detective Cunningham had told her to do earlier.

I just need to check the calendar—that's all. Still, her mouth was dry and she wanted to get out of there as quickly as possible. She pushed away her trepidation, ignored the strange shadows in the corners, and headed into the kitchen. The calendar was on the fridge, just as it had been that morning. She began thumbing through the months, heading for January to find Anne's birthday and touching only the very edges of the thick paper. October, November, December—then nothing. A sliver of light shone in from the streetlamp outside, barely enough for her to read by.

"What?" she said quietly, scrunching her eyebrows together. And then she realized that like most calendars, this one ended in December.

Okay, she said to herself, *I'll look at last January.* She had to take the calendar off the fridge in order to thumb backwards. She reached January and clenched her teeth—it was completely blank. She moved forward one month at a time. Everything was blank until March—the month Anne had moved in. She hadn't brought the calendar with her, she'd bought it when she moved in.

"Doggone it," Sadie muttered. She put the calendar back on the fridge and was heading for the front door, dejected, when the bookshelf near the fireplace caught her eye. Remembering the book Anne had checked out and then paid for before it was overdue, Sadie stepped toward the shelves. There was something about that title that had been familiar to her, but she wasn't sure what it was. She wondered if she had seen it at Anne's house sometime. Or maybe she was just being fanciful to think it was somehow important. It was a romance novel for heaven's sake.

As her eyes adjusted to the darkness it was easier for her to read the titles if she squinted enough. She had scanned three of the four shelves when she saw it: *My Father's Eyes.*

Bingo!

She pulled the book from its shelf. On the back it still had the sticker for the Garrison City Library. Anne *had* kept it. But why? It looked like an ordinary paperback novel. What made this one any different from the other books Anne had checked out? And then she remembered why the title had struck a chord. Just a month or so after Anne had moved in, the two of them had gone for a walk and Anne had asked Sadie how to dry out a book.

"What kind of book?" Sadie had asked.

"Just a paperback," Anne had said. "I dropped it in the tub last night—I guess that's what I get for reading in the bath." When they returned from the walk, Sadie had gone to Anne's and inspected the book. It was an older book, shelf-worn and still damp, with a dramatic cover Sadie hadn't looked at too closely. Some of the wrinkled pages had already stuck together. She'd recommended that Anne lay it outside in the sun, going out every few minutes to turn the pages, then she should press it between other books to help flatten it once it was dried out.

"It won't ever be as good as new," Sadie had said. "But it might be legible. Then again, for a little paperback like this it's probably worth the six dollars to buy a new one."

"It's been out of print for awhile," Anne had said. "I bet it's hard to find, but it's a great book."

"Oh, well, if the drying doesn't work, you can always check the library—they have a very extensive inventory for such a small town and can do special orders from Fort Collins if you want to pay a couple dollars for interlibrary loan."

Sadie had never seen the bathtub-book again, and they hadn't talked about it. But it had been important to Anne. Sadie tried to read the description printed on the back, but gave up after just a few seconds. Without her reading glasses the small type was impossible, especially in the dark. She'd have to take it home, secretly glad that her breaking and entering hadn't been for nothing.

She headed back toward the door. Her hand was on the doorknob when she thought about all the notes she wrote on her own calendar at home. Phone numbers, appointments, family birthdays. She turned and looked into the darkened kitchen. Maybe Anne did the same thing.

She knew she couldn't simply sit down and go through it right now. But what if she took it home and looked at it? She could bring it back as soon as she finished—and she might find something that would be important. *I'd be removing it from a crime scene*, she told herself. But if the police hadn't taken it, then they must not have wanted it. Besides, she was already stealing the book. What was one more item? After only a few more moments of hesitation she hurried toward the kitchen. She was just steps away from the fridge when a band of light crossed the floor in front of her.

Sadie froze and she snapped her head up to see the source of the light. The corner of the doorway prevented her from being able to see the windows or the sliding glass door at the back of the house. The light waved past again and she flattened herself against the wall, keeping herself out of range of what she realized must be a flashlight. Were the police looking for her? Did they know she was here? The light disappeared and for a moment she thought she'd escaped, then she heard a key in the lock.

CHAPTER 20

No! She screamed in her head for the second time that day, clenching her eyes closed. *Not again!* She opened her eyes to find herself staring down the hallway, straight into Anne's bedroom. Not knowing for sure if she'd been seen or not, she headed for the first hiding place she could think of.

By the time the back door slid open, she was hiding under her second bed of the day—and the last three decades. Impossible.

Luckily Anne's bed was not only higher off the ground, but since it had also been pushed against the wall on one side, Sadie felt much more secure. She tried to avoid the area where the filing cabinet had been, not wanting to interfere with the indentation, and scooted as far away from the edges of the bed as possible, glad that Anne didn't keep as much stuff under the bed as Ron did. In fact, other than a few socks, some candy wrappers, and a toy car, it was uninhabited. And the dust wasn't nearly as thick—something her sinuses thanked her for. But she pulled the sweatshirt to her nose just in case—not impressed with all the tricks she'd learned about hiding under beds.

The footsteps were nearly silent. Unlike Ron in his own home that afternoon, this person was being cautious, careful, taking his or her time. She wondered who it was. Detective Madsen? Did he know she was here? Or maybe it was Ron coming back for something. Whoever it was had a key; she had thought she was the only one with a spare. Who else would Anne have trusted with a key to her house?

She'd barely finished the thought before two shoes appeared at the end of the bed, in front of the small closet. Men's shoes. Black leather. The door to the closet opened, creaking on its hinges, and then stopped as if the intruder—the other intruder beside herself—was waiting to make sure nothing answered to the noise. After a second, the door creaked opened even further. The sound caused Sadie to shiver. She knew better than to hold her breath this time and focused on keeping her breathing even in hopes of keeping her anxiety at bay. She hated hide-and-seek! How come she kept being forced to play?

A voice in her head reminded her that if she would mind her own business she wouldn't be in this situation. *Too late.* This *was* her business, and besides, now was not the time to reflect on her own stupidity.

She heard the shuffling of boxes, the movement of hangers on the rod, and wondered what the intruder was after, grateful it wasn't her. Several boxes tumbled to the ground, and the intruder cursed. It was a man's voice, though too much of a whisper for her to determine if it was Ron or not. One by one the boxes were picked up, but just as the last one was moved out of sight, another pile crashed to the floor, and this time the flashlight fell with it. It spun around until it was facing her, staring at her—ratting her out.

Sadie held her breath, staring at the eye of light that was giving her away. She backed closer to the wall and squinted against the bright light. A hand, a man's hand with the cuff of a blue dress shirt showing at the wrist, reached down and grabbed the flashlight, a glint of gold flickering quickly in the light. A ring? She hadn't seen enough to tell for sure, but if it was a ring then this man wasn't Ron.

She wished she could have been able to tell for sure if it had been a wedding ring—but what other kind of ring did a man wear? Could she have been mistaken and it was a watch? She began to breathe again once the spotlight was off her face, and she tried to remember everything she knew about whoever was in the room with her—a ring or a watch, black leather shoes, a blue dress shirt, and she knew he was a man.

The boxes continued to disappear from view. She could make out that one was an old shoe box, another was a used priority box from the post office—she wished she could read the address it had been sent from. Another box, the biggest one she could see, had once contained a waffle maker. She shook her head. Why had Anne kept that—or any of the boxes? Being a pack rat was completely at odds with being a good homemaker.

She watched as the waffle box was lifted up, but instead of it being put in the closet with the others, she heard a different sound. Like the box being shaken. And there was definitely something inside. The bed squeaked as the intruder sat down. Because of the box springs, she didn't lose any space this time. She could hear the box being opened, and then she assumed it was turned upside down because several photographs and papers fell to the ground. *Anne kept pictures in a waffle box?*

Two hands appeared, quickly gathering up the pictures—what Sadie wouldn't do to have them. But she knew what she wouldn't do—anything. She was terrified of being caught by this new threat. She kept perfectly still and hoped that the pictures were what he was looking for so he would leave. She thought she saw a wedding ring again on one of the hands gathering the photos, but with so little light it was impossible to be certain.

Apparently the items in the box were exactly what the intruder wanted. He quickly replaced the box in the closet and, much faster than he had entered the room, he hurried into the hallway where he stopped. She watched the light from the police spotlight scan the room and marveled that the cops didn't know there was not one, but two people in the house. They definitely should have done a better job at surveillance. A few minutes passed and she heard footsteps again, heading toward the back door. The sliding glass door opened, then shut, and he was gone. She'd dodged a bullet twice today.

After waiting a few minutes to be sure she was alone, she pulled herself out from under the bed. The intruder had left the closet open and she realized that if she could find a way to tell Cunningham she knew someone had been here, he might be able to lift fingerprints from the door handle. She looked into the darkened closet, trying to find that priority mail box in hopes of reading the return address. But without a flashlight of her own she couldn't tell which box was which and she didn't want to get her own fingerprints on anything the intruder might have touched.

Maybe I can come back tomorrow, she thought as she straightened the bedspread that had been ruffled when the other intruder had sat down—then stopped short. *Am I insane? Planning to come back again?* She hurried toward the front door, the book held tight against her chest, anxious to get out of there before someone else stopped in—then she remembered the calendar.

Pausing at the door for the second time, she considered her options. If she found a way to tell Cunningham someone had been here and the police then found that the calendar was gone, they'd assume the intruder took it. But it would be in her possession, which could make things very bad for her. But to be this close to maybe finding some answers?

She ran back to the kitchen and grabbed the calendar.

CHAPTER 21

She was home in less than a minute and slammed the door shut behind her, her back pressed against it, still breathing hard.

"Mom?" Breanna asked from where she sat at the kitchen table, a big thick textbook open in front of her. "Are you okay?"

Sadie forced a smile. "Uh, yeah . . . it's just kind of dark out there." She peeked out the small oval window set into the oak of the front door to see if anyone was running after her. The sidewalk was clear. She'd gotten away with it. She turned back to face Breanna and then heard an engine. Were the police back already? After stepping to the picture window she saw that it was just Jack coming back. She wondered where he'd gone.

"What's that?" Breanna asked, looking at the calendar and book in Sadie's hands.

"Oh, uh, just something I got from Mindy." She couldn't believe she'd just lied to her daughter. Terrible. She placed both items casually on the countertop. She was searching for something to say when Breanna saved her from herself—at least for the moment.

"Detective Cunningham called. I didn't think it was my place to tell him about Ron but I told him you'd be right back and he said he'd come over."

Sadie smiled but her heart was thumping in her chest. What if he found out she'd been in Anne's house? Would he be able to tell just by looking at her? Police were trained to see the slightest detail in the way a person talked or held their head. And what about the other intruder? There had to be some way to tell Cunningham about him without incriminating herself.

"He's coming right now?" Sadie asked, glancing anxiously at the calendar. She needed to hide it, but didn't want to draw Breanna's attention to it again. She left it there for the moment.

"He said it would be around 7:30, so you've got more than half an hour. Why don't you go take a shower or something? No offense, but you look awful."

Sadie glared at her daughter. "How am I supposed to not take offense at that?"

Breanna shrugged, still grinning. "You're the one who's always said taking offense is like taking a hand grenade—it's up to you."

"Humph," Sadie said, smoothing her hair dramatically.

"Okay, fine, don't shower, see if I care." Breanna tsked and shook her head. "Some people's parents."

"Thin ice, my dear, thin, thin ice talking to me that way."

"I've got some studying to do, Mom, and then I'll clean up the kitchen."

"You'll do dishes voluntarily?" In truth Breanna was very helpful around the house, but Sadie hated to let a good banter session go to waste. And she had to admit that a shower sounded marvelous. Between the applesauce this morning and the bed-hiding of the afternoon and evening, Sadie felt perfectly filthy. But it didn't overcome her motherly sensibilities. Sadie sat down across the table from her daughter. "Thank you for coming down, Bre, but I know you have a very demanding schedule right now. I don't want you to feel obligated to stay here." And yet, she really wished she would. Though Sadie sometimes judged Carrie harshly for her determination to hold on to her children too tight, Sadie had found her own children's adulthood hard to take as well. She missed the years when she had them in her home every day.

Breanna bit her lip and Sadie was glad to see she was considering it. "I don't want you to be alone," she said. "Ron's out there and no one really knows what happened. If I get up early I can make the drive before my first class."

"When the detective comes I'll tell him about Ron," Sadie said, dreading the conversation already. "He'll know what I should do about it, and I'll be okay here by myself. I'm good at being alone." Sadie patted Breanna's arm. "What classes do you have tomorrow?"

"Well," Breanna said slowly, as if not having planned to reveal this. "I actually have a midterm at 8:00 and then a lab in the afternoon." Her voice sped up as she continued. "But

Trina hasn't called to go back and it doesn't seem right to leave you here alone. I'm sure that I could do the midterm another day."

"Not unless college has changed a whole lot since I was a student." She smiled reassuringly at her daughter. "I promise you I won't be stupid." Breaking into Anne's house notwithstanding, but it's not like she was going to do that again. "I'll be okay."

"I'd feel better if I knew someone was staying with you."

"Not if that means you miss your classes," Sadie reiterated. "If I have to I'll go to Carrie's, but it's your senior year—no time to start slacking now."

"Well, maybe I'll call Trina and see what her plan is. I know she has a midterm tomorrow too. But either way you need a shower."

"Do I smell that bad?" Sadie asked with mock sincerity.

Breanna laughed. "I'm a zoology major, Mom. My sense of smell is extremely acute."

Sadie laughed, finally gave up, and went to the bedroom. The shower was as divine as she'd thought it would be and she used up all the hot water before she got out—only then realizing how long she'd been under the steady beat of water, mentally running through her day. She threw on a pair of yoga pants and a white T-shirt, then wrapped her head in a towel. When she got back to the living room, Breanna was wiping down the countertops. Her books were packed up and her backpack was sitting by the door. Sadie's heart sank, and yet she was relieved to know she wouldn't be the cause of forfeiting her daughter's education.

"Trina's going back too?" Sadie asked.

Breanna turned to look at her and nodded. "Yeah, it's sure weird over there though."

"What do you mean?"

"Well, Aunt Carrie answered the phone and said Trina couldn't talk, so I asked her and she said Trina was staying, but then Uncle Jack was, like, all mad in the background. So she said she'd call me back and a few minutes later Uncle Jack called and said that Trina was going back with me as soon as I was ready to go. So I guess she's coming over in a minute."

It was unhealthy for Carrie to put so much of her security into her children. Out loud, Sadie said, "Carrie really misses her."

"Ya think?"

Sadie gave her a reprimanding look, but agreed completely. "Did Jack say if he was staying over there tonight?"

Breanna shook her head and laid the washcloth over the divider in the sink. "He didn't say."

Just then there was a knock at the door, reminding Sadie of Detective Cunningham's arrival. She reached up to find the turban on her head and panicked.

"Tell him I'll be right there," she said, running toward her room, then turning around and grabbing the calendar and book from the counter, earning an odd look from Breanna before she bolted for her bedroom again.

She was fingering some gel through her wet hair to bring out her natural curl—she didn't have time to dry and straighten it right now—when Breanna showed up in the doorway.

"It's Uncle Jack and Trina. We're going," she said. Sadie rinsed her hands, dried them on a hand towel hanging next to the sink, and pulled Breanna into a tight embrace.

"Thank you so much for coming," she said, closing her eyes and reminding herself it was best that Bre go back to school.

"I'm supposed to work Saturday morning, but maybe I can find someone to cover for me so I can come home this weekend."

"That would be wonderful, but if you can't, that's okay."

"I'll try," Breanna said again as she pulled back. "You call me if you need anything, okay?"

Sadie nodded. "I will."

"And keep your phone on," Breanna said with mock reprimand.

Sadie saluted. "Yes, ma'am."

"Love you, Mom," Breanna said as she turned and disappeared.

"Love you too," Sadie called after her. She heard voices in the living room, the door closed, and then the darned silence settled back into the house. She swallowed the emotion and told herself she would be okay.

Turning back to the mirror, she noticed how tired she looked. She also remembered that Detective Cunningham would be arriving any minute. She didn't want to put on makeup this late in the day, so she settled for moisturizer, some foundation, and just a touch of lipstick before fluffing her hair with her fingers one last time, frowning at the old lady look it gave her.

She wondered what it would be like to be one of those women who just looked great all the time—like her daughter. In truth, though, an active life and a good diet—Sadie liked to believe homemade sweets were much healthier than their processed counterparts—had kept her looking good for her age. She couldn't even blame her hips on childbirth or getting older; they'd always been wide, but Sadie didn't think they were necessarily unattractive. Sure she had wrinkles and her hair might be totally gray if not for home-coloring kits, but compared to other women her age, she was doing just fine. With that thought she turned off the lights and left the room, and the mirror, behind.

The doorbell rang before she even made it to the end of the hall. She took a deep breath and opened the door. To her relief, Detective Cunningham was alone. She was glad he hadn't brought Detective Madsen with him, sure the younger man would have carted in his own lie detector test or drug-sniffing dog.

"Your message said you had some things to tell me," he said, not smiling or saying hello. The masked expression on his face told her that he was not entirely pleased with her and her stomach sank. Detective Madsen had probably told him what happened at the library.

"Yeah," she said sheepishly, moving aside to invite him in. "Can I get you anything? Some herbal tea, hot cocoa—apple juice?"

"No, thank you," he said, holding her eyes in such a way as to make her feel as though she were shrinking.

She swallowed and realized the moment of truth had arrived. "There's something I didn't tell you earlier."

He raised an eyebrow. "Only one something? That's not what I've been hearing."

CHAPTER 22

"That's all you have to tell me?" Detective Cunningham asked a few minutes later after she told him all about Ron—his being with Anne last night, the toys at his house, the scene at the restaurant. The tone of Detective Cunningham's voice reminded Sadie of the questions she asked her children when she already knew the answer. She wasn't sure how to respond.

After a few seconds of silence Detective Cunningham spoke again. "And what about the information you got from Susan Gimes?" he asked, tilting his head.

He knew about that? She said nothing out loud as he continued to stare her down. Even when he was annoyed, he was a very distinguished-looking man.

When she stayed silent, he continued. "Susan and I have worked on cases together before. She's a good attorney, a smart woman—smart enough to tell me the truth when I asked her if you'd come by today. She can get in a lot of trouble for giving you any information."

"She said it was okay," Sadie explained. "That it wasn't confidential."

"Confidential or not, she told you information that was meant only for the police."

"That was not my fault," Sadie said, suddenly in a hurry to defend herself. She wondered how Susan Gimes had explained it. "If Detective Madsen hadn't bullied her then she wouldn't have told me anything."

"Bullied her?" Detective Cunningham asked before flipping open his notebook and reading as if their conversation was casual.

This gave her courage to keep going. "You should have heard him. He was telling her that if he came back with a warrant he'd trash her office. She said she'd dealt with him before and couldn't stand him." She remembered what she'd learned about Madsen that afternoon and pushed forward. "I think I understand more of what's going on with the two of you now, though."

"Meaning what?" Cunningham asked, his attention on his notes as if her opinion didn't matter much.

"She told me about the attorney general and how Madsen ended up in Garrison. I bet that drives you crazy." She smiled, hoping he'd soften into the Detective Cunningham she'd known that morning.

He looked at her with a steely gaze. "What really drives me crazy, Mrs. Hoffmiller, is when I give people the benefit of the doubt and they betray my trust. It not only impedes our investigative work but it makes me look very foolish."

Sadie straightened in her chair and blinked. It didn't seem as if she'd made much headway to the let's-work-as-a-team option as she'd been vying for.

Cunningham leaned forward. "I responded to the call about Ron Bradley this afternoon at Baxter's restaurant, but after talking to him, and being assured the man he assaulted didn't want to file charges, I let him go because I had no other reason to detain him since I hadn't yet talked to Susan Gimes."

Sadie swallowed and berated herself for not coming clean sooner.

"Had I known all of this, I wouldn't have let him leave. That means he's still out there, on the street."

"You think he did it?" Sadie asked, leaning forward. "You think he killed Anne?"

Cunningham let out a breath in frustration. "You do," he said bluntly. "And the rest of the investigation is moving very slowly. It's likely the best lead we've got—ten hours late."

"I'm really sorry," Sadie said, looking at the carpet beneath her feet. She thought about the intruder at Anne's house this evening and felt even worse. Whoever it was wasn't Ron, but how would she tell the detective that?

"Is there anything else you would like to tell me?" he asked.

"I got some papers at the library," she said, standing slowly and heading to the computer desk where she'd left them. She picked up the papers and brought them to the detective. She sat down and waited until he had scanned each paper. "I also sent an e-mail to the human resources person at Riggs and Barker in

Boston asking about Anne—that company is the same one Ron works for—and I thought maybe they would—"

"Yes, I know."

Sadie gasped and Detective Cunningham looked up to meet her eye. "You seem to believe that while you've been looking for answers, we've been doing jumping jacks in our back office." His voice was tight, his hazel eyes slightly narrowed. "But in fact we have been investigating this—and we spoke to the head of human resources at the Boston office this evening. When your e-mail came in she called us; it seemed suspicious to her in light of Anne's death, which the entire office had already heard about. But we'd already let Mr. Bradley drive away from Baxter's and he hasn't gone back home. We have, as they say, lost him."

"I—I'm so sorry," Sadie repeated. Cunningham said nothing, but his expression showed his displeasure. Sadie cleared her throat, hating how uncomfortable all this had become. "I'm only trying to get answers," she said lamely. "I'm not trying to get in the way."

"Mrs. Hoffmiller," Detective Cunningham said, sitting forward and stretching his back. She wondered if he was sore but doubted now would be a good time to offer him a massage, not to mention it was a rather forward thing to do seeing as they were alone. "An investigation is like a living thing, with rhythms and routines. In order for the police to be effective, we need people to not interfere with those rhythms. I understand that your intentions have not been malicious. But they are causing problems—do you understand that?"

Sadie nodded like a child receiving a reprimand. She pushed all thoughts of the calendar and book from her mind. He'd likely arrest her if she admitted to breaking into Anne's house and taking the items. The guilt was overwhelming.

"Problems not only with this investigation, but with my *partner.*" He seemed to emphasize the last word and it confused her. She was certain that Detective Cunningham and Detective Madsen were pitted against each other. Detective Cunningham continued. "You witnessed something between Madsen and me this morning that you should never have seen. The irony is that you were at the root of it."

"Me?"

"Since we first spoke to you, Detective Madsen felt you were, at best, a threat to our investigation, if not a suspect. I disagreed. Based on the reputation you have in this community, and the times that our public service has crossed paths, I brought you into this investigation and when Detective Madsen questioned my choices, I dismissed them as overly suspicious."

Sadie tried to swallow the lump in her throat.

"However, it's my *job* to be overly suspicious, and as Detective Madsen pointed out to our captain just a little while ago, I have not been doing my job. He was right."

"Madsen set me up at the library," Sadie added, but it was a weak argument. "He gave me the books then followed me and made all kinds of accusations when the library gave me some of Anne's things."

"As I said, he was doing his job. I am grateful for the help you have given us. But will you please stay out of this now?"

She nodded before considering whether or not she planned to stay out of it. But she hated that he was angry with her. She wanted to ask if they knew where Trevor was, if they had made any determinations about the cause of death, but she didn't. He wouldn't tell her anything now.

Detective Cunningham closed his notebook and slipped it in the inside pocket of his coat. "Is there somewhere you can stay tonight?" he asked. "Until we can bring Mr. Bradley in for questioning you shouldn't be home alone."

"I can probably stay with my sister-in-law," Sadie said, though she really didn't want to. Then again, she wanted to be home alone waiting for Ron even less.

"That would be a good idea," Detective Cunningham said, standing and heading for the door. With his hand on the knob he turned to look at her. She stood and shifted her weight, hating the tension she had caused.

"I really am sorry," she said again, promising herself right then that she wouldn't keep anything else from him—and she'd think about how she could tell him about the second intruder without getting herself in more trouble.

"I'll wait in my car until I see that you're safely at your sister-in-law's. And I still need to talk to Mr. Henry."

"Do you want me to go with you? He might be more open . . . to a . . . familiar . . ." She let her words vaporize at Cunningham's cold look and shuffled her feet clad in pink slippers. "Okay," Sadie finally said, nodding.

She let him out and then called Carrie on the cordless phone, hating the pit in her stomach at having upset Detective

Cunningham. He seemed like a really nice man. She only wished he'd try to understand her situation a little better. She couldn't just do *nothing*. Carrie's phone rang and rang. Sadie hung up and dialed again, certain they were home. She headed into the bedroom to get Anne's book and calendar. Finally, on the sixth ring, a frazzled Jack answered the phone.

"Hello," Jack said with impatience.

"Jack," Sadie said, putting the book and calendar in the bottom of a small bag and covering them with her vitamins, slippers, and fingernail clippers. It was only overnight, but she'd hate to forget something. "It's me. Can I stay there tonight?" She added an extra pair of socks, just in case, and a small first-aid kit—you never knew when it might come in handy—a shower cap, should she decide to take a shower in the morning, and her own towel.

Jack paused. "Stay here?" he repeated as if the words she'd used were long and hard to understand.

She realized she hadn't told Jack anything about Ron. Did she dare tell him now? Did he already know? She was tired of keeping secrets. Taking a deep breath, she said, "The police are looking for Ron, to bring him in for questioning." In her mind they would definitely arrest him and throw him in jail. "They don't want me home alone."

Jack was silent and Sadie waited for him to ask why the police were looking for Ron, but he didn't. After a few seconds he spoke again. "I'm, uh, just leaving, but I'm sure Carrie would be glad for the company. I'll be back later."

"Okay, thanks," she said, though she dreaded going to his house now more than ever. He must know about Ron. Otherwise he'd have asked more questions. Her heart sank as her earlier ponderings on who she could trust came blazing hot into her mind. She grabbed her bathrobe, some clean under-wear, face cream, clear nail polish, and another pair of socks. "I'll just be a couple minutes."

"Make it at least ten," Jack said. "We're finishing up some . . . things. I'll tell Carrie you're coming."

"Okay," Sadie said, hoping she wasn't interrupting some kind of reconciliation. "Ten minutes."

When Sadie had locked her front door—after grabbing her pillow, her address book, and an extra pair of pajamas in case she spilled anything on the set she'd already packed and after securing all her windows and doors and turning out the lights—she hurried down the steps. The chill of the day had warmed some, despite how late it was and she wondered if that meant it might snow. If it had snowed last night there might have been footprints at Anne's house. She'd seen a show where the police caught a bad guy by matching up his shoe tread. As she hurried along the sidewalk to Jack and Carrie's she ignored Detective Cunningham's car idling further down the circle and looked at the sky. It did look like snow and she wished she'd brought her coat and put some salt on the steps just in case. Jack's truck was no longer in the driveway.

Carrie let her in and Sadie noticed she looked absolutely exhausted. Maybe she'd been right when she'd said that Sadie wasn't the only one who'd had a difficult day. Or maybe she was sick.

"You can take the guest room downstairs," Carrie said, turning toward the kitchen. "I was just straightening up, then I was going to get into a bath."

"Thanks, I really appreciate you letting me stay," Sadie said. A few months ago Carrie's oldest daughter had surprised Carrie with a home makeover inspired by a community education class she'd taken on interior design. She'd repainted the living room in a shade called "Desert Rose." Sadie thought it looked more like bologna left on the counter too long. But Carrie had liked it so Sadie had simply smiled and nodded. Paired with an old sage-green sofa set and several family portraits in mismatched frames, the room was really quite sickly looking. There was a fire in the fireplace, filling the room with heat too thick to be comfortable. Sadie was glad she didn't have to sleep on the couch.

"So, Ron, huh?" Carrie said. She glanced up at Sadie quickly, then went back to straightening the counter in the kitchen.

Sadie wasn't in the mood to talk about it anymore. "Yeah," she said simply. "It's been a long day."

"Yes," Carrie said slowly. She looked toward the kitchen window to her left and seemed distracted for a moment. But then she looked back and raised a hand to brush her recently dyed blonde hair from her face—the new color didn't suit her fair complexion. She didn't have any makeup on and looked rather washed out. She'd never put as much into her appearance and personal development as Sadie did, and it showed, though Sadie didn't mean to judge her too harshly. To each her own.

Carrie said good night and turned toward her bedroom; Sadie took note of just how much weight her sister-in-law had lost. Daily gym visits had made quite a difference and Sadie wondered how much she planned to lose. Already she looked like the Carrie she'd been after just the first two girls, when she'd still been fairly active. Sadie also wondered, for the thousandth time, if there was any hope that Carrie and Jack could resolve their differences and try again. The fact that Jack had come over tonight was a good sign.

Sadie went downstairs. The guest room was painted stark white, and cluttered with mismatched leftover furniture pieces from the kids. A bookshelf had been painted a brilliant green, whereas a cast-off dresser was covered in bumper stickers with phrases like "Jimmy Buffett for President" and "Go Navy." However, outside of looking like a pathetic secondhand store showroom, it was more comfortable than the meaty walls upstairs. As soon as the door was shut on the little room with a queen bed and an old quilt Sadie's mother had sewed decades earlier, she opened her overnight bag and pulled out the book she'd taken from Anne's bookshelf, *My Father's Eyes*.

Even in full light Sadie couldn't read the back cover. It took her a moment to find her reading glasses in her bag, next to her cough medicine, and try again. She sat back against the headboard, pulling the quilt over her legs—it was chilly down here. The back cover seemed to be an excerpt from the book.

"You're ending this?" Marci said, her heart seizing in her chest as she placed a hand on her belly, pregnant with the life their love had created. "What about our family? What about me?"

"I'm sorry," he said with tears in his dark brown eyes. He reached out and pulled her against his chest one last time and she thought about how much she'd miss his tight embrace. Memories of their nights together washed over her like ocean waves intent to drown her in their depths. "I love you," he continued, "and you've given me more joy and passion than any other woman ever could. But she's got money, Marci, and an impeccable reputation that can further my career. At least this way I can support you—and our child. What else can I do?"

But Marci's heart would not be denied. How could she convince the man she loved, the man she'd given her heart to, that being his mistress wasn't enough for her? She would stop at nothing to prove to him she was all he'd ever wanted. Her daughter would know who her Daddy was—and they'd live happily ever after . . . one way or another.

Sadie's eyebrows went up and she read the pathetic excerpt again. She turned the book over and looked at the cover. It was a picture of a man, an older man judging by his gray hair even though he was built like a teenage lifeguard. He gazed into the adoring eyes of a young woman holding a child.

"Oh my goodness," she breathed as several pieces fell into place and the significance of this particular book became apparent. "Anne, what did you do?"

CHAPTER 23

It was almost 1:00 AM when Sadie finished the book. She stared at the final page for nearly a minute.

Sadie could hardly believe it, but it was there—in black ink on mass-market paperback pages, riddled with dangling participles, an obnoxious indulgence in adverbs, and sappy descriptions.

In the story, the character Marci had a two-year affair with a man who'd been engaged to another woman. When she became pregnant he refused to call off the wedding. So a few months after the baby was born and the man was married, Marci moved to his hometown. Everything other than the marriage fit—even down to Anne's friendship with Sadie, who seemed to be the substitute for the fiancée-turned-wife character in the book. In the story, the wife—who was in her forties—befriended the much younger mistress, who then learned all the details of taking care of the man she loved.

But Anne had died before her story finished. In the novel, the man eventually realized he couldn't live without her, but only after she'd proven herself capable and determined to have him in her life. He eventually left his wife and came to the mistress, promising a lifetime of love and devotion to her and her alone. Because of community property laws, when he divorced his rich wife, he also got half her fortune. Sadie was sure that would never hold up in real life, not when he was such a scoundrel, but that was romance novels for you.

As far as story lines went it was weak, immoral, and in Sadie's mind, completely ridiculous. But obviously Anne had seen something of merit in it. Enough that she'd lived it—even used it as a blueprint. She'd tried to resurrect the copy of the book that had been ruined, and when that didn't work, she'd stolen another copy. Sadie felt sick to her stomach at how orchestrated it all had been.

All this time she'd been some pawn in Anne's game to get Ron? Or had Ron gone along with it like the man in the book? Maybe it was even his idea. And Sadie was stupid enough not to notice. She heard the front door shut upstairs. Was it Jack? Footsteps crossed the floor above her head and then stopped. She listened for a few more seconds but heard nothing but voices muted by the floorboards above her.

Sadie hadn't left the room since opening the book, and hadn't eaten since Breanna's Alfredo in the early evening. Throwing back the covers, she changed into her pajamas, robe, and slippers before heading upstairs in search of something to eat—a glass of milk if nothing else. But she also tried to think of what she could say to Jack. She had to know if he had been in on Ron's deception, if he'd been keeping it from her too.

The imagined heartbreak of his treachery was almost too much to bear. As she reached the top of the basement stairs she realized what she really wanted was some sympathy, some understanding. Jack was her brother, he'd always taken care of her and she longed to have him pull her into his arms, smooth her hair, and say "Ah, Sadie-Sadie, I'm so sorry."

When she reached the kitchen she could hear Jack and Carrie's voices, only whispers, but they were arguing, which made her hesitant to interrupt and somewhat irritated that her opportunity for comfort wasn't going to happen as she'd hoped. She considered returning downstairs but she was so close to food—not to mention her insatiable curiosity as to what they were arguing about. She wondered if they were rehashing Jack's decision to send Trina back to school that evening. Carrie had wanted her to stay, but Sadie mentally sided with Jack on this one, even if he was possibly a secret-keeping louse of a brother. She tiptoed into the kitchen, scanning the countertops for something edible. It was dark except for the light above the sink that cast just enough light for Sadie to see around the room.

She spied her pan of brownies, half gone, and her mouth began to water. She moved as quietly as she could and put two brownies on a napkin before tiptoeing to the fridge. She couldn't have brownies without milk.

"I know," she heard Jack say in a louder voice. She stopped and leaned closer toward the door. *What* did he know?

Carrie said something in reply but she whispered and Sadie couldn't make it out. She took another step closer to the kitchen doorway. When Jack spoke again his voice was softer, but she made out the word "Sorry."

It annoyed her that Jack would give into whatever it was Carrie was haranguing him about. Couldn't she see that the fact that he was here meant they had a chance to make things better with their relationship? Sadie took another step and the floorboards creaked under her foot. The voices stopped and she hurried across the kitchen as the door to the master bedroom opened. The family calendar was tacked on the wall next to the sink and she pretended to be absorbed in the comings and goings of her sister-in-law. There were work hours written on the last week, and for the next two weeks, bringing to mind the fact that Carrie hadn't gone to work even though the schedule still seemed in place. She also noticed that Trina had had an appointment on Monday—but didn't she have school that day? Sadie's back was facing the doorway when she heard someone enter the kitchen.

"You're up," Jack said.

Sadie turned to look at him, raising her eyebrows as if surprised he was there. She busied herself by getting a third brownie even though she couldn't possibly eat that many. She still hadn't gotten any milk. "I'm sorry, I'm just starved. I'm going back down." She met his eyes again and opened her mouth to ask about Ron, but the words abruptly congealed in her throat.

Jack wasn't dressed for bed. He still wore his work clothes and she suddenly felt dizzy. The house was dark, but the light above the sink glinted off his wedding band—just inches below the blue cuff of his dress shirt.

The brownies fell to the floor and she just stood there while Jack moved forward to pick them up. They'd landed facedown, but he put them back on the napkin and stood. "Ten-second rule," he said, with the hint of a smile on his otherwise sad face.

Sadie stared at him. *It was Jack!* He had been at Anne's house. She couldn't breathe and didn't know what to say. He handed her the brownies and she took them and pulled them to her chest, crushing them in her napkin.

"Are you okay?" he asked.

In her mind she was talking herself out of it. It couldn't be. Why would Jack go to Anne's house? Why would he have a key? She looked into his eyes. "Jack?" she asked. Other thoughts and details tried to push their way into her mind, but she refused them, overcome by her unexpected realization.

"What?" he countered.

"I—" She paused and looked back at his hand. "I didn't know you still wore your wedding ring."

He looked down at his hand but he said nothing. After a few more seconds of silence, he headed for the front door.

"Where are you going?" she asked, taking two steps toward him.

"Sadie," he said quietly, now too far away for her to see his expression as he turned to face her. "Ron's a good man and I know he truly cares about you. I know no one understands this, but I never stopped loving Carrie."

CHAPTER 24

Sadie didn't know how long she stood there before she heard footsteps in the hall. Carrie stood in the doorway of the kitchen and Sadie looked at her. "What's going on?" Sadie asked.

"Nothing to concern yourself with," Carrie said in a voice far too calm for what Sadie had just heard. "Go back to bed, Sadie. Things will be better in the morning." She turned and went back to her room.

Sadie stayed rooted to her place in the middle of the kitchen, brownies in hand. *Did Carrie know?* But she couldn't mentally go down that path for long before bigger thoughts yanked her mind back to her brother. She couldn't ignore it any longer. Could *Jack* be Trevor's father?

Sadie refused to accept it. She had misunderstood. She was putting together clues in the wrong order. Jack was helping Ron. That had to be it. That's *all* he was doing, all he had done. But what did that have to do with never having stopped loving Carrie?

Almost trancelike she went back downstairs, put the brownies on the dresser, turned off the lights, and climbed into bed. She stared at the darkened ceiling with the covers pulled up to her chin. She was awake when dawn inched its way into her room, that is, if she ever slept—she wasn't sure. She hadn't had such a horrible night's sleep since the first few weeks after Neil's death. Why couldn't Neil be here now? Even after nineteen years she missed him most when she had big decisions to make. How she had loved to ask his opinion over biscuits and gravy, just talk about life, and have someone to line her thoughts up with.

Since Ron had entered her life it hadn't hurt so bad to be alone, but right now she ached for the man she'd loved so much, the father of her children, the person she had trusted most in the whole world. She dressed slowly in the clothes she had packed the night before, listening for any sounds of movement upstairs. It was silent. She padded up the stairs, anxious to get back home. Maybe things would make more sense over there.

Carrie was still asleep or gone—either way Sadie was relieved not to have to talk to her. She was sick over the thoughts still coursing through her mind. The living room windows revealed that, just as she'd expected, the mildness of yesterday had given way to a flurry of snow and wind. She scowled, remembering she hadn't brought a coat. She'd packed *everything* else. She wrote a quick note, thanking Carrie for letting her stay and put it on the kitchen counter.

At the front door she took a deep breath, pulled her bag close to her chest and hurried out into the blizzard-like conditions. She didn't look at the other houses in the circle, she didn't see if there were any cars at Anne's. She didn't want to know. All this meddling had left her sick to her stomach.

It felt good to be home, but the pit in her stomach was still there. She brushed the snow from her hair, knowing it was frizzed out and horrid-looking now that she'd slept on it. She vowed to style it later and then went about making herself some hot cocoa, still processing everything she'd heard last night.

Jack's words, "I never stopped loving Carrie," rang through her ears and she shuddered. There was no way Jack could be the one! And yet, Jack had been the intruder at Anne's house last night. He must have come from the back field. She'd seen his truck leave when she was hiding in the vacant lot. He must have gone to the far end of the fields and walked up from the back, waiting for the police to go by just like she had. And then he'd driven back to the house a few minutes later. Could he have done the same thing the night before? Could he have killed Anne?

"Slow down," she told herself. Then she grabbed a pad of paper and started making a list of everything she learned yesterday—and what was left to be followed up on. When she finished she had a whole list of things she could look into. Only now, she wasn't looking for proof it was Ron, she was looking for proof it *wasn't* Jack. And Trevor. Her stomach clenched like a fist. Where on earth was Trevor? It had been twenty-four hours.

She was still looking at the list, trying to think of anything she'd missed, when the phone rang, making her jump. She took a deep breath and read the caller ID. It was a blocked number. Did she dare answer it?

Unfortunately, she didn't know what else she had to lose.

"Mrs. Hoffmiller?" Detective Cunningham said into the phone.

"Yes?"

"Could you come down to the station? We have some questions and we need to ask you for an official statement."

Sadie nodded, even though he couldn't see her, but her stomach sank. They'd never asked her to come into the station for questions and it validated the changes that had taken place since yesterday. Everything was worse now. "I'll be right there," she said. "Is there any particular reason I'm coming down?"

"We have the coroner report back from the autopsy, and you were right about the time cook on the oven. Anne was killed sometime between 2:00 and 5:00 AM. And the body was moved. We need to ask some specific questions in regards to some other things we found . . . and we've . . . had a confession."

CHAPTER 25

It took exactly eight minutes for Sadie to reach the police station and run inside. Detective Cunningham and Detective Madsen were waiting for her and led her to an office rather than the mirrored rooms she'd seen on cop shows. The office was on the small side, with a window running the length of one wall, allowing them to look into the inner workings of the police station.

"Did you find Trevor?" she asked, choosing her focus.

Cunningham shook his head but said nothing. She tried not to give Detective Madsen a dirty look, but it was hard not to. He just rubbed her wrong at every turn. Detective Cunningham sat down in the chair behind the desk, and Detective Madsen stood by the side of the desk near the door as if making sure she didn't run out. As if she would do something so undignified!

Cunningham began by asking her if he could record the conversation. She agreed, at which point he turned on a tape recorder and began with many of the same questions they had asked her yesterday. She answered with absolute honesty and tried to ignore her growing curiosity about the confession he'd told her about on the phone. She wondered for a moment if he'd only said that to get her down here.

"The coroner has made some determinations in regard to the murder weapon," Detective Cunningham said.

Sadie swallowed. Ron and Jack's faces appeared in her mind, but she forced Jack's away. She knew she was ignoring facts, that she was being completely subjective, but her mind would not allow anything different.

"I wonder if you could describe the missing tieback for me? In detail," Cunningham asked.

"Um, like I told you before, the pattern was floral. I'd actually used it for a quilt we made for a young woman at church—she was getting married. When Anne lamented being able to find a suitable tieback in the store, I went through my fabric—I've got quite a collection you know—and found it. I was thrilled to—"

Detective Madsen cut her off from where he stood with his back against the wall. "We need size and shape. We don't care what it looked like or how you found it." He gave the impression that he had no interest being there at all and was simply waiting for permission to leave.

She scowled at Detective Madsen. She did not like him one little bit, but did as he said and got right to the details. "It was just under a yard long—36 inches of fabric—but you lose some length when you sew the seams. It was about three inches wide, with a pressed seam on the interior."

"A pressed seam?" Detective Madsen asked. She noticed a look pass between the two men.

"Yeah, I made the tieback by sewing a six-inch wide piece of fabric in half the long way, then I pressed it so the seam was on the inside. It's very unflattering to have the seam on the outside, where people can see it. If people would understand the part that seams play in the finished product, they would realize how imperative an iron is to the overall process of getting the right lines when it comes to even basic sewing."

Detective Madsen pulled out a notebook and began making furious notes; she wondered if he was a closet seamstress at heart. Cunningham just looked at her oddly. Then he nodded and let out a breath. It took a few seconds before she registered his expression. She thought back to yesterday, when she'd wondered if Anne had been strangled. Sadie clenched her eyes shut, but that just put the imagined scene in her head. She forced them open. "She was murdered with my tieback?"

"*Your* tieback?" Madsen repeated, leaning forward slightly, pen poised above his paper.

Detective Cunningham glowered at the other man before looking at her again. "We're not sure," he said. "But there are other considerations we need to understand. Did you see Anne on Monday?"

"I watched Trevor while she was working," Sadie said.

"And she was okay? Uninjured?"

"Uninjured?" Sadie repeated. "What do you mean?"

Cunningham continued to stare at her. "Her body showed signs of trauma, a bad fall maybe, or someone having been violent with her."

"Don't tell her that!" Madsen spat, shaking his head and turning away from them as if trying to get control of himself. He put his hands on his hips, and the sides of his suit jacket fanned out like wings. He let out a deep breath. Both Cunningham and Sadie ignored him completely.

"No," Sadie said slowly, picturing Anne's body in the field again. Twisted and contorted. "She was fine when I saw her. She borrowed a lemon. . . . I guess for the lemon tart she made that night. She'd forgotten to pick one up from the produce section after work." She wondered again what that tart was for. "Lemon zest makes all the difference."

Madsen turned back toward them and they all went quiet as Sadie swallowed and looked at her hands. "You said there was a confession," she continued, steeling herself to hear it. *Please let it be Ron,* she said to herself.

"Yes," Detective Cunningham said. "I'm very sorry. The man who confessed to the murder of Anne Lemmon is Jack Wright."

Sadie remained frozen and tested out the words in her mind. *"The man who confessed to the murder of Anne Lemmon is Jack Wright."*

Nope, it didn't take.

There wasn't one part of her that could even consider such a thing. Madsen's eyes were dancing, as if he loved every minute of this. She refused to look at him anymore.

"It can't be Jack," she said resolutely with a sharp shaking of her head to emphasize the implausibility. "It's just not possible."

"Why not?" Detective Cunningham asked, leaning forward and seemingly genuine in his interest.

"Because . . ." She stopped. "Because I love him and trust him and he just wouldn't do this!" It sounded naïve and brimming with nepotism, but it was true. Jack couldn't have *killed* Anne.

Detective Madsen rolled his eyes. "Oh, please," he said in a long-drawn-out grunting voice. "This is so ridiculous!" He turned to look at his partner. "Get her out of here, we're finished with her anyway."

Cunningham slowly met his partner's gaze. "We're not finished."

Madsen groaned again. "Well, do what you want. I'm going to file the paperwork on this thing." He stomped to the door—really, he stomped like a child—and left the room.

Detective Cunningham made no reaction to his partner's tantrum, but his face seemed to relax just a little bit once he'd left. He leaned back in his chair. "Mr. Wright confessed, Mrs. Hoffmiller. There isn't much argument in that." But his voice wasn't hard and militant as it had been last night. In fact, Sadie sensed a kind of challenge behind his words.

"Let me talk to him," she said with a crisp nod. "I'll get the truth from him. He didn't do this."

There was a tapping on the glass to their left. Sadie looked toward it and saw Madsen and another man gesturing to Cunningham.

"Just a minute," Cunningham said as he stood up and left the room. Once alone she put her fingers to her temples. *Think,* she told herself. There had to be a way to prove Jack didn't do this. There had to be something she could do.

Larue! She fumbled in her coat pocket for her cell phone and was almost surprised to find it, but although the police had taken her purse they hadn't searched her before leading her into this room. She quickly dialed directory assistance. She usually called a free service since she was charged seventy-five cents for every directory assistance call, but the free service was full of ads and she didn't have time to be frugal.

"I need the Garrison office of Riggs and Barker."

They transferred her and she asked for Larue Adams.

"Larue," she breathed, grateful that though their acquaintance was limited, she had made it a point to get to know Jack's receptionist. "I need to ask you a few questions about the convention this week—questions about Jack."

"What for?" Larue asked, trying to laugh it off.

"Something . . . horrible happened Monday night and I need to know if you know anything about where Jack was that night."

Detective Cunningham came in and scowled at her. She held up one finger and listened, asked a few more questions, and then nodded. "Thank you, Larue, now I need you to tell that exact same information to Detective Cunningham. Here he is."

It only took a minute for Detective Cunningham to learn what Sadie had just found out. He finished by asking Larue to come into the office and make an official statement. Then he hung up the phone and handed it back to Sadie.

"You can't stay out of this, can you?" he nearly growled.

She ignored his question. "Jack couldn't have done this, and she just verified it."

Detective Cunningham shook his head. "He confessed."

"Then why were you asking me so many questions about how Anne looked, and what the tieback was like? Surely a confession would make all those points moot. Please let me talk to him. I can get the truth out of him, I swear it."

He clamped his lips together, telling her without any words that he wasn't as convinced by the confession as he wanted her to believe. He held her eyes for a long time but she refused to blink. Finally he stood up. "I'll be back."

More waiting. She wished she'd had her purse and the book hiding in it, but then she looked at the giant window on the wall and realized she wouldn't want anyone to see her reading it. The waiting, however, was horrendous.

Finally Cunningham entered the room.

"Did you get permission for me to talk to him?" she asked, standing up, her nerves making her completely on edge.

"Yes," Cunningham said, leading her out of the room. "But we'll be watching and listening to everything. He's being brought up right now, and he's been told that it's all being recorded. Only his legal counsel gets to talk to him privately."

Sadie thanked Cunningham before following him further down the hall. They stopped in front of a very ugly door. It'd had at least two shades of gray paint slapped on it sometime in the last forty years. It looked awful. She turned to look at the detective.

"I owe you an apology," she said nervously. She licked her lips though her whole mouth had suddenly gone dry as she imagined Jack on the other side of that door. Why was he doing this?

"You already apologized for e-mailing the Boston office and poking your nose in too many places."

She shook her head. "That was for what you *knew* I'd found." She swallowed and forced herself to hold his eyes. "There's more." It came out as more of a squeak. "And when I'm in there I might say stuff that gives it away so I want you to know first of all, that I'm really sorry—I really, really am. And that I'll explain everything when I get out. Okay?"

His face was hard and she had no doubt he wanted to bop her on the head for doing this to him. Finally, he nodded. A female officer stepped forward and told Sadie to remove her coat and put her arms out.

"Why?" Sadie asked though she did as requested, her coat hanging from one hand.

"You're meeting with a confessed murderer," Cunningham said, taking the coat. "We need to make sure you're not giving him anything."

She held her arms out. "What, like a weapon? You think I'm . . . packing?"

The left side of Cunningham's mouth pulled up in a grin, and Sadie flinched as the woman patted her in places that made Sadie blush. She felt horribly violated, even more so to go through this with Cunningham watching, but she told herself it was the woman's job and that not everyone who came into a police station was the kind of upstanding citizen Sadie was.

The woman finished and stepped back. "She's clean," she told Cunningham and headed back down the hallway. For a moment Sadie thought the woman meant she had showered, then realized it meant she didn't have any switchblades hiding in the waistband of her underwear.

"Okay," Cunningham said, nodding toward the door. "You can go in."

Chapter 26

Sadie straightened her shirt and turned back to the badly painted door. She wondered why people didn't pay more attention to details and just repaint the thing all one color—surely she wasn't the only person who'd noticed.

Once inside the room, however, all thoughts of paint and other people's attention to detail were forgotten. Jack sat at the table in the center of the cinder-block room, dressed in what looked like bright green hospital scrubs. His hands were cuffed in front of him and he stared at the top of the Formica-covered table. The office she'd been questioned in was imposing, but this room was downright dreary. Sadie let the door shut behind her and tried to repress a shiver. It was cold in here and she wished Detective Cunningham hadn't taken her coat away.

Drawing a deep breath she walked to the table and pulled out the only other chair in the room. Jack didn't look up at her. She sat down and folded her hands in her lap. She was aware of the mirror behind her but tried not to think about

Cunningham standing there listening. Watching. The next few minutes were about Jack, and what he said he'd done.

"Jack," she said. The whisper sounded loud in the barren room.

He took a breath and finally lifted his head. The tears she'd been holding back filled her eyes at the look of hopeless sorrow on his face. On impulse she reached across the table and took his hands—needing to reach out to him any way she could. He wrapped his large fingers around her smaller ones and held on tight. It made her cry even harder. *Maybe this was a bad idea,* she thought as a sob shook her chest. And yet she tried to push through the emotion and get down to the task at hand— proving her brother's innocence.

"I'm so sorry, Sadie," he said, tears dripping down his cheeks. "I'm so sorry."

Sadie didn't know what to say to that so she remained silent.

Jack continued, "I don't know how it happened . . . everything just got so crazy."

"Jack," Sadie said again after several seconds of silence. Jack let go of her hands and wiped awkwardly at his eyes with his cuffed hands, but the tears continued to fall. It just didn't make sense and the more she looked at him the less sense it made. She knew this man, he was her brother—her protector. With their parents gone, and their sister living several states away for the last twenty-five years, he was the person on this earth she knew longer and better than anyone else. She couldn't have misjudged him so much. Looking at him, broken and crying, she couldn't accept that he'd killed a woman. It just couldn't be true.

"Why are you taking the fall for this?" There—she'd said it! She'd vocalized what had brought her in this room.

Jack's head popped up and his eyes went wide. "What are you talking about?" he asked, an edge of panic in his voice.

"I know about the bank account and what Ron did—and I know he's your friend. But, Jack, you can't throw your life away for him. That isn't justice for anyone. You have no reason to do this."

Jack let out a breath and looked back at the table. "All Ron did was try to help me—that's all he's ever done for me. I did this. I did all of it."

"I called Larue," Sadie said. "She saw you Monday night in the bar—though you know better than to hang out in places like that." She paused and told herself not to get distracted with lectures that didn't matter right now. "She said it was after midnight when she left you and the other people there, but you were at breakfast the next morning. Anne was killed in the early morning—you couldn't have made the two-hour drive to Garrison, killed Anne, and gotten back to Denver in time."

Jack was silent, but he didn't give in. "She's wrong," Jack said, squaring his shoulders—an action Sadie found odd. Why take a defensive stance with her? "There were a lot of people there. She was mistaken—probably drunk. I got back just in time for the breakfast."

"And laughed and joked about life insurance fraud in your opening class? You wouldn't do that after just killing someone.

Besides," she paused and took a breath, "Ron is Trevor's father, not you—you have no motive." It was her last holdout, but it sounded jagged and vaporous once she said it out loud.

Jack shook his head. "No. I'm Trevor's . . . father," he said strongly, though his shoulders slumped again. "Ron set up the account for me—I couldn't have it showing up on a credit report. What if Carrie saw it?" He looked Sadie in the eyes, hard and deep and she couldn't breathe for fear of what she'd hear next. The silence stretched like a rubber band.

"Anne was hired as a receptionist at the Boston office three years ago," Jack said, looking into the mirror behind Sadie's shoulder, as if he were talking to the detectives back there rather than talking to her. "I met her when I went to the spring conference that year." He let out a breath and Sadie almost felt as if she were intruding on his memory, one that obviously brought him both guilt and reluctant pleasure to relive. "She was only twenty-two years old, and yet she seemed so mature, so grown up. Carrie and I . . . well, you know better than anyone how our relationship was, how it's always been. The older girls had moved out—something I had always thought would precede a repair in our relationship. It didn't. Things were as bad as ever and Carrie was holding on to Trina as if she was the only joy Carrie had left in her life. I was just so unhappy." He stopped.

"*You* had an affair with Anne?" Sadie asked, desperately needing to hear him say it. Her brain was still processing slowly, throwing out excuses and justifications like birdseed. She wanted so badly to have another explanation to all this.

"Oh, please, Sadie," he said, frustration lacing his tone. "Don't judge me. We can't all be saints."

Sadie pulled back, but bit her tongue. This discussion wasn't about her and she wasn't going to let him change the subject.

Jack lifted his hands to his face. "I'm sorry," he said. "This isn't your fault."

They both went silent again; Sadie couldn't think of a single word to say. *Jack* was Trevor's father? The idea nauseated her.

Jack finally let out a breath and continued. "It was months after I met her before I . . . we . . . then the guilt nearly ate me alive." He took his hands down and Sadie studied his face, disheartened to see the honesty in the lines around his eyes. He was telling her the truth. "I didn't know what to do with a young, beautiful woman pursuing me, listening to me, admiring me. It was more than I could handle."

She swallowed and nodded for him to continue while praying for help in knowing what to say, what questions to ask. She wished she'd just given her statement and gone home.

"I love Carrie," he said with resolution. "For better and for worse—I love her. She's my wife." His voice cracked. "She bore me three wonderful daughters and she was always true to me, always took care of our home, always took care of the girls. Many men would love to have a wife such as her."

Sadie kept her thoughts to herself. Yes, Carrie had her strengths, but she had her faults as well—faults that came out most often with her husband. Though it disgusted and disappointed Sadie to no end that Jack—gallant and devoted

Jack—had strayed. Carrie was not generous in her affection or affirmations toward her husband. *That* part wasn't Jack's fault.

He continued. "And I broke our vows, I put asunder the covenants I'd made to her and to God. After just a few weeks of clandestine weekend trips with Anne, I put an end to it."

Sadie licked her lips and found her voice. "Did Carrie find out? Is that why you broke it off?"

"No," Jack said with a shake of his head. "I was very . . . discreet. And the affair was short-lived. But I felt awful. I thought I would get over her fast, and Carrie and I would carry on as if nothing had happened."

"But Anne was pregnant," Sadie inserted.

Jack nodded and his face, already slack, fell even more. "I managed to avoid Boston for six months. I wouldn't take her calls; I blocked her e-mail. When I finally went to Boston, her condition was obvious. She pulled me aside and told me to leave Carrie, to be a dad to this baby. I couldn't believe she expected me to disregard my entire life so easily, but she did. She'd been waiting for me to come to her—she'd been waiting all those months to say those things to me in person. And then, when I explained I couldn't do what she wanted—wouldn't do it—she threatened to call Carrie herself." He took a breath. "I couldn't let her do that, so I offered her money. I cashed in a portion of my retirement. Twelve thousand went directly to Anne and the other eight was specifically for the baby's college later on. Then I agreed to pay her $500 a month in child support—Ron set up the accounts."

"Ron," Sadie breathed, not realizing she'd spoken out loud until the word escaped her lips. Her mind accepted the fact that Trevor wasn't his son but she wasn't sure how to go back to unsuspecting him of the murder—and yet Jack still had more talking to do.

"He was divorced," Jack continued, seeming as if he was now in a hurry to divulge the secrets he'd worked so hard to protect. "Ron didn't have a wife who would be suspicious about an extra bank account or two. It made sense to have him as the middleman, keeping Anne and me from having to deal with each other, and he was willing to do it—he's the executor for the college fund and a cosigner on Anne's account. I didn't want her to have access to all the money." He looked up and met Sadie's eyes. "Don't hold this against him, Sadie, he was only trying to help a friend. It was all set up before he even met you. I guess, once it got started, it just seemed like it wasn't such a big deal. I felt like we'd fixed everything. Anne would stay in Boston, I would help financially, but I wouldn't have to watch my family torn apart because of what I'd done."

Sadie tried, really tried, to give Ron the credit Jack wanted her to give him, but it wasn't working. "Ron went to see her that night, Jack. He was in her house. Setting up those accounts wasn't all he did. He's part of this deception—that speaks of his character in big loud words—and now Anne's dead." She didn't have to say that it spoke to Jack's character even louder.

"Sadie," Jack sighed. "You're a good person. It's no wonder that this doesn't make sense to you. I even told Ron that—"

"Why do you keep saying that? That I'm a saint, that I'm a good person. Do you think because I *choose* to see the good in the world, the good in people, that I can't understand this?"

Jack's eyes softened, showing his love for her and how much he hated telling her this. His sympathy only made her more upset. He should have told her everything a long time ago. She'd have helped him fix it. She'd have talked to Carrie, talked to the pastor of their church, even talked to Anne. Why hadn't he asked for her help instead of treating her as if she were too delicate for reality?

He continued, "I think . . . you have a good heart. It's not in your nature to be deceiving and selfish. I think it's very hard for you to understand what motivated me, or Ron for that matter."

"That's lovely, Jack," Sadie said, sitting back in her chair and crossing her arms over her chest. "Does it make you feel like some kind of intellectual to talk down to me? I understand loneliness," she said. "Better than you do. And I understand hopelessness, and wanting more than you have. I can see what drove you to be with Anne—not that I in any way approve or justify it—but I also know the difference between right and wrong. And so do you."

Sadie paused, took a breath and reminded herself, again, that this wasn't about her. She could not afford to get side-tracked. "So, you said you had it all figured out. What went wrong?"

"It got complicated, but that wasn't Ron's fault." He paused and then spoke again. "After Trevor was born, Anne sent me pictures of him. A son." Tears filled his eyes again. Jack had always wanted a son.

Sure, he'd never said so out loud, but with each of Carrie's pregnancies he seemed to be holding his breath. He loved his girls, and would have doted on them if Carrie hadn't gone over-board and left so little parenting for him to participate in. Instead, he'd become very close to Sadie's son, Shawn. Jack was the one who did scouting with Shawn, talked to him about the birds and the bees, showed him how to sack a quarterback, and took Shawn to his cabin for hunting weekends. The love for that cabin was something only those two could appreciate—another thing that bonded them together—and Sadie had often pondered on what a blessing Shawn was in Jack's life. In many ways Jack was closer to Shawn than he was to his own daughters. And Anne gave Jack a son of his own. How terribly, horribly ironic.

"I tried to stay away," he said, "to pretend it hadn't hap-pened, but the next time I went to Boston I called her. And the next, and the next. I made it clear to Anne that our rela-tionship was over, but I wanted to see Trevor. I was able to see him every few months, watch him grow. Finally, when Trevor was fourteen months old I realized he was getting old enough to remember me between visits. My staying in his life would make things harder for everyone. It broke my heart to do what I had to do, Sadie, it was awful, but I paid Anne more money based on her promise to leave me alone. Dad died a few weeks later and I told Carrie I only got half the inheritance he really left for me, the other half went to Anne to pretend I had never been a part of her life. That Trevor was not my child."

Jack let out a breath and wouldn't meet Sadie's eyes. She had the feeling that he didn't want to talk anymore. She wasn't about to let that happen. "You're lucky I never talked to Carrie about the inheritance," Sadie said. As executor of their dad's will, Sadie knew Jack had received almost eighty thousand dollars—same as she did. "I could have clued her in without knowing it."

Jack nodded and gave her a repentant look. "I'd managed your investments long enough to know you weren't one to talk about money."

Well, that was true. She'd always felt that finances were a personal matter, which was why so few people knew that she was so well off. "But Anne came to Garrison anyway," Sadie said, getting back to the topic at hand. "Why did she do that?" But Sadie had read the book. She knew exactly why Anne had come to Garrison.

Jack shrugged and wiped at his eyes again. "I hadn't spoken with her for months, not since sending her the money. Then I came home from work one day and Carrie starts telling me about this woman who had just rented the Tilly house. That night I take the garbage to the curb, and who should meet me with Trevor in her arms? She said that Trevor needed a father and if I refused to go to her, she'd come to me." He paused. "I begged her to leave, I offered her more money. She didn't want it."

An instant picture entered Sadie's mind. It was May, she was helping Anne plant some tomatoes in the backyard. The ground was warming up and Anne was excited about growing something all her own. The day was warm, with a breeze that kept blowing their hair around their faces. Trevor was kicking a ball—sometimes directly at them—but mostly against the back of the house, then running after it. Sadie had teased Anne about using her fresh tomatoes to lure in a good man come fall, when the harvest would be on. Anne had smiled to herself and tucked a strand of highlighted hair behind her ear.

"I'm just waiting for Mr. Right, Sadie. He'll come around."

Mr. Right—Mr. Jack *Wright* to be exact. Anne was waiting for *him*—waiting for him to come to her. In the meantime she was taking seriously her education on how to care for a home and family the way Jack would want—with Sadie as the teacher. It wasn't the book, not exactly, but it was close enough.

Even now Sadie could see Anne's face from that day, see the smile Sadie had interpreted as longing and dreamy, rather than secretive and contemplative. She had to shake her head to get rid of the vision, afraid that her feelings of betrayal would overshadow the sense she needed to understand what Jack was telling her.

"And then you left Carrie a few weeks after Anne moved in. Had she found out?" Sadie asked, bringing herself back to the present.

"No," Jack said, a little too fast. "She didn't know until I confessed everything last night. But back then, once Anne had moved in, I knew it was only a matter of time. I'd run out of cards to play and fate was catching up with me. So I left—I left both of them. I couldn't bear seeing Anne, seeing Trevor— seeing what I'd done. I hoped that if I left, Anne would leave too."

Sadie watched his face. He wasn't looking her in the eye anymore. Instead he had a distant look on his face while his eyes were blankly fixed on the tabletop. "But then you changed your mind and came back to kill Anne months later?" Sadie asked. Up to this point she believed him. Not that the story wasn't utterly fantastic, but the emotions that played across his face weren't feigned. He meant what he said. But there was no way he killed Anne. He wouldn't work so hard to take care of her and Trevor and then murder her. It was ludicrous. "And what about Trevor? What did you do with him?"

Jack was silent for a long time. Sadie was patient. He skirted the question. "Anne called some old coworkers in Boston and got a job at the office here in Garrison. I saw her when she came in for her interview on Friday. She actually came into my office and gave me a key to her place. She said I'd be wanting to come see her soon and she was trying to make it easy for me. She was invading my life—stalking me. I couldn't take it anymore."

"And Trevor? Where is he?"

"He's . . . safe."

"He's alive?"

Jack's head snapped up. "Of course he's alive."

Sadie shrugged as if they weren't discussing the life of a two-year-old boy. "Well, you'd kill his mother, why not assume you'd kill him too? Destroying the evidence, so to speak."

"He's my son," Jack said in short, clipped words, looking horrified. "I would never hurt him."

"And killing his mother isn't hurting him? Where is he?"

Jack looked back down at his hands. "The police will find him soon," he said.

The cryptic response took her by surprise. What did that mean? "Tell me where he is and I'll go get him."

"No." It was a solid no, a "there is no way in heck I'll ever tell you" kind of no.

"So let me get this straight," Sadie said, wiggling forward in her seat and putting her arms on the table, shortening the distance between them. His story was beginning to unravel. "You won't risk telling your wife about your infidelity and illegitimate child, but you'll kill the mother of your only son?"

Jack wouldn't meet her eye. "I finished the Monday classes at the convention and came back to Garrison to talk to Anne. I had hoped she would take more money and disappear. But she wouldn't. She was as obstinate as ever and so I . . . I killed her."

"What about Ron? He was there that night."

Panic crossed Jack's face, but he quickly repaired it. "Ron came with me, but then I told him to leave when she became so difficult. I did this, Sadie."

"You took two cars? Ron drove separately?"

"Ye-es," Jack said.

"Why? If you're both going to the same place for the same reason, why take two cars?"

"It seemed better that way."

He was such a liar! She didn't even bring up the fact that both Ron and Jack then returned to the conference *without* a toddler.

"And why did you go back to her house last night?" She was leaning forward, staring at him so as not to miss a single nuance of his face. He startled, furrowing his eyebrows for half a second.

"Uh, I . . . didn't." He glanced at the mirrored wall as he answered.

"You did," Sadie said. "You went to the closet, fumbled through some boxes and stole some pictures."

"How do you—"

Sadie waved a hand as if parting smoke from the unseen fire she imagined coming from Detective Cunningham's ears on the other side of that glass. "Why were you there?"

Jack looked at the table again and eventually let out a breath. "I gave Anne a gift, in the beginning. It was silly, really." He paused and Sadie feared she'd see some kind of calm look of reminiscence on his face, but instead his pain intensified. "The first time we . . . went out, we went to a waffle house. The next time I went to Boston I bought her a waffle iron. She loved it, and it made me feel like some kind of hero for spending thirty bucks on a kitchen appliance. There was a recipe in the instructions and we made Belgian waffles together a few times—funny, Carrie never lets me cook. She didn't want me to mess up her kitchen." He let out a strangled breath. "When I saw Anne a year or so later, after Trevor was born, she brought the box for the waffle maker out of her bedroom. In it she'd collected all the e-mails we'd sent back and forth, a card I sent her with some flowers, and a few pictures I didn't even know she'd taken. She'd used the box as some kind of hope chest. Last night I . . . I knew I was going to turn myself in and I didn't want those things found, I didn't want to hurt Carrie with them. So I took them and threw them in the fireplace when I got back home." He met Sadie's eyes. "But I still don't understand how you know—"

Sadie cut him off again, remembering the fire in the hearth at Jack and Carrie's the evening before. "It's hard for me to believe that such a cold-blooded killer would be so worried about his wife's feelings."

"I'm also an adulterer and a liar," Jack said softly. "I'm not the man you thought I was, Sadie. I'm a monster."

Sadie chilled at the word "monster" and knew that regardless of whether or not he convinced her of it, he truly believed it about himself. "If you really want me to believe this—that Jack Wright, my friend, brother, and neighbor—the coach of my son's little league team, the man who mowed my lawn, fixed my appliances, stood up at my son's eagle court—if you really want me to believe you did this, then you have to tell me what you did."

Jack was silent and tears filled his red-rimmed eyes again. Sadie ignored the tears on her own cheeks and didn't break her gaze. She needed to *see* him tell her this—see him lie to her about it.

"I killed her," Jack said, his voice a whisper.

"You strangled her," Sadie said pointedly. "You didn't just kill her—you need to tell me that you strangled her." She paused and then spoke again, her words deliberately slow as she watched every movement of his face. "You put your hands around her neck and killed the woman you once loved, the mother of your only son."

"Yes," Jack said, his voice cracking. He couldn't hold her eyes any longer and looked at the table. "I put my hands around her neck and killed the woman I once loved, the mother of my only son." His voice choked and his chin trembled as he said it. "I did this, Sadie. I did all of it."

CHAPTER 27

"Did you catch that?" Sadie said to Cunningham once the ugly gray door closed behind her. What she wouldn't give for a paint scraper and a Sherwin-Williams clearance sale. The detective looked at her with a guarded expression and nodded. Madsen wasn't in the observation room with them, which meant luck was on her side—sort of. There was still the pesky matter of Jack taking the blame for something he didn't do.

"He doesn't know she was killed with a drapery tieback. He didn't do it," Sadie said, fully assuming that their interest in the tieback earlier meant that the coroner's report had been rather specific. She looked through the glass and watched her brother, head in his hands, slowly rocking back and forth in his chair. Misery exuded from him and her throat got thick again. Sadie was suddenly grateful that the tragedies in her life had not been directly related to choices she made. How did someone live with the guilt of having put events in motion that ended like this?

"Then who did?" Cunningham asked, the challenge in his voice showing his frustration. "And why did he confess?"

"To protect Ron," Sadie said. It was obvious. There had been a momentary hope during her discussion with Jack that Ron wasn't the man she felt she'd discovered him to be—but that hope had gone now. Ron may not have been Trevor's father, and there was some relief there—though if she'd had to choose, she'd have picked him over Jack to have fathered the child—but regardless, she had little doubt that he was, in fact, Anne's murderer. He was there that night around the time the coroner's report said Anne had been killed. Jack felt guilty for having involved Ron and felt this would be his penance.

"Your fiancé?" Cunningham asked, watching her closely.

"Just call him Ron," Sadie said. She attempted a small smile, though she couldn't take the sadness from it. "The engagement is off."

"Your brother would go to these lengths to protect him?"

Sadie furrowed her brow. It was obvious, and yet, ridiculous at the same time. "You heard what he said," she reminded him. "He said 'I did this.' He feels like it's his fault. He was the one who had the affair and pulled Ron into it, and Anne died as a result so now he feels as if he's somehow responsible."

"Would you do that?" Detective Cunningham asked. She looked up to find him watching her, his eyes seeming to take in every detail of her face. "Would you give up the rest of your life and plead guilty to a murder of someone you cared for simply because you made a mistake?"

Sadie looked back at her brother. A guard was helping him to stand. Jack shuffled out of the room, his back bent, and more than his forty-six years showing in the slump of his shoulders. Even his hair looked older, duller. "I don't know," Sadie said as the door closed without Jack looking back. "I've managed to keep myself from having to make those kinds of decisions."

"Yet you broke into Ms. Lemmon's house last night, didn't you? And you've been withholding information again." His eyes were stones in his hard face as he stared at her. "You're interfering with a police investigation," he said. "I should arrest you."

Sadie knew her pleading showed in her eyes. "Please don't," she breathed. "Please, I'm helping, I'm gathering information—"

"You're causing a great deal of trouble, the very least of which is trying to convince me that the man confessing to this murder didn't do it." His voice lowered and he leaned forward slightly. She suddenly wondered if it was appropriate for them to be alone in the observation room together. "I've asked you," he said in a tone stretched between warning and compassion, "to please stop, to let us do our job. You have put me in a very awkward position."

Sadie was not intimidated and pulled herself up to her full height. "You have put me in a very awkward position as well, Detective. You are accusing a man I know to be innocent of a serious crime. I have no choice but to do what I can to prove his innocence."

They stood there, him bent slightly over her as she stood tall, refusing to concede her position. Finally, he straightened, the stiff lines of his shoulders relaxing just a bit. "I will consider this a final warning. You need to back out and let us take care of this."

"Have you ever had English trifle, Detective?" she asked, surprising him with her out-of-the-blue and completely off topic question.

"English trifle?" he repeated with a blank look.

"It's delicious. I make it every Christmas Eve. It's cake and custard and Danish dessert layered with fruit and whipping cream. I once assigned six different women at church to make it for our Christmas social. I got back half a dozen completely different variations. One woman added pineapple, another used chocolate cake instead of ladyfingers. One woman stirred it all together so it looked like soup. We were all doing the same thing, making the same dish, but they were all done so completely different."

"And the point of this little culinary lesson?"

"We all go about things in our own way," she said. "I won't tell you how to make your trifle if you don't tell me how to make mine. Jack's my brother. I will mind my Ps and Qs, but I will not stop looking for a way to clear him."

"Then you should go to jail."

"Madsen," she said, noticing the way Detective Cunningham stiffened when she said his partner's name, "would put me in jail. But you won't, because you know that beyond all your procedures and policy and possiblys, that I *am* helping you." She cocked her head and narrowed her eyes. "And you know Jack's innocent. You can't prove it, and neither can I, but you know he is. And you're a good enough cop—a good enough man—to find it impossible to ignore that."

They were silent for a few seconds and she watched his eyes, the only part of him that slipped through his training enough to show just how right she was. He couldn't say it, he wouldn't say it, and in truth, he shouldn't say it. But he knew. And he was going to let her go.

Cunningham finally snapped his gaze away and abruptly headed for the door and pulled it open for her. "What a tangled web we weave," he said as she passed through the doorway. Their moment was over, but their understanding was sealed. She would do what she had to do, within reason, and he would allow her the freedom to do it.

Once outside of the small room she turned to him. "You will keep investigating though, right?" she said. "I mean, you see the inconsistencies. You have to take those seriously, don't you?"

Cunningham let out a breath. "It's not my decision," he said, his voice almost sounding apologetic. "We have a confession and that's not something my captain takes lightly."

"But you still have to find Trevor," she reminded him, sidestepping the whole Jack-is-innocent argument since she knew he was fully aware of it. "That will keep you on the case, right?"

"Trevor," Cunningham said, sounding like a grandfather lamenting his own grandson. "Jack won't tell us anything about him. He won't say where he's been or who he's with now. All we have is his comment that we'll find him soon."

"Is the Amber Alert still in place?" Sadie asked. She hadn't turned on the news today, so she didn't know what was being reported. She should have TiVoed it.

"It is," Cunningham said, following her down the hallway, carefully shepherding her out the door. At the glass doors she turned to face him and moved to tuck a strand of hair behind her ear before remembering it was a messy mass of curls. Oh, the humiliation! She felt strangely vulnerable, knowing she didn't look like herself. She hated that people—including Detective Cunningham—might think she was a dowdy woman.

"Will you call me when you find something out?"

He raised one eyebrow, quite a nice eyebrow. "Would you?"

Sadie blushed at the reprimand. His face was stoic once again, as if their silent exchange of connected allegiance was nothing more than a memory. But then she wondered if he was simply keeping up pretenses, having to live up to the big-bad-cop image he'd spent a lifetime earning.

"Go home, Mrs. Hoffmiller. Stay home. Knit something if you have to, but my request that you stay out of this is still in force."

He turned and walked away from her as she put her hands on her hips in response to his rudeness.

"I don't knit," she said to no one but the inebriated man sitting on the bench to her left. "Those pointed needles are a safety hazard."

CHAPTER 28

It had long been Sadie's habit that whenever she found herself passing a grocery store on her way home, she searched her mind for anything she needed. There was nothing quite as frustrating than walking in the door after a long day and realizing you were out of laundry detergent, cream of tartar, or something equally important. Albertson's grocery store was on her way home from the police station and despite everything, old habits die hard, and she automatically asked herself if she needed anything.

Lasagna noodles.

She'd used the last of them on Sunday and would hate to get a hankering and be unable to fulfill it. Though never a very good dieter, she'd found a rule of thumb that kept her from blimping out as her metabolism slowed with age—eat what you want, but not all of it. So, if she wanted cheesecake, she made cheesecake, had a slice, and took the rest to a friend or someone in her church in need of a pick-me-up. If she wanted pot roast, by George she'd have pot roast and freeze the leftovers for a night when she craved a good stroganoff or beef soup. So far the system worked for her—she enjoyed food but didn't overindulge and could still fit into styles that made the most of her curvaceous hips. However, she became very cranky when a craving drove her to the pantry only to find she had neglected to stock her shelves correctly. She pulled into the parking lot while mentally scanning her cupboards to make sure there was nothing else she needed.

The morning snow had stopped, leaving a steely gray sky and a few inches of snow behind—another reason to get her groceries now, in case the snow came back later. It was only as she scanned the parking lot to find a space that she remembered this had been the store where Anne worked. It wasn't the grocery store Sadie frequented; it was a chain and she preferred to support Sammy's on Mount Ridge since it was locally owned. She slid her car into a space between a Cadillac and a Pinto and paused with her hands still on the steering wheel.

What could she possibly gain from talking to the people Anne worked with? There was no real answer—she could learn a lot or she could learn nothing. All she could do for sure was her best. She did feel the tiniest bit of apprehension, but the memory of Jack being handcuffed made it hard for her to swallow as she got out of the car. A blast of cold wind took her breath away and she shivered, glad she hadn't left her jacket at the police station.

She hunched her shoulders and peered at the sky, wondering if it would snow any more today, or if the weather was just taunting her.

It took less than five minutes to find the lasagna noodles and remember that she also needed some nutmeg and a few lemons—Anne had used her last one for the mystery tart. Then she got in the express lane and began putting her items on the conveyor belt. She knew the clerk, though they didn't have a good history. Melba Browton's son was quite likely the worst student Sadie had ever taught. It had only taken one parent meeting to realize he'd inherited his mother's personality charms. His name was even Damien, which she believed meant "devil" in Italian, or maybe Portuguese. Regardless, it was fitting. Sadie scanned the other check stands but knew it was too late to choose a different lane. Picking up her items and moving would be overtly rude.

"How are you guys holding up, Melba?" Sadie asked sweetly as the clerk scanned her first item.

Melba looked up, staring at Sadie from behind her glasses. She was a thick woman, with middle-aged skin to go with her middle-aged figure. Her red hair was tightly curled and looked as if it were glued to her head. It had been a decade since Sadie had taught Melba's son, but Melba still wore the exact same hairdo. "Holding up?" Melba repeated.

"Well, with what happened to Anne Lemmon," Sadie said. Wasn't it obvious? They'd lost a comrade, a fellow employee. Surely it stung a bit.

Melba shrugged. "I said I wasn't gunna take any of her open shifts," the woman said. "She weren't nobody that ever tried to help me out."

Sadie stiffened. Was there no respect for the dead at all? "Oh," she finally said, opening her purse and pulling out her wallet. "So you two weren't friends?"

"Hardly," Melba said. "She was nice enough to the customers, but she let us know from the start that this weren't no career for the likes of her." She snorted and hit the total button. "Last I heard she was quitting anyway."

"She wasn't, uh, close to any of the other clerks then?"

Melba looked up at her this time and eyed her with suspicion. "Why d'you care?"

"I'm just curious." Sadie handed over a twenty-dollar bill. "It's been a long time since Garrison had a murder is all." The last one was a teenage kid almost eight years ago who killed his girlfriend and then himself. People still talked about it—usually when their daughters were dating a boy they didn't like.

"Yep," Melba said. She opened the till, counted out Sadie's change and handed it back to her. "Y'all have a nice day," she said without a smile before moving onto the next customer—an order well over the ten-item limit. Melba glared at the customer who was breaking the rule.

"You too," Sadie said. She retrieved her grocery bag and looked around the store, trying to think of anything else she could do, anyone else she could talk to. To her surprise another clerk in the next lane was watching her. As soon as Sadie met her eye, however, the girl looked away. But there was something in her expression that caught Sadie's attention. The girl was close enough to have heard the exchange with Melba.

"Doggone it," Sadie said out loud. "I forgot I was going to cook up a roast tonight." She turned to Melba. "Can I leave my bag here while I go back for it?"

"I don't care," the woman said. Sadie got her roast and was in the other girl's line before Melba had finished with her over-the-limit customer.

Though they were a chain store, Albertson's had always been good about employing otherwise difficult to employ people in the community. Mason Dillies, a local man with Down syndrome, had recently been featured in the paper for having worked as a bagger at Albertson's for fifteen years. Their philanthropic disposition was enviable. However Sammy's did the same thing, she preferred their produce, and the owners went to her church. The clerk for this new check stand didn't have Down syndrome, but she had a breezy disposition that seemed to make time move slower in her lane.

The girl was young, early twenties Sadie guessed, with shoulder-length brown hair. She had a fair amount of acne scarring, a general look of naïve unkemptness, and jack-o'-lantern earrings that dangled from her ears even though Halloween was three weeks away. When she said "Good morning," her words were slow and not fully sounded out.

Sadie smiled brightly, wanting to put the girl at ease. "Did you know Anne?" she asked directly.

"Yes," the girl said as she picked up the roast and slowly pulled it over the eye of the scanner. It didn't take. "She gives me rides home so I din't have to take the bus."

Sadie smiled and realized how hungry she was to hear something positive about Anne. Until this moment she hadn't known how badly she needed the reassurance that Anne wasn't just mean and manipulating. Sadie had seen worth in her; surely she hadn't been completely wrong in her judgment. "She was very nice, wasn't she."

The girl nodded, her nod as slow as the words she'd just spoken. She didn't offer Sadie any other information as she pulled the roast over the scanner a second time. This time the cash register beeped and she put the roast in a plastic sack.

"Did she get along with anyone else here?" Sadie asked, wishing she'd grabbed more items so as to extend the conversation. She grabbed a pack of gum from the rack behind the conveyor and put it down. "Or were you her only friend?"

The word "friend" made the young girl smile, which relieved Sadie even more.

"She was my friend," the girl said. She looked up and met Sadie's eyes. Underneath the scarring and softness of her expression, she was a beautiful girl, with wide green eyes and high cheekbones. Sadie hoped she had wonderful parents who cared for and loved her dearly. She picked up the pack of gum and swiped it across the scanner. This one beeped on the first try.

"I know," Sadie said, imagining Anne waiting for this girl to finish her shift and ushering her to her car. Good for Anne. Sadie searched for something else to say. "She got along with the customers?" Melba had already said as much, but Sadie wanted it from another source.

"Customers like Anne," the girl continued. Her eyebrows furrowed. "'Cept the one in the pink shoes."

"Oh," Sadie asked, trying not to sound too interested. "What happened with the one in the pink shoes?"

"Well," the girl said. She stared at the conveyor, concentrating hard. "Anne was givin' me a ride home, and a lady stopped her car in front of us. Anne stopped fast and I hit my hand." She lifted her hand as if to show an injury Sadie couldn't see, though she frowned sympathetically. "And the lady jumped out and yelled mean things." She shook her head as if still upset about it.

"How horrible," Sadie said. "Then what happened?"

"Anne yelled too." The girl looked up and met Sadie's eyes. She leaned toward Sadie and lowered her voice. "She said bad words."

Sadie made a face. "That's not good."

The girl shook her head slowly and straightened. "Then she took me home."

That's it? Sadie thought. "Um, what did this woman say, the one who stopped her car in front of you?"

"She said Anne was a home breaker."

"A home breaker?" Sadie asked, searching her mind for a definition of the term. "Oh, you mean a home wrecker."

"Right," the girl said, smiling as if embarrassed. "Home wrecker. And she said Anne had to go away forever." The girl's eyes went wide to illustrate the seriousness of such a demand.

"Forever?" Sadie said, keeping the tension up though her thoughts were moving a million miles an hour now. If Jack was the father of Anne's baby, only one person would be accusing Anne of being a home wrecker. "That's a long time," she said, swallowing and forcing herself not to cover her ears as yet one more person she loved came into focus.

"And then Anne said the bad words I was telling you about. I can't say them."

"Oh, no," Sadie assured her. "I wouldn't want you to. Um, what did this lady look like?"

"Pink shoes," the girl said bluntly. "With light hair." She looked triumphant, as if that explained everything.

"What did her car look like?" Sadie asked, trying to imagine Carrie wearing pink shoes, but finding herself not wanting to think on it too hard even though she couldn't get Carrie's newly blonde hair out of her mind. The denial she'd been wresting with in regards to both Ron and Jack was back full force. *These things don't happen in real life!* she lamented. *Not to me.*

"White," the girl said. "With black tires and a fish on the back." Carrie's car to a T. Sadie swallowed as the clerk continued. She seemed to have warmed up to Sadie. "I have a fish, too, you know. She's a molly fish and I named her Polly. Get it?"

"Polly the Molly," Sadie said, though she wasn't sure how much longer she could pretend her whole world wasn't spinning out of control. "That's very cute."

The girl smiled broadly and nodded.

"Was Anne upset when she got back in the car?"

The girl furrowed her brow and then shook her head. "No, she said the lady was crazy but I was scared of that lady."

"I bet you were," Sadie said, reaching over to pat the girl's arm sympathetically.

Someone standing behind Sadie cleared her throat. Sadie turned to look. "Oh, sorry," she said to the little old lady who'd already loaded all her groceries on the conveyor. She turned back to the clerk. "Thank you for talking to me," she said with a smile. "Say hi to Polly for me."

She was a few feet away when she remembered something else. She stepped back, earning an unhappy look from the customer in line.

"When did this happen?" Sadie asked. "The mean lady and the bad words."

"Um," the girl said, her eyes drifting to the ceiling. "Monday."

"Monday?" Sadie asked bleakly. "You're sure?"

The girl nodded. "I never work on Sunday and I came back on Monday. Anne was s'posed to pick me up on Tuesday after lunch." Her face fell and a confused expression took residence behind her eyes. "But she didn't call and she didn't pick me up. Mama said she's in heaven now. I bet she's a pretty angel."

Sadie tried to swallow the lump in her throat and give the girl a final smile. "I'll bet she is too."

CHAPTER 29

H i, Sadie."
Sadie smiled brightly at Mr. Henry who stood just inside his doorway. He regarded her with complete boredom. She could hear a television coming from the darkness behind him and tried not to shiver in the wind that was still blowing. The junipers he had planted around the doorstep helped shield her from the worst of the wind, but it was still very cold. It didn't surprise her that he didn't invite her in. That's why she'd grabbed her heavy winter coat on her way out the door.

He was the only neighbor she hadn't talked to and she wanted to make sure she'd left no stone unturned before she allowed her suspicions to blossom into a full-grown garden. Already the shoots of such newly planted seeds were pushing up through the ground, making themselves difficult to ignore. When she'd seen his car in the driveway and realized he wasn't working today she knew she couldn't resist.

"Hi, Frank," she said. Using his first name felt strange on her lips, but she was pretending they were bosom friends who told each other everything, and she'd never call a bosom friend "Mr. Henry." She held out the plate in her hands. It was still warm and she was hesitant to let it go. "I made you carrot cookies," she said, smiling widely. The first thing she'd done when she got home was start the cookies. While they baked she took a shower and did her hair—finally—and she'd even put some makeup on and enjoyed feeling like herself again.

He stared at them with longing, then looked up at her with narrowed eyes. "I don't eat sugar anymore, Sadie. Doctor says I have prediabetic symptoms."

"Oh," Sadie said, her voice showing far more disappointment than was warranted. She'd just spent forty minutes baking these cookies. For nothing? "I'm so sorry," she said. "I didn't know."

He shrugged and began closing the door.

"I could make some soup," she said quickly, not wanting to lose the opportunity. "I make a fabulous beef-and-barley—no sugar and limited starches. I could bring some over later, it takes about two hours to simmer so—"

"What do you want, Sadie?"

Hmmm, so she wasn't fooling him. "I . . . just wanted to be a good neighbor."

He rolled his eyes. He actually *rolled* his eyes at her attempts of service! "You want something," he summed up. "What?"

Sadie straightened up and looked aghast at him as a gust of wind blew against her back, causing her hair to blow forward.

She wrestled with the now tousled strands, trying to get them back in place. "I am just trying to—"

"Sadie Wright Hoffmiller," Mr. Henry said. "I've got your number, okay? I've known you for, what, eight years? And in all that time you only show up with food when you either need to borrow something or want to find out who was visiting me for the weekend." He stopped and smiled just enough to offend her even more as she raced for an explanation. "Your Christianity is lovely, and the fact that you're a terrible busybody doesn't bother me in the least, but I've got a show I'm in the middle of and my TiVo ain't workin', so just get on with it."

Oh, fine, Sadie decided, finally lowering the plate and her facade. "Did you see anything yesterday morning or the night before?"

"Nope. Same old stuff as always, 'cept Carrie."

"Carrie?" Sadie asked as she tried to pull everything she'd heard about Carrie over the last two days to the forefront of her mind. It was weird that the topic she was hoping for more information on was the very thing he would bring up. Could it be fate?

"Yeah, she was loading a suitcase in the car when I left for work—I went in at five to get ready for an audit."

Suitcase. Someone else had said something about . . . that's right, Mindy had talked about Carrie taking a trip. Sadie had forgotten all about that. "At five in the morning?"

"That's what I thought. Funny thing about it," Mr. Henry said, his eyes dancing as he leaned forward slightly. She'd never seen him so animated and found it a little disgusting that he'd take so much delight in the ugliness of all this. And Mr. Henry had never liked Carrie. Not since the time at the block party that he mentioned he was against war and she called him an anarchist. People don't generally like to be called anarchists and Mr. Henry was no exception. He'd stood up from the table in Sadie's backyard and walked away without a word. That was five years ago, and he hadn't come to a block party since.

"The car left last night but she didn't, darn my luck. I was gettin' all excited about her holiday."

Sadie turned to look at Carrie's house. Her car wasn't there. She tried to remember if it had been there last night. All she could remember was Jack's truck—but it wasn't there either.

"When did the car leave? Who took it?"

Mr. Henry shrugged. "I saw your girl's car on the street. The next time I looked out the window both cars were gone. At first I thought Carrie was gone too—I was about ready to celebrate—but then I saw her out talking to Jack for a little while."

Sadie stared at the porch. "Did you tell all this to the police?" she asked.

He shrugged. "I didn't pay it much mind till the car was gone and the dragon lady wasn't. The police haven't been around for me to tell them anything today and I don't think it matters to them if Carrie goes out of town or not." Mr. Henry began shutting the door again. "Ain't my business, Sadie. If you ask me, it ain't yours either."

"Trevor is Jack's son," she said quickly, needing the upper hand and knowing that kind of information would give it to her. Mr. Henry startled and his eyebrows jumped up. He pushed the door open a little wider.

"What?" he asked slowly.

She summed up the whole sordid situation in about half a dozen sentences. Mr. Henry looked appropriately shocked and just a teeny bit impressed. She'd have slapped him but she knew full well that wouldn't help her get any more information. "He didn't kill Anne," Sadie said sharply. "I know he didn't."

"Then who did?" Mr. Henry asked, watching her carefully as if afraid she might spontaneously combust with all the stress and pressure.

Sadie turned away from him without giving a direct answer, shrugging her shoulders slightly. "If you remember anything else will you let me know?"

"Sure," Mr. Henry said as she headed down his front walk, the cookies still in hand.

Suitcase.

In the trunk.

"Frank," she said, turning to face him and knowing he'd be there because she hadn't heard the door close. He was watching her. "What color was the suitcase?"

"Black, I think," he said. "And heavy. If it had been anyone else I'd have stopped to help. As it was I enjoyed watching her struggle."

What a gentleman. "And did you happen to notice if she was wearing pink shoes?"

"Pink?" Frank said. "Only good witches wear pink, Sadie, and Carrie ain't never been a good witch."

Sadie nodded and turned away, closing her eyes for a moment as she caught her breath. She was worn out from all the suspecting she'd been doing. She crossed the cul-de-sac, the north wind destroying all the hard work on her hair strand by strand, but she wasn't paying it much mind. She peeled back the plastic from the plate long enough to grab a cookie and shove the whole thing in her mouth. The orange-glaze frosting filled her mouth as her cheeks puffed out while she chewed.

A suitcase.

A heavy suitcase.

A heavy black suitcase.

Anne's missing filing cabinet?

She should have asked Mr. Henry if he'd had his glasses on when he saw Carrie, but it wasn't a stretch to imagine that in the darkness of early morning a two-drawer filing cabinet could look an awful lot like a big heavy suitcase. Without the car here, presumably with the suitcase or filing cabinet in the trunk, there wasn't much she could do on that front. But she felt an increased urgency to get some answers. She felt so close, both physically and metaphorically. So much had happened right under her nose. It felt as if the only way to validate that she wasn't a complete idiot for not realizing just how much had been happening was to find out exactly what those happenings were.

With her free hand she pulled out her phone and once she reached the sidewalk in front of Carrie and Jack's house she began typing a text message to Breanna. She'd have called, except Breanna never answered her phone during class. It took an inordinately long time to type with one hand, even using a few abbreviations. Although she was hesitant to involve her daughter, she needed answers.

Did T drive C's car home last night? Call ASAP

She put the phone in her pocket and found herself looking at Jack and Carrie's house. The shades were drawn, the porch cluttered, as had been its state the longer Jack had been away. Sadie wondered how many secrets were held inside that quiet house.

Inside, she repeated. That's what she needed to do. Get inside!

She'd try doing it the right way first.

She headed up the front steps and knocked loudly on the door, deciding she'd offer the cookies and tell Carrie she'd left something in the guest room. That would give her a reason to be invited in, and once there . . . she'd come up with another plan.

No one answered.

She knocked again and waited. Nothing. The heavy curtains—too heavy for an entryway, in her opinion—made it impossible to see through the front windows. Entryways should be light and welcoming, not shut out visitors. Sadie tried the door—locked. She went back down the porch steps and around the side of Carrie's house. The windows were all closed tight, the curtains drawn.

I have a key, she told herself, then remembered that she'd given Jack and Carrie's key to Detective Madsen. She briefly wondered what he was going to do when he found out the mistake, then pushed that thought from her mind. As she rounded the back of the house she decided to try the back door. If it was unlocked, she could go in and . . . look around. Should Carrie come home, Sadie could use the same forgotten-item excuse to explain her presence there. However, the back door was locked, and try as she might to peek through the mini-blinds of the kitchen window, she couldn't see a thing.

"Fine," she said as if giving in to an argument, though she wasn't giving up. She would get into this house one way or another, but she'd have to get creative or wait until Carrie got home. Sadie headed down the back steps, then paused on the last one with her foot in the air. Her eyes were drawn to the garbage cans lined up against the garage. In two seconds she was standing over the green Rubbermaid containers, but she didn't have to open them to know what was inside. Her nose was sending out an urgent alarm even as she tried to talk herself out of it. But a mother never loses the ability to diagnose certain things. There are simply some smells that remain embedded on her senses for the rest of her life.

Sadie was willing to bet the entire plate of carrot cookies still in one hand that she smelled diapers.

Carrot Cookies

1 cup butter
3/4 cup sugar
1 egg
1/4 teaspoon orange extract
1 cup cooked and mashed carrots (Steam carrots in microwave until
    soft—don't use baby food—bleck!)
1 teaspoon grated orange zest
1 teaspoon baking powder
1/2 teaspoon salt
2 ½ cups flour
1 cup chopped walnuts (optional)

Icing
2–3 teaspoons orange zest
3 tablespoons orange juice
Powdered sugar to consistency

Preheat oven to 375 degrees. Cream butter and sugar. Add egg,
extract, carrots, and orange zest. Mix well. Add the remaining
ingredients and mix until combined. Roll into walnut-sized balls and
press flat with fingers or a fork on a greased cookie sheet. Bake
10 minutes.

For icing, mix zest and juice then stir in powdered sugar until
icing is slightly thicker than a glaze. Drop by teaspoonfuls onto warm
cookies so icing melts into cookies.

Makes 2 to 3 dozen.

CHAPTER 30

Inside the garbage can was a white plastic bag knotted at the top. Sadie moved to the porch and put down the cookies before returning to open the garbage bag. Not only were there a few dirty diapers, but also a shoe box. Sadie picked the box out of the bag, thinking about the pink shoes that she still couldn't picture Carrie wearing. Then again, she couldn't picture Jack dating Anne either, or Ron lying to her for months, or Anne being strangled—yet she knew those things had happened. Pink shoes didn't seem too far-fetched in comparison. But the box was a child's shoe box, the picture showing Spider-man shoes with Velcro tabs and lights in the heels. She pictured Trevor's shoes sitting by the back door of Anne's house. The little boy had been barefoot when he left the house. She also reviewed the trips to the store Carrie had taken yesterday—as she pulled out a box for children's Benadryl. Would Carrie actually drug a toddler in order to force a nap so she could run errands? Had she kept him downstairs so that in

265

case he woke up, no one would hear him? It was hard to imagine, and yet impossible to ignore the possibility.

There was one other thing in the garbage can that got Sadie's attention and she pulled the green hanging file from the bag, snagging the metal end on the plastic. There was nothing unique about the file. Sadie had the same kind in her own filing cabinet, but she'd seen stacks of them just yesterday and that image was fresh in her mind. Scattered around Susan Gimes's office had been dozens of similar files. Anne's file had been missing.

Susan's voice from yesterday filtered back to her, "We're shorthanded today."

Carrie's calendar also came to mind. She'd marked working hours for the next three weeks, but she hadn't worked on Tuesday.

Susan had verified with her receptionist that K through M was supposed to have been scanned in on Monday—Anne's file should have been among them.

What are the chances? Sadie asked herself as she flipped the file open. It was empty, except for the plastic tab that Sadie assumed had once been attached to the top of the file.

LEMMON, ANNE

Sadie's hands began to shake. Carrie's temp job must have been at Susan Gimes's office. Carrie had found the file and put things together much faster than Sadie had, but somehow had come to the conclusion that Jack, not Ron, had been involved with Anne. Sadie wondered what it was that had made Carrie figure it all out. Maybe she knew about Jack cashing in his retirement, or only admitting to half the inheritance. Maybe she'd seen him talking to Anne that one time and somehow put everything together. But the newest facts marched through Sadie's brain at a steady pace, not allowing her to focus on Carrie for long. Sadie couldn't seem to catch her breath and it had nothing to do with the wind that was blowing directly into her face.

Trevor was here.

Carrie knew about the affair before Jack said she did.

Carrie confronted Anne.

Jack's taking the fall for her.

"I did this," Jack had said at the police station. "I did all of this."

"Dear heavens," she said out loud. Were the documents still in Carrie's house? It would tie everything together.

Jack is innocent.

I have to talk to Detective Cunningham!

Sadie dropped the file back into the garbage can, picked up the plate of cookies from the porch, and with hurried steps, moved to the side yard closest to her house, already thinking of how to explain this information to Cunningham. The side yard was about ten feet wide, with Jack and Carrie's white house siding on their side, and Sadie's cedar fence on the other. Jack had always talked about fencing in his own yard, but he never seemed to get around to it, leaving only Sadie's enclosed. She was almost to the end of her fence line, where she could cut left for her front steps, when she heard an engine shut off. A car door opened and then shut. She stopped just shy of the corner of the house and pressed her back against the cold siding. *Is it Carrie?* she wondered.

Sadie could see her own house from the corner of Jack and Carrie's house, the black walnut tree close enough to the sidewalk that it didn't block her view from this angle. She was close, but she couldn't talk to Carrie right now and trying to cut from Carrie's yard to her own front door would make that inevitable. She'd just wait until Carrie went inside, then run for her own house and call Detective Cunningham.

Sadie moved to stand against the side of Carrie's house, straining to hear footsteps heading for the door of the house, so she could make her escape.

"Mrs. Wright?"

Sadie couldn't see him, and he had to be several feet away, but she knew it was Detective Madsen. She growled low in her chest and came as close to swearing as she'd been since the time Shawn and Breanna had a chocolate syrup and ketchup fight in the kitchen almost six years ago.

"Do you know where Mrs. Hoffmiller is? I understand she stayed with you last night."

Sadie's heart leapt into her throat and she held the cookies tighter against her chest. Why did he want to talk to her?

"I've been running errands," Carrie said, though her tone sounded the tiniest bit nervous. Sadie could imagine that hiding so much information from the police would make anyone anxious. Carrie continued. "She was gone before I got up this morning."

"Is she here now?"

"No," Carrie said. "I came back to pick up some things a while ago and she was gone. Her car is in her driveway though." Sadie wondered what Carrie was driving. Had she picked Jack's truck up from the police station or did she have her car back?

"She isn't answering her door," Madsen said with annoyance. "So you haven't seen her?"

"No," Carrie said. "If I do, I'll tell her you're looking for her. I've got an appointment, Detective. Can I go inside now?"

There was a pause and Carrie's cat, Pouches, came around the corner from the back of the house. Sadie shooed at her, trying to get her to go away, but instead Pouches continued out a few more feet—in full view of both Sadie in her hiding spot and Carrie and Madsen in the driveway. Pouches sat down, cocked her striped head at Sadie and meowed.

Sadie looked at her sternly. The last thing she needed was the cat giving away her hiding place. "Go," she mouthed—as if the cat could not only understand the English language, but read lips as well. Pouches stretched her front paws in front of her and laid down, still staring at Sadie.

"Meow."

Pouches had distracted Sadie from the conversation between Detective Madsen and Carrie, but she tuned back in as soon as she realized it.

"Do you recognize this?" Detective Madsen asked.

"That's my house key," Carrie said with alarm. "The one I gave to Sadie. What are you doing with it?"

Sadie made a face. He'd discovered the key. Shoot. How on earth was she going to explain that? And Carrie thought she'd just handed it over to the detectives. Doggone it, why didn't she give the right key in the first place? Then she remembered she wouldn't have been able to break into Anne's house last night if she'd handed over the real key.

"You don't need to worry about that," Detective Madsen said. Instead of being angry, he seemed quite pleased with himself. One more reason for him to suspect Sadie. She wondered if Cunningham knew about the key and could imagine the lecture awaiting her if he did. At what point would they stop threatening and actually arrest her for interference? Sadie had a sudden image of herself in the green scrubs she'd seen on Jack a couple hours earlier. Green had always washed her out.

Pouches rubbed against her leg and she nearly screamed. Looking down, she scowled at the cat again, who was purring loudly and mewing at her. It was true that Sadie sometimes bought canned cat food for Pouches as a treat—Carrie would only buy the bargain dry food and even cats deserved a little something extra on special days—but now she wished she'd never spoiled the feline. It lay down on her feet, and turned its sea-green eyes toward her.

"Meow."

She removed a carrot cookie from the plate and tossed it a few feet toward the back of the yard in hopes the cat would follow. Pouches looked at it, then back at Sadie. Apparently carrot cookies looked and smelled nothing like fish.

"Meow."

Sadie shook her head, waiting to hear Carrie muse aloud why her cat was acting so funny. But Carrie hadn't seemed to notice just yet.

"I sure *am* going to worry about you having a key to my house!" Carrie said loudly. "I want it back." The anger in her voice surprised even Sadie, who was used to hearing Carrie go off about something or another. But it made sense for her to freak out. Based only on the things Sadie had found in the garbage can, the idea of the police being able to go inside her home at will must be horrifying.

"I'm sorry, but it's part of a police investigation," Detective Madsen said. "It will be returned to you when we're finished with it."

"Finished?" Carrie repeated. "Then give it to me now. You have your confession, the case is over."

Everyone was silent. Even Pouches who was lying on Sadie's feet—weird cat. The flippancy in Carrie's voice was shocking.

"So you're aware of your husband's confession?" Detective Madsen said carefully.

Sadie leaned toward the voices, but Pouches protested loudly, so she kept her feet steady.

"I know all about it," Carrie said, and the calmness in her voice was more of a shock than her anger had been a few moments before. "He told me last night, before he turned himself in. Now give me my key."

Last night?

Sadie knew Carrie had known about Jack at least twenty-four hours longer than that.

"I'm sorry, ma'am," Madsen said. "I can't give you the key."

She continued to argue about it, and he continued to refuse until Carrie stormed up the steps and slammed the door, clicking the lock into place once she did so. Sadie tried to listen for Madsen's retreating footsteps, but couldn't hear them over the rustling leaves, then realized he'd see her if he decided to knock on her door again. She'd have to go through the back, which meant walking to the end of Carrie's backyard and using the gate Jack had put into the fence when they had all their kids at home.

She nudged Pouches off her feet, no longer worried about the cat's protests, and walked quickly, picking her steps along the grass carefully, well aware that Carrie was on the inside of the wall she was using as a guide and Madsen could take a few steps to his right at any time and see her shirking away. When she was around the back of the house and under the kitchen window she finally allowed herself to breathe.

Water ran in the sink above and behind Sadie's head. Wasn't there somewhere else Carrie could go for just a minute? Sadie looked down the length of the yard. The gate was on the right side, just past the apple tree. If she headed for the fence now, Carrie would see her from the kitchen window. She couldn't take that risk. Not only could she not afford Carrie's suspicion of what Sadie knew, but Carrie was mad about the key. And Sadie did feel very bad about that.

After a couple minutes of listening to Carrie move around in the kitchen, Sadie heard Carrie start humming.

More than anything else she'd put together in the last hour, the humming made Sadie's blood run cold. Carrie killed her husband's mistress, allowed her husband to take the blame, and now she was in her kitchen, doing dishes—humming as she did so. What kind of woman had Jack married?

Even more important than that—where was Trevor? He'd been here, but she didn't think he was anymore. If Sadie had only been able to get into Carrie's house!

The humming stopped and Carrie spoke. It took a few words before Sadie realized she must be on the phone.

"Hi, dear, how is everything? . . . Good, that's exactly right." Her voice moved out of range as Carrie left the kitchen. Despite her curiosity about the phone call, Sadie ran for the back gate as fast as she could, wishing she could just keep running and leave all these unwelcome thoughts and feelings about the people she loved behind her. But she couldn't outrun any of it. She went through the gate and came to a stop when she reached her own side of the fence. She rested her back against the wood and took a deep breath, nearly screaming when her cell phone rang in her jacket pocket.

She fished the phone out of her pocket with her free hand, the plate of cookies still in the other one, and saw it was Breanna.

"Oh, Bre," she breathed once she answered, resting her head back against the fence. "I'm so glad you called. You got my text?"

"Yeah," Breanna said. "I got it as soon as I finished the lab. What's going on?"

Sadie searched her mind, trying to remember what it was she'd wanted to ask Breanna about. Oh, yeah, Trina. "Did Trina drive Carrie's car home last night?" She was careful to keep her voice down so as not to draw anyone's attention.

"She did," Breanna said. "Uncle Jack explained it after we left the house. I couldn't figure out what the big deal was, and why they were in such a hurry to leave if we were taking separate cars, but he said he was worried about Trina driving back by herself and wanted to make sure I followed her until we got back to town."

Now Sadie understood why Jack was so hesitant about her coming over last night. They must have sent Trevor with Trina, using the darkness to cover up what they were doing. And they couldn't have buckled Trevor in a car seat or else Breanna might have noticed. How horrible—and irresponsible, especially in regard to Trina's emotional state at the time. Sadie wondered where Trevor was now—hiding in Trina's dorm room? It didn't seem likely, but what else would she do with him? She tucked the information away and returned to her questions.

"Did they, by chance, open the trunk?" Sadie asked, still trying to catch her breath for a multitude of reasons.

"No," Breanna said after a short pause. "Why?"

Sadie closed her eyes and argued with herself. The last thing she wanted to do was get Breanna involved in this, and yet the clock seemed to be ticking faster. "I need a favor," Sadie said. "I need you to look inside that trunk. I think Carrie loaded a two-drawer black filing cabinet into the back of the car." She paused. "It belonged to Anne."

She and Breanna briefly discussed what Sadie had learned. Once Breanna felt sufficiently informed, she promised her mother she'd call as soon as she learned anything. Sadie put the phone back in her pocket and headed up her back porch steps, her feet and her heart heavy. She had her hand on the doorknob when she remembered Trevor. Could he have been in the car with the filing cabinet? Sadie was pretty sure he hadn't been at the house last night.

So many questions.

Once inside, she shut the door quietly, not wanting anyone to hear it slam. She let out a ragged breath and after a few seconds, headed toward the phone in the kitchen so she could call Detective Cunningham.

She was stepping past the bathroom when a movement caught her eye. She automatically turned to look into the darkened room only long enough to see the light reflect off his hair. Before she could do anything else, his hand was over her mouth and the plate of cookies fell to the floor as she was pulled against him.

"Don't scream," Ron said in her ear as her heart raced all over again. "I need you to understand that I didn't mean to do it. It was an accident."

CHAPTER 31

"Y ou won't scream?" Ron asked after a few seconds.

Sadie shook her head. He hesitated a moment, then removed his hand from her mouth, but he immediately grabbed her arm and held on tight. Sadie knew panic should be coursing through her, sending a rush of adrenaline, but she barely reacted at all. Ron had been waiting for her, she still believed he'd been involved in Anne's death—in fact he'd just said as much—and he was wanted by the police for questioning. Big deal.

"I'm not going to run, either," Sadie said, rubbing her mouth where she still felt the pressure from his hand.

She turned her eyes on Ron, who now stood a few feet away, carrot cookies at his feet. He didn't look anything the part of the cold-blooded killer she still thought him to be, but he didn't look like the man she'd been planning to share her life with either. His deception and his anger at the restaurant clouded the vision of the future that had at one point seemed so clear. Instead he was shifting his weight, running the hand not clamped to her wrist through his hair. There were bags under his eyes and the lines of his face seemed deeper.

"I'm not going to run, Ron," she said again.

His face reacted at her use of his name and it showed her that she still had some power. She wondered how much he knew she knew and yet the details she thought she understood an hour ago had shifted thanks to the information she'd gathered about Carrie. But at least she was finally in a place where someone was going to offer her some answers. "What do you mean it was an accident?"

Ron finally relaxed his hand, but his face was tight, his eyes full of turmoil. She kept a distance between the two of them and couldn't stop her mind from reviewing all the possible fire escapes she and the kids used to drill through once a year in case she had to make a break for it.

"She was threatening him—both of us really."

"Both of you?"

"She was going to tell you," Ron said, turning his tortured eyes on her. They were still standing in the hallway; she realized he was likely hesitant to go into the living room with so many windows. Being in a small space forced his face closer to her than she'd have liked. "She was slowly cornering us, Sadie. She'd already found a job at Riggs and Barker, and she was going to start next week. Jack had dipped into his 401(k) and done all he could. He felt there was nothing else to do but to tell everyone the truth. But he wanted to wait until after the conference to do it."

Sadie said nothing, but continued to hold his eyes.

"It wasn't just about Carrie," he continued, his tone rising. "He's got three grown daughters. He has neighbors, friends . . . you."

"Me?" Sadie said. "Jack knows that if anyone is going to stand by him no matter what, it's me."

Ron's expression showed a moment of frustration, as if his being so familiar with all the details made her unfamiliarity with them hard to understand and empathize with. "But he didn't want you to have to stand by him, Sadie. He was humiliated, and full of so much remorse for all of it—for everyone. He'd tried so hard to set something up where he was the only one that suffered, but it was falling apart. On the way to Denver he said he was going to call his kids and have them come down on Saturday. He'd tell Carrie first, of course, but he felt he needed to let everyone know. I think . . . he was almost relieved to finally have an end to it. He seemed lighter."

"But you went to Anne's house Monday night," Sadie said, realizing his visit would have been several hours *after* Carrie confronted Anne in the parking lot.

"She called me," Ron said. "Monday evening. She called and said she'd waited long enough. She demanded that Jack come see her that night." His shoulders slumped and he shook his head slightly as his arms hung limp at his sides. "I didn't even tell Jack. He had a presentation in the morning, and he was already under so much pressure getting ready to tell his family. I thought maybe I could reason with her one last time, help her understand that he wasn't giving her any more money—he couldn't." He shoved his hands into his pockets and continued to stare at the floor. "She was so unreasonable," he said. "She finally admitted to me that everything she'd done wasn't about the money. She wanted to be a part of his life. When I told her that wasn't going to happen, she lost it. She said that in the morning she was going to tell you first thing. She felt that once you knew, Jack would be forced to come home right then and face everything and everyone—her, Carrie, his kids."

But Carrie already knew, Sadie said in her mind. Ron didn't know that. Did Jack?

He looked up and met Sadie's eyes. "I was horrified, Sadie. I knew you wouldn't understand."

It was the most insulting thing she'd heard all day—and she'd already been told by Cunningham to go knit something. "Why does everyone keep thinking that I somehow live on a different planet?" Sadie interrupted, throwing her hands up in the air for emphasis. "For heaven's sake, I'm not an idiot." Though a quick review of all the things she'd missed challenged that pronouncement. "If you all had been honest this would have taken care of itself, and for a man who asked me to marry him, you had an awful lot of secrets. I don't know how to rectify that."

"I know," Ron said, looking down at the ground. "It seemed so straightforward in the beginning when I agreed to go along with Jack. It made so much sense. If Anne had just stayed in Boston . . . if she'd have just stuck with the original deal, none of this would have happened."

Sadie stiffened. "This is not Anne's fault," she said evenly, pointing her finger at him as though he were a student. "She was a young woman trying to do her best with—"

"She was not some kind of hero, Sadie. Don't put her on a pedestal just because she's dead."

The harshness of his words silenced her and she dropped her hand. She didn't know what to think or how to feel. One minute he was explaining it as if he had been a victim in all this, and the next minute he was angry and spiteful. Could both sides be true?

"And why is she dead, Ron?" she asked calmly, reminding herself of all the questions she needed answered. "What happened?"

His face went slack, a haunted expression flashing in his eyes just before he looked away. "We were arguing, and she was being completely unreasonable. She was demanding—"

"I don't want to hear how she deserved it, Ron," she yelled, surprising herself that her voice could even get that loud. "What happened?"

"She fell down the stairs," Ron said and his eyes stared over Sadie's shoulder. "We were arguing in the kitchen and I tried to grab her arm so she'd stop walking away from me, but she pulled away real fast and lost her balance at the top of the stairs."

Stairs? Sadie repeated in her mind. But the family room was cleaned up. And the tieback? She reflected on what Ron had told her yesterday, that Anne was alive when he left her.

"And you left?" Sadie breathed, unable to comprehend how he could have not gone for help.

"She was alive," Ron said, tears filling his eyes. "She was breathing and she had a strong pulse, but she was unconscious and I didn't know what to do. She started coming around, moaning. I panicked and I ran. I should have called the police, I know that, but I reacted on instinct and drove straight back to the conference. In the morning, I used a pay phone to call the police to go check on her."

Ah, so *Ron* had called in the tip—one mystery solved—but she had little time to ponder on it. Sadie's instincts would never allow her to leave someone like that. How could he be wired so different? "You must have known she was dead when you called the police, otherwise she'd have implicated you."

"She *wasn't* dead," Ron said quickly. "And I planned to come back to Garrison later in the day—after I talked to Jack. I needed to take care of a few things and tell my side to the police."

"If she were still alive, you mean. You had to know that there was a chance she didn't survive the fall down those stairs, yet you waited until it was *convenient* for you to call the police."

He couldn't looked at her and she was reminded of the quote that said a person's character was proven in the split-second decisions they make when they think no one will ever know. Ron had chosen to leave, and that said a lot about his character. She felt the last shreds of hope and commitment for their relationship to work disappear from her heart. Jack was her brother, they had been connected their whole lives, but who she married was up to her and she would not choose this.

"I called in the tip from a pay phone, then I went to wait for Jack to finish his class. I was wandering around the hotel, sick to my stomach, trying to come up with the right words when I walked past a security guard. He was on the phone, talking to someone else about a dead girl in Garrison he'd heard about on the scanner—he said something about an Amber Alert for the kid. It was too much of a coincidence and I jumped in the car and drove to Garrison as fast as I could, trying to figure out what to do, afraid you'd seen me that night."

"And Trevor?" Sadie asked before he had a chance to break off the dialogue.

Ron paused there. Did everyone forget about Trevor in this?

"I don't know," Ron said. "I left. I don't know what happened to Trevor. He was asleep when I got there. It was after midnight."

Sadie regarded him and tried to line things up. Everything she'd learned about Carrie's involvement was directly tied to Trevor. Had she simply taken Trevor? Gone over after Ron left? But why? And where was he now? How did Anne get into the field? Why would Ron tell her this story if it wasn't the truth and so easily disproved? There was so much to sort through.

After a few seconds, she looked up at him. "I need you to do me a favor," she said, using the exact same words she'd spoken to Breanna a few minutes earlier. She walked past him toward the phone and picked it up. "Call Carrie," she said. "Tell her that Jack asked you to call about Trevor. That you're supposed to help her."

"Carrie?" Ron asked. He was still standing in the shadows of the hallway, hesitant to step into the wintry light. "What does Carrie—"

She pushed the phone closer to him. "I think she has Trevor somewhere, but I'm sure she won't talk to me."

"I don't want to get any more involved in this than I already am," Ron said, taking a step backward. "The police are watching my house. I've been afraid to go to work, to drive more than a mile over the speed limit. I'm going to turn myself in, Sadie. I know I have to, but I wanted you to know the whole story first."

"Do you know that Jack confessed this morning?"

Ron's eyes went wide and he visibly started. "What?"

"He says *he* killed Anne. I thought he was covering for you, but now I believe he's covering for Carrie. Anne wasn't killed by the fall, someone strangled her and dragged her body into the field."

"But I—"

"You owe me this," Sadie reminded him. "After all the stews and steak dinners I have made you while you were lying to me, hiding something this big, the least you can do is make one lousy phone call in the hopes of saving this boy whose mother you left to die."

Finally, Ron took a few steps forward. Sadie dialed the number and handed it to him before hurrying to the extension in the bedroom. She shrugged out of her coat—she was sweating. She picked up the phone carefully, and one ring later, Carrie answered the phone.

"Carrie?" Ron asked, his voice higher than usual. Sadie hoped Carrie didn't pick up on it. "I, uh, need to ask you some questions. Jack wants me to help with Trevor. He asked me to call you and find out what you need me to do to help."

Carrie was silent for a few moments and Sadie held her breath. "Jack wanted you to call?" she repeated.

"Yes," Ron said. "He was, uh, worried about you doing . . . it all by yourself. I want to do whatever I need to do to help. I won't tell anyone."

"Is that so?" Carrie asked, her tone superior. Sadie was confused. "Then why are you calling me from Sadie's house?"

Oops.

CHAPTER 32

Three things happened at once.

Someone knocked at the door, Carrie hung up, and Ron swore—another strike against him.

Sadie was frozen as the triple play took place and in the next instant Ron appeared in the doorway of her bedroom with an angry look on his face. "What now?" he asked in a fierce whisper.

"Answer the door," Sadie said as she sprang off the bed and headed for the back door. She knew it was Detective Madsen knocking. She also knew that she had to confront Carrie herself, and she had to do it fast. "You said you were going to turn yourself in and now is your chance. Tell him everything."

"But," he said as Sadie bolted past him in the doorway. She pulled open the back door, stepped outside, and shut it quietly before Ron had a chance to say anything else. She walked fast toward the back gate, glad for the privacy fence that would protect her from being seen from the street, at least as long as she was in her own yard. She was halfway to Carrie's back door when she heard an engine start up. She increased her pace, but half a second later, Jack's truck passed the black walnut tree on its way out of the cul-de-sac.

Carrie was on the run.

Sadie sprinted back to her own yard and fumbled in her pocket for her car keys. Twenty seconds later she was squealing out of her driveway. She slammed the gearshift into drive and sped after Carrie, paying no mind to the irate detective bounding down her front steps. She blew past the stop sign and turned left after catching just a glimpse of Jack's tailgate ahead.

Once she straightened out she could see the back of Jack's truck ahead of her. Her heart was thudding in her ears and she fumbled for her cell phone in her pocket.

"Detective Cunningham," she said to herself, holding the steering wheel with one hand as she held the phone up to her face. She'd called him on her cell phone before, hadn't she? In between glances at the road, she scrolled through dialed numbers, but none of them jumped out at her. "Shoot," she said before calling directory assistance for the second time that day. She did not look forward to her bill this month.

"Yes, I need to be connected to the Garrison Police Department."

"Is this an emergency?"

"Yes," Sadie said, needing this woman to hurry. She rounded the corner Carrie had taken seconds before.

"I'll connect you with 911."

"91—wait. It's not that kind of—" But it was too late.

"911, what is the nature of your emergency?"

She grunted and hung up. Carrie was at least two hundred feet ahead of Sadie when Sadie was forced to stop at a red light. She tapped her fingers on the steering wheel, afraid to blink for fear Jack's truck would disappear. Her phone rang and she quickly answered it, hoping it was Detective Cunningham somehow sensing her need to talk to him. Carrie turned right at the next light.

"Hello?" Sadie said as her light turned green and she hurried to catch up.

"Mom, it's me."

"Breanna," she breathed. "Did you find out anything?"

"Yes and no," Breanna said. "Trina's not home, in fact she hasn't been home since last night when we got back to Fort Collins. *And* all she did was run in and pack a bag. She told her roommate she was going back to her parents'."

"She's not there," Sadie said even though Breanna already knew that.

"I know," Breanna said while Sadie took the same right-hand turn she'd seen Jack's truck make, scanning the cars ahead of her. Sadie thought she saw the truck way ahead, and squinted in hopes of making out the details better, but she couldn't be sure it was Carrie.

Breanna continued. "Her roommate said Carrie picked up Trina Sunday after Trina got off work. Trina said she'd be back Monday night—because of midterms she didn't have class on Monday. But then Trina didn't come home until Tuesday morning after nine o'clock. Aunt Carrie dropped her off and Trina went right to bed, skipping two midterms she had that day. She only came out when her mom called that afternoon. Then Trina called me for a ride back to Garrison."

Thoughts and ideas swirled through Sadie's mind all over again. Trina had been in Garrison Monday night? In an instant she pictured Carrie's calendar, the one she'd pretended to be reading when Jack had come out of the bedroom last night. She'd seen an appointment for Trina just before Jack interrupted her. If Trina was in town then she might have known her mother found the documents at Susan Gimes's office. The number of people who knew about Anne's deception was getting bigger by the minute.

"Oh my word," Sadie breathed into the phone. "Breanna," she said sternly, her hand clenching the phone. "Trina's shoes," she said quickly, as if she might run out of time to get the words out. "What kind of shoes was Trina wearing when you saw her last night?"

"Tennis shoes, I think," Breanna said, a question in her voice as to why this detail was important.

"Does she own any pink shoes?" Sadie asked, praying Breanna would say no. Trina was only twenty years old and she'd struggled to find a life of her own. Sadie did not want to heap anything else upon the poor girl's shoulders, the least of which were undeserved suspicions. But ever since talking to the girl at the grocery store she'd been stuck on the idea of Carrie wearing pink shoes. "Does Trina ever wear pink shoes?"

Breanna paused, a pause that seemed to reflect that she knew this was an important question. Finally she answered.

"Yes," Breanna said quietly. "She has a pair of pink Converse sneakers. Carrie gave them to her for her birthday last month. Last night was the first time I'd seen her without them in weeks."

CHAPTER 33

The silence on the line was thick as Sadie absorbed what Breanna had said. *Not Trina*, she pleaded, *not her too*. She continued forward through an intersection, looking for a glimpse of Carrie while simultaneously wondering what she'd do if she lost her sister-in-law. She must be going to find Trina and Trevor.

"Where would they go?" Sadie said out loud. "A hotel?" Maybe she should call Karen Thorgood who worked for Holiday Inn; surely she could call the other hotels in the area to ask if any of them had seen Trevor. Sadie had taught Karen's three sons when they came through the second grade, and she had no doubt Karen would help her out if she could.

"People would see them, and she'd have to use a credit card," Breanna added.

"That's true," Sadie said. And she couldn't imagine Trina checking into a hotel when her nerves were already so frazzled. "But if not a hotel, then—"

"What about the cabin?" Breanna interrupted. "If I were going to hide someone, that's where I'd go."

"The cabin," Sadie repeated.

It was Jack's cabin. Carrie had always hated it, saying it was too cold, too run-down, and too dirty. Sadie didn't disagree with her much on those points. It was an old hunting cabin Jack bought twenty years ago, and in Sadie's opinion calling it a cabin was giving it far too much credit since it was basically a one-room shack in the mountains. It had plumbing that continually backed up, a sink, and a stove, but no water heater.

Jack and Shawn used to go there for a week each year when the deer hunting season opened, but over the years it had become more of a retreat for Jack than anything else. When Carrie was making him crazy, or if he just needed a break, he'd disappear for a day or two, returning with a skin thick enough to withstand Carrie's faultfinding once again. Sadie hadn't been there herself for years—not since the time she went up with the kids and killed ten spiders in half an hour before heading home. To imagine Trevor being there gave her the chills, but she couldn't deny it would be a good hiding place.

"I wonder if I can remember how to get there," Sadie said, making the instant decision to check it out. "I think it's off the Grass Canyon exit."

A reflecting sliver of red and then blue played across Sadie's dashboard and she was confused until she looked in her rearview mirror.

Detective Madsen sat in his blue unmarked car directly behind her. Just below where his rearview mirror was attached to the windshield were alternating red and blue lights. His face was pinched and he pointed to the right and mouthed, "Pull over."

"Breanna," she said quickly as she realized she couldn't outrun Madsen and she didn't have much time. "This is very important. You must call Detective Cunningham at the Garrison Police Department. Tell him everything I've told you and everything you just told me about Trina." She felt silly for making this request since Cunningham's partner was pulling her over, but she didn't trust Madsen and she wanted Cunningham to know she'd tried to give the information to *him*. She pulled to the curb and watched Detective Madsen jump from his car as soon as they were stopped.

"Call him right now, Bre, right now!" She clicked off the phone and quickly put it in her pocket as Madsen banged on her window. She looked up into Madsen's irate, and yet somewhat pleased, expression.

"Get out of the car!" he yelled.

With a resigned sigh, Sadie opened the car door. He grabbed her arm and pulled her the rest of the way out.

"Hey," she said as she stumbled to the side of the car. He grabbed her left arm and twisted it behind her. "I have a bad shoulder," she said, cringing against the pain. It was a lie, but she didn't feel guilty for it because he shouldn't be treating her this way.

He loosened his grip and she managed to pull out of his grasp while turning to face him. She took in the handcuffs he was holding in one hand.

"You're arresting me?" she asked, her cheeks flushing with embarrassment.

"For interfering with a police investigation," he said, reaching for her arm again. She hit at his hand and then, realizing his intent, decided not to make a scene in hopes of keeping some control in the situation. She put her hands forward, wrists together.

"Behind your back," Madsen said, grabbing her arm and attempting to turn her around. No way was she going to have her face mashed into the top of her car with all these people driving by.

"And ignite my bursitis?" she asked. "I don't think so."

She held her wrists up even higher. "Surely you can make an exception for a fifty-six-year-old woman, or do you think I can take you down?"

His eyes narrowed, but he finally snapped the first cuff on her right wrist.

"For heaven's sake," she muttered as he finished binding her wrists. "I want to talk to Detective Cunningham," she said, trying not to look too closely at the cars whizzing past. Surely she knew some of these people. How embarrassing.

Madsen laughed. "He's done about all he can do for you," he said as he pulled her up and pushed her toward his car. "In the meantime, you have the right to shut up."

CHAPTER 34

Madsen shoved her, none too gently, into the same back seat he'd held her prisoner in yesterday afternoon at the library. Then he moved her car to the parking lot of the post office. When he returned, he was stone-faced and offered little by way of explanation for having arrested her; something she was sure was illegal. To say nothing of his telling her to shut up. She added it to the list of things she planned to report to Cunningham. Maybe she'd file a great big lawsuit against the entire police department for mistreatment or something like that. Yet, even as she thought about it she knew she wouldn't. She was not a supporter of frivolous lawsuits, but then again she'd never been treated so . . . well, frivolously.

"I thought the investigation was over now that you have a confession," she said.

"There are still loose ends to tie up—like you."

She let out a breath and would have rolled her eyes but for the anger she felt at his wasting any time at all with her. "Every minute you spend with me is a minute taken away from the real investigation."

"The investigation is over," Madsen said. "Just like you said. We've got our man."

"But you don't have Trevor. And if it's over then why were you at Carrie's? Why were you asking her questions? And why am I being arrested for interfering with an investigation that isn't really happening?"

His eyes met hers in the mirror. "Stop talking," he said blandly before his eyes returned to the road. "You're giving me a headache."

"What about Trevor? Aren't we still trying to find him?"

"We?" he repeated, meeting her eyes again. "*We* are doing nothing. *You* are going where you can't cause any more problems."

His eyes went back to the road and Sadie adjusted her position—handcuffs were blasted uncomfortable but she offered up a quick prayer of thanks that her hands were bound in front. How would she sit at all if they were wadded up behind her?

Madsen made a right-hand turn and Sadie searched for Jack's truck on the roads around them. The steely afternoon sky spoke of more snow to come. Carrie was long gone by now, however. It made Sadie's stomach ache to think what could be happening right now. While she was stuck here, falsely accused, was Carrie headed for the cabin? What were her intentions with Trevor? "I'd like to talk to Detective Cunningham. Will he be at the station when we arrive?"

Madsen muttered something under his breath.

"It's terrible manners to mumble," she reminded him sternly, fed up with his arrogant rudeness. She reflected on most of her day, realizing she'd been short and snippy with several people—quite out of character for her. Then again, she didn't usually live under so much pressure. Surely she could be excused for being a little tense.

Madsen sighed. "I said, 'I'll just bet you would.' You seem to think you've got Cunningham in your pocket."

Sadie snorted. "Hardly," she said, thinking of the very un-pocket-occupying treatment he'd been giving her, though she was curious as to his unofficially telling her to continue with what she was doing. Almost as if he was prevented from doing what she could still pursue. She found herself rubbing her mother's ring again, searching for calmness, and tried to come up with something she could say. She stared at the back of Madsen's head, reviewing all their experience with one another, looking for something to make sense of his ongoing poor treatment of her. Something came to mind that didn't add up just right.

"So what happened to your hearing yesterday?" Sadie asked. He seemed to be taking the long way to the police station.

Detective Madsen stared straight ahead and said nothing—a reaction she hadn't anticipated. It sharpened her awareness of him, the tightness of his shoulders, the deep breathing. He was taking her into the station, getting her out of his hair. Why was he so tense?

"What are you talking about?" he asked after several seconds. "I went to the hearing."

"No," Sadie said, "you didn't." Feeling cocky for catching him in a lie, her eyes narrowed and she forgot about the police station for the moment. "You said you were going to one, but then you showed up at . . ." Her sentence trailed off as she realized he might not know she'd been at Susan Gimes's office. Detective Cunningham knew, but it seemed as if they were working separately now. That was something else that grabbed her attention. Why was Madsen alone? Why wouldn't he know she'd been there if Cunningham knew? What kind of partners withheld information from one another? *Distrustful ones,* she answered her own question.

The plot thickened.

He stopped at a red light and turned to look at her over his shoulder. "How do you know where I was?" he asked incredulously.

Sadie gave him a cocky smile; he looked nervous as he turned to face the front again. A shiver of recognition ran through her at the expression on his face. It was so similar to the look Ron had yesterday morning. Madsen was hiding something and whatever it was had caused a breach between him and Cunningham, had necessitated Madsen's lie about the hearing. She took a breath. Everyone's secrets were wearing her out, but she was determined to figure out what *his* secret was. To do so, though, she needed to keep him talking.

"So what brought you here from Denver?" she asked with feigned casualness; she already knew the answer thanks to Susan Gimes and her family history lesson.

His jaw stiffened and the tension rolled off of him in waves. Like a shark in bloody water, her senses heightened even more. He said nothing.

Her phone!

She'd forgotten she had it and maneuvered her hands to the side so she could dig it out of her pocket. But she needed him to keep talking so he wouldn't notice what she was doing.

"You came from Denver, right?" she pressed as they passed Harmony Street, the route that would take them to the police station. Her heart began thudding in her chest as they headed further toward the outskirts of town and she paused in the retrieval of her phone. He wasn't taking her to the station after all. Even more alarming, the tension seemed to be leaving him and his arrogance returning. Her movements quickened and she finally had her phone in her hands. She was attempting to flip it open when it slid out of her hands, bounced on her knee, and landed on the floor. She stared at it in horror.

She was trying to scoot it back to her with her foot when instead she sent it under the seat at the very moment Madsen's voice broke the silence. "Boston, actually."

If not for the cars and the road still moving outside her window, Sadie would have thought the world had frozen in place.

Boston?

Anne was from Boston, it was where she met Jack, where she had worked for Riggs and Barker, where Trevor was born.

In an instant all her moments with Madsen and his incredible arrogance and determination to find her guilty flashed through her mind. Like a kaleidoscope, all the colors shifted and a whole new pattern appeared before her. It wasn't often that Sadie Hoffmiller found herself at a loss for words, but she couldn't think of anything to say.

Madsen seemed to count her silence as a victory and continued without prompting. "I'd had some trouble in Denver, so I went to Boston to stay with a friend of mine. Horrible city, if you ask me," he said, shaking his head slightly. "Not only is it full of boring history lessons I already had to sleep through in high school, but it's big and smelly and under continual construction. But it's got a nice night life if you're into that kind of thing." He met her eyes in the rearview mirror and smirked. "I don't imagine you are though."

Sadie felt her mouth moving but she couldn't make any words come out. Her head was buzzing again as all the pieces of the puzzle she'd been working on seemed suspended in the air: filing cabinet, dirty diapers, Trina's appointment, Jack's wedding ring, Anne's book, pink shoes. None of them had anything to do with Madsen. She felt cheated for having given so many things so much attention for no reason.

Madsen continued, the more he talked the more relaxed he became. Sadie had read about that. Serial killers seemed to make a habit of it in suspense novels—wanting to boast of their exploits. *Is Madsen a serial killer?* she wondered.

"There was this one club, The Barracks, on the north end. Nice place; catered to military and police. I met a girl there, hot little number. We danced, and had a few drinks every weekend for a couple months. She had a kid at home, but hired a babysitter for Friday nights. After awhile she starts telling me about the kid's dad, some old guy, married, living in my home state of Colorado. He totally ditched her, but was coming around sometimes, still wanting the best of both worlds, ya know."

"You?" Sadie finally said as everything else she'd already learned funneled through her brain. Carrie . . . well, probably Trina had confronted Anne in the parking lot just hours before Ron had caused her to fall down the stairs. More details rushed through her mind: the lemon tart, a child's shoe box in the garbage can, Carrie telling Mindy she was taking a trip. Nothing made sense, as if she had taken pieces from eighteen different puzzles and was trying to make something out of them anyway. "You . . . but . . . Anne . . ."

Madsen laughed. They were outside of Garrison now, heading east on the highway which just happened to be the same direction as Jack's cabin. "It was my idea to have her move out here, ya know. I got hired onto the Garrison force, which wasn't hard to do with idiots like Cunningham taking up space, and then we waited for a house to come up for rent in Jack's . . . well, I guess it's your neighborhood too. Can you imagine the stroke of luck when it was two houses away from Jack?" He shook his head and Sadie had to fight back tears as she absorbed what he was telling her. He was so cold, so uncaring about the whole sordid story. "Almost seems like it was meant to be, doesn't it?"

"How could you do that?" she said quietly, almost in a whisper. "How could you ruin the lives of all these people?"

He glared at her. "Guilty people, Mrs. Hoffmiller, adulterous, lying, deceitful people who thought they could get away with it."

"Like you plan to?" Sadie replied, leaning forward. "Have you no shame in the fact that Anne is dead because of your plan?" Sadie spat out. He met her eyes again, narrowed in the rearview mirror.

"That wasn't my fault!" he roared, making her flinch and pull back into the upholstery of the seat. "We just wanted money. I was sick of playing the politics of law enforcement. I found this place in Costa Rica where, with a couple hundred thousand dollars, we could have a good life together. We were moving toward that goal and then Anne had enough. When I called her on Monday she was acting weird and she didn't want to talk to me. I knew something was wrong and she finally admitted Jack was coming over that night and that she would get the money. He'd been so *generous* in his attempts to keep her quiet, we had little doubt he'd do it again."

It wasn't making sense. Ron hadn't said anything about Anne making those kinds of demands. She hadn't said anything about money that night, just that she was going public and wanted Jack. In fact she specifically said she *didn't* want money. And then a few of those hovering puzzle pieces snapped into place.

"Oh," Sadie breathed as she saw things a bit more clearly than she had—than Madsen had too. "Oh," she said again, managing a low chuckle. "Did she play you or what?"

His brows furrowed in the mirror and she laughed, thinking about the book she'd read; the way the woman kept trying to be a part of the man's life. It wasn't about the money for the woman in the book and it wasn't about the money for Anne either. Anne was a far better player of this game than anyone had ever expected her to be.

"Carrie already knew about Trevor when you called Anne on Monday," Sadie told him, watching his eyes closely as they hardened. "The blackmail angle was gone and Anne knew it before she demanded Jack meet her that night. *You* wanted the money, but even after everything that happened, all Anne ever wanted was Jack." She paused, aligning her understanding; the clicks of everything coming together was almost audible in her head. "And the lemon tart," she mused. "My mother used to make that recipe for Jack and me when we were little. It's been a favorite of his all his life and Anne had asked me how to make it right after she moved in." There was silence for the space of two seconds as the implication of it all settled, reminding her that everything had been so calculated and yet she'd had no idea. "Jack was coming to see her, or so she thought, and she expected him to stay. She even set the tart to finish cooking so it would be ready when they started a new day—a new life together. Only Jack didn't come Monday night like she planned, Ron did." She wasn't sure yet, however, what part

Madsen played in that. But it was coming, she could feel the details lining up in her mind.

Madsen's knuckles turned white against the steering wheel but he said nothing. Sadie felt her panic rising again as even more questions entered her mind about where they were going, but she tried to keep them at bay. She needed to keep the dialogue going.

"Your boyfriend pushed her down the stairs before she had a chance to tell him," Madsen said. "That's all. He ruined everything. That stupid tart isn't the lynchpin."

"But it is," Sadie said quickly. "It was the symbol of the woman she was becoming for him, the proof that she could take care of him better than Carrie, better than any other woman in his life." She paused. "Wait, how did you know about the stairs?"

Ron had only told her half an hour ago. If *only* Ron and Anne had been in that house Monday night and Anne was found dead in the field and Ron had only told Sadie . . . "Unless, *you* were there!" She leaned forward as more and more pieces of the gruesome puzzle fit themselves together. "That's it, isn't it? You were there, in the house, and Anne didn't know because if she had known you were there she'd have had to follow your plan and demand the money. But you figured it out, didn't you? From where you were hiding in the closet, or maybe downstairs, you heard the whole thing and you—" Ron's words came back to her, *"She was alive when I left her."*

"You killed her for betraying you," Sadie summarized, shocked at her own words, at the picture they created. "You strangled her with the tieback."

Madsen was looking ahead now, though she could feel his anger. His whole attitude made sense now, the reason why he'd targeted her from the beginning, why he'd followed her to the library, and why he had confronted Susan Gimes. All along he'd been protecting himself, hiding his own sins while inflating everyone else's. And now she was his only secret keeper; she was the only one who knew the part he played. In one sense it was absolutely terrifying, and yet in another way, a whoosh of relief washed through her. It wasn't Jack or Ron or Carrie or Trina. No one she loved had killed Anne. The relief of that realization was overwhelming enough that it tempted her to relax and accept that it was over and she could stop thinking such dark thoughts. Then Madsen took the Grass Valley exit off the freeway—the exit that led to Jack's cabin. Everything shifted again.

"Where are we going?" she asked. Hadn't she figured out enough? What was left? Was it a coincidence that he had taken the same exit?

"We're going to your dear brother's cabin," Madsen said. "Carrie's meeting Trina's boyfriend there—she thinks he's going to help her figure things out—another loose end." They reached the fork Sadie remembered. Jack's cabin was to the right. Madsen turned left.

Sadie had to clench her lips together to keep from asking the next question out loud. But Madsen followed her line of thought anyway.

"No, Carrie doesn't know I'm the boyfriend and Trina doesn't know that the guy she's been seeing is also a detective on the case. Neither of them know that this guy has been asking dear Trina subtle questions for months about her family, more specifically her father. How much money does he make? What kind of investments does he make with his money?" Madsen shook his head and met Sadie's eyes in the rearview mirror, his eyes cruel and confident once more. "No offense, but your niece isn't the brightest girl I've ever met. And I think I know more about Jack's finances than Carrie does."

"You're a terrible man," Sadie said, trying to catch up with this new information. "Trina took Trevor?" Sadie asked, almost to herself.

Madsen laughed and Sadie would have slapped him for being so delighted with what he had to say if not for the handcuffs chaffing her wrists. "Dumb girl," he said, shaking his head. "I knew she was at her parents' house so I called her after I left Anne's. She thinks I work as a security guard on the night shift. I often call her late and she *always* takes my calls. That's when she told me about her father's affair, that she'd found out that afternoon and confronted the hussy—that's what she called her, is she eighty years old or what?" He laughed and Sadie considered boxing his ears for his callousness . . . after she slapped the grin off his face. "I got her all pumped up and told her a hundred other things she should have done. When I suggested she go over right then and confront Anne with the demand that she leave and never come back, she was all over it. She called me an hour later, hysterical. She'd found Anne's body in the field. I expected her to call the police."

"And because of the confrontation that afternoon she thought they'd suspect her," Sadie filled in. Poor Trina. "But what about Trevor?" she mused, yet even as she said it, she knew the answer. Trina was a girl, but she had a woman's heart.

"That was stupid," Madsen said, shaking his head. "Taking that boy was the dumbest thing they could have done. She was supposed to call the police and get it over with. Even if Trina told them about me, she thought my name was Randy Sharp and that I worked for Aglimate Security—they'd never find me."   ·

"But they couldn't leave Trevor home alone," Sadie said, this part making perfect sense. No woman could abandon a little boy late at night after his mother had been murdered. "And they didn't call the police because they were terrified Trina would be a suspect." She paused, still sorting through all the information in her head. "The filing cabinet," she said under her breath, then understood. "They thought maybe they could hide everything, make sure no one ever knew Jack was Trevor's father. Carrie had already taken the papers from Susan Gimes's office and then took the filing cabinet, just in case."

Madsen shrugged Sadie's assessment off as if Trevor and the filing cabinet were incidental issues. "Stupid."

This man was a sociopath. "Why didn't you find Trevor right away if you knew who had him?"

He shrugged again, causing heat to rise up Sadie's spine. "It was kinda fun seeing people scramble, and I wondered how far Cunningham would get—about as far as I predicted. He's a lost cause. I figured they'd come up with nothing and the case would go cold—I sure didn't expect it to get this dramatic."

His superiority complex, his thinking he was so much smarter then everyone else, was infuriating. And yet she realized that in the right circumstance it could possibly be used to her advantage. She filed it away for later.

"Jack's expecting Trevor to be found," Sadie reminded him, wondering how much Jack knew. Surely he knew Carrie had Trevor, but what were her intentions with the child? What did she plan to do with him? Sadie understood that the panic amid everything else Carrie had learned about her husband and his life could keep her from thinking rationally. She'd proved that already.

"He will be found," Madsen said. "By me. What Jack doesn't know is that Carrie's agreed to pay me—or rather, Randy Sharp—a large sum of money to keep Trina out of this, to drop Trevor off where someone can find him and not trace him back to Trina or her mom. When they find out that Randy Sharp is really me, the money will become even more important in order to ensure Trina isn't implicated. It's all falling into place."

Madsen made eye contact with her again. "You, however, have become a real problem."

Sadie knew there was no way he would keep her alive after telling her all of this—he had too much to lose. Sadie scanned the back seat, looking for . . . something. But of course the back seat of a detective's car wouldn't have anything in it she could use as a weapon. She was left with only her ingenuity—something she feared was not quite up to this challenge.

The road they were on was no longer straight, winding one way and then another, causing her to sway with each bend of the road. Huge trees stretched upward on both sides of the car and Sadie's mouth went dry as she realized how secluded this area was. In fact, they hadn't passed a single car since leaving the highway. He was going to kill her and leave her in the woods. As if aware of her suspicions, Madsen turned onto a side road, not nearly as well maintained as the other road had been. Sadie was bouncing on the seat like popcorn.

"You killed her, didn't you," she said again, straining for him to confirm it once and for all. She pressed herself against the door for stability.

Madsen said nothing, but suddenly pulled over to the side of the road so fast that she flew forward and hit her chin on the front seat, unable to brace herself with her hands still cuffed together. Madsen turned in his seat to face her. He drew a gun from underneath his jacket and pointed it at her face, causing her to pull back. "We're getting out of this car and then we're going to take a little walk."

Sadie stared at the black chiseled metal in his hand. It could have been a child's toy, something she'd have bought for

Shawn when he was younger. "Why on earth would I go willingly when we both know you're going to kill me?"

"Who says I expect you to go willingly?" he said, half his mouth pulling up in a sadistic smile as though he anticipated her putting up a fight and it made this experience all the sweeter for him. At least she knew now why he'd rubbed her wrong from the beginning, though her own skill at judging character provided her a very small amount of bittersweet satisfaction. Had she figured this out just fifteen minutes earlier, she'd have run into oncoming traffic before she'd have let him put her in the car. It was unnerving how much could happen in fifteen minutes.

Madsen continued, causing her to look away from the gun and meet his eyes. "But as you said, we both know you've done all the damage I can allow you to do. And we also know that an old lady like you is no match for a man like me."

CHAPTER 35

O ld lady, she repeated as he got out of the car and pulled open her door. She was barely fifty-six years old—and felt a good fifteen years younger than that even if she was a bit old-fashioned at times. She glared at him and drew upon all the fury and anger of a lifetime—those things she usually refused to dwell on. But she called them up and felt them begin to ball up in her chest as she prepared herself. *This* was something he didn't have, a lifetime of fortitude a punk kid like himself could never muster. Rather than panic, she felt calm and began taking measured breaths, sending all the oxygen to her muscles and tissues. She balled her fists, still locked in the handcuffs, and got out of the car on her own accord, scanning the ground as she did so.

There was nothing but trees and pine needles covered with half an inch of snow from this morning. He grabbed her arm and began pulling her toward the trees. He didn't seem to think this would take long enough for him to bother locking up the car. That meant he didn't expect much—a point in her favor.

She noted that he'd left the key ring full of keys—including a small key she assumed was for the handcuffs—in the ignition.

She dug her heels into the frozen top layer of forest floor, prepared to fight it out here and now, but he simply pulled on her arm more sharply, causing the metal cuffs to cut into her wrists. She determined to be more patient—not one of her greater virtues—and wait for the right moment. Good conquered evil all the time. Surely God could spare her a moment or two of his intervention to help her right now. She tried to remember exactly where Jack's cabin was. If she got away and didn't make it to the car, could she find her way to the cabin? She didn't like her odds so she abandoned that idea. She'd *have* to make it to the car.

Other than their feet moving through the snow and leaves on the ground, there was hardly any sound, save for a rustling wind that caused the tops of the trees to sway in a very languid, peaceful motion that seemed a betrayal of what was happening to Sadie at this moment. They'd gone perhaps fifty yards to where the trees thickened so that there was barely a skiff of snow on the ground, and approached a downward slope. She looked at the incline he was pulling her toward and the tangle of brush at the bottom—the perfect place to hide a body. No one would find her until spring, if they found her at all.

Madsen was a foot or so ahead of her, pulling her forward, when she stopped suddenly and pulled back hard. He didn't let go of her arm as she'd hoped.

"Don't make this more difficult than it needs to be," he said in a droll tone, tightening his grip and yanking her forward, nearly pulling her off balance.

"I plan," she said, pushing her feet into the ground, "to make this as difficult as possible." She pulled again, but when he planted his own feet for leverage she took a step, not backward as he expected her to, but forward, throwing him off balance as she pulled hard, managing to get her arm out of his grasp.

"I don't have time for this," he growled, forced to take a step back to rebalance himself. The split second his emphasis was not on her, she kicked his hand that held the gun, taking him completely off guard. Thanks to her once-a-week yoga classes she was pretty flexible. Especially for an *old lady*.

Madsen craned to watch the gun disappear into a pile of leaves and then turned back to her, his face twisted in rage. He immediately lunged forward, and she lifted her handcuffed hands as high and fast as she could, catching his chin with a hard snap and sending him reeling backward down the embankment. Then she turned and ran for all she was worth. She broke out of the trees, stumbling and almost losing her balance, but she caught herself and with her hands held to her chest she focused on her destination. The car was only ten yards away when she heard him behind her. She didn't dare glance back, intent on the door handle ahead of her.

Oh please, oh please, oh please, oh please, she repeated as she got closer and closer. Madsen was shouting behind her but she could barely hear him over the rushing blood in her ears. She didn't know how far behind her he was, but she knew he could run much faster than she could, even if her hands weren't cuffed. She braced herself for a gunshot, but knew he'd have had only moments to decide whether to shuffle through the ground cover to find the gun or run after her. Since she could hear him, and she had no bullet holes through her body, she assumed he was without his weapon.

In her mind, she choreographed what she needed to do to get inside the car, amazed at how detailed she could review the plan in the remaining yards and ignore doubts that it might not work. It had to work! She'd only have one chance.

When she reached the car door she pulled up on the driver's door handle with both handcuffed hands, then used her foot to kick it open before turning to jump backward into the driver's seat. The turn afforded her the first glance of Madsen since she'd sent him careening down the embankment. He was less than a dozen feet away and looked as if he could take one leap and grab her. She practically fell into the car, landing hard on the seat. The steering wheel caught her right shoulder but she leaned forward, grabbed the armrest of the door—he was literally three feet away—curled her fingers around it, tucked her feet inside, and threw herself backward across the front seat to slam the door.

She expected a slam of molded door fitting into molded metal made just for its connection. The crunching of bone and Madsen's agonized scream took her completely by surprise. With her feet wedged at odd angles between the seat and steering wheel, she felt her stomach drop as she realized that in his attempt to keep her from shutting the door, he'd managed to catch his hand in it.

He looked at her from the other side of the glass, pain thick in his wild eyes as he pulled at his trapped hand. It wasn't coming out, vised in the door. It made her stomach roll to imagine the crushed skin and bone, but she took advantage of his panic to lock the doors before he realized she hadn't done so yet. Oh, but she felt horrible. In any other circumstance she'd have done all she could to help a man in a situation such as his—she'd been first-aid and CPR certified for the last thirty years and didn't take such training lightly. But considering that he had just minutes earlier admitted that he planned to kill her, she felt justified to leave him screaming on the other side of the glass. His feet kicked wildly at the loose ground cover, and he twisted and pulled as if a new position would help his plight. She couldn't look at him.

It was awkward maneuvering around the car's interior with her hands still cuffed and she fumbled the keys from the ignition, feeling through them with her fingers to identify the small one she suspected would open the handcuffs. She muttered a prayer as she wriggled her hands around, then poked around for the lock on the cuffs. She felt like singing the Hallelujah Chorus when the ring around her left wrist sprung open.

She righted herself in the seat, her shoulders aching from her acrobatics, and looked at Madsen. He was staring at her, not with the glaring arrogance she was used to, but with the absolute shock of his situation, begging her to help him. "I'm so sorry," she said as in one fluid motion she unlocked and opened the door so fast and so hard that not only was his hand released, but the door caught him on the side of the head and propelled him to the ground a few feet away. She pulled the door shut, locked it again, and turned the key in the ignition. Without looking back at the man struggling to his feet, cradling his grotesquely misshapen hand, she punched the gas and U-turned sharply. She regained the road and, with the hand-cuff still dangling from her right wrist, managed to put on her seatbelt. Safety first.

She was back on the dirt road in mere seconds and felt secure enough to start pushing buttons surrounding a CB radio thing as the main road came into sight. She held the wheel with her left hand and picked up the speaker thing, the hand-cuff banging against the console of the car.

She pushed the button on the side of the radio, then released the button and listened to the static for a minute. "Hello?" she asked. Someone had to be there! She glanced in the rearview mirror to see if Madsen was behind her and though she'd only driven a few hundred yards, the road was empty. Her hands and voice were shaking as she pushed the button again. "This is Sadie Hoffmiller. I just got away from Detective Madsen. He admitted to me that he killed—"

The radio tumbled out of her hand and fell to the floor. She groaned before leaning forward and grabbing at it with her still shaking right hand—taking her eyes from the winding road for a moment as she searched the floor for the radio.

The impact threw her forward for a split second before another force—a big white billowing one that felt like concrete—threw her back against the seat. She heard crunching metal and felt the loss of level ground beneath the car's tires. Pain shot through her face, head, neck, and shoulders. The entire world spun as that charging force pushed all air from her lungs, leaving her choking on her own tongue and gasping for air that no longer seemed to exist. The air bag deflated just as her lungs had done a moment before, leaving her crushed against the seat, moaning and trying to remember where she was. Her face burned and she could barely open her eyes, but when she did, she could see the trunk of a large tree that seemed much too close. The windshield was intact, but had it been gone she felt sure she could reach forward and pull off a strip of mangled bark.

She'd run into a tree? She'd never hit anything in her life—well other than Shawn's bike when he was ten and parked it behind her car, but she didn't count that. It was nothing like this. The stinging in her eyes persisted and she continued to try to blink it—whatever it was—away.

A disembodied female voice seemed to be speaking to her from the floor of the car. "Do you copy? Mrs. Hoffmiller, please give us your location, do you copy?" The voice faded into static.

Copy what? she thought to herself as she continued to blink, trying out the muscles in her body to see if any of them still obeyed her. Most of them did, though not without laborious protesting. Where was the voice coming from? She looked around and saw a black speaker attached to a curly wire dangling from the dashboard. Her chest still felt as if it were being crushed into the back of the seat. She reached for the speaker, but something was wrong with her depth perception and she simply brushed through air.

Air! She took a breath, a gasping, painful breath, and was reminded of the moment she'd stood on Anne's back porch and heard the police say they were calling in a homicide unit. She'd had to suck in air then too, but that was based on shock, not physical inability. The memory filtered through and she wasn't sure if that had happened yesterday, last year, or this afternoon. Her brain still seemed to be bouncing around in her head.

And then another voice sounded from the speaker still on the floor. This one she recognized and with that recognition the last hour of her life came back to her recollection with startling clarity that caused her newly rediscovered breathing to come fast and erratic.

"Mrs. Hoffmiller!" Cunningham screamed from the floor mat, his voice draining away into static then rising again. "Where are you? Where did he take you?"

"I'm in the mountains," she said in a gasping voice, still fighting for air. "Off the Grass Valley exit. Jack's cabin is around here somewhere and Trevor's there." Then she realized she'd have to pick up that speaker and push a button in order for him to hear her. She reached for the speaker again, this time catching the cord with the chain of the handcuff still swinging from her hand. The handcuff reminded her of Madsen. The reminder of Madsen made her realize she likely hadn't made it half a mile before hitting the tree.

He would have heard the crash, which meant . . . she had to get out of there. Now!

CHAPTER 36

Her chest still felt as if it were strapped down in duct tape, but her legs seemed to work well enough. She grabbed the keys out of the ignition and ran for the trees instead of the road, only realizing twenty yards later that she never told her position to Cunningham. Her brain wasn't working very well. She found a large tree—an oak she thought, due to the fact that there was no growth underneath the branches and the trunk was wide and thick. She leaned against it, leaning forward slightly as she tried to catch her breath. She was nauseated and dizzy, two things that did not help her come up with a plan.

As she stared at the ground, her eyes moved beyond the tree and she saw the thin layer of fresh snow. She didn't dare look behind her but knew she'd left tracks. Luckily, it was a very thin layer and patchy beneath the thick trees, but still, it wouldn't take Madsen long to follow her trail. She looked around and began picking her way deeper into the trees, stepping on the bare patches of ground to hide her tracks, moving away from the car until she found another oak tree, a good fifty yards from the first. The wide trunk was on the edge of a copse of aspens and scrub oak, making it a good hiding spot for the moment. "Think," she said to herself, just as she heard Madsen's first call.

"I know you're here," he yelled in the distance. She assumed he was at the car. "And I know you couldn't have gone far, not with that air bag having gone off in your face. I'll outlast you, old woman, I swear to you I will. But if you come out now, I'll leave the rest of your family alone. If I have to chase you, I'll take it out on the people you love. I swear I will."

You're already taking things out on the people I love, Sadie thought, trying to keep her breathing slow and quiet. He was allowing Jack to take the fall for Anne's murder. . . . Her thoughts came to a stop. Why was Jack taking the fall for *Madsen?* But she instantly knew he wasn't. Jack must think he was taking the fall for Carrie—and Carrie had let him believe it. Shame for her sister-in-law, sympathy for her brother, and fear for her circumstance dog-piled inside her head. She had to get out of here, she had to get to the cabin.

"Your nosy nature is going to get them killed. Maybe I'll start with your daughter—Trina told me all about her."

There was no time to sift through the details that were finally making sense—though a twisted kind of sense for sure. A single word came to mind, keeping her in the moment, keeping her focused on getting out of here. Trevor. She was the only one who knew where he was, and who had killed his mother. Her heart rate increased and she swallowed. Oh, why didn't she pay more attention to her driving? How could she have hit that tree?

"Ah," Madsen yelled, his voice a bit closer. "Look at this, tracks in the snow."

She looked down to make sure she hadn't left tracks in the last few dozen yards. Her shoes caught her attention and she had an idea. Bending ever so carefully, she began undoing her laces. The handcuff on her right wrist clanged against itself and she quickly quieted it, then removed the keys from her pocket and undid the cuff. She stowed the handcuffs in her pocket; they might come in handy. She went back to work taking her laces out of her tennis shoes, barely able to see them through her burning eyes. She was well hidden and the wind in the trees and his steps in the leaves seemed to mask the sounds she made.

When both laces were free, she tied them together with a square knot and scanned the area, finally finding two scrub oaks close enough together to anchor her self-made trip wire, but far enough apart to make sense as an escape route. As she carefully made her way to the trees she questioned her ingenuity but silenced her own doubts with the fact that she hadn't been able to come up with anything else.

By the time she finished setting the tripwire, Madsen had been silent for several seconds and she wondered if he'd gone another direction after her tracks had disappeared. She was terrified to move for fear he was sneaking up on her, but she managed to turn around slowly, checking every direction. All she could see through her still-foggy vision were the trees around her. Her swollen face burned in the cold and the wind.

Should she stay? Should she run?

What she wanted to do was make it back to the car and call Cunningham to let him know where she was, but did she dare? What if Madsen was waiting for her at the car? She bit her lip and peered around the tree once more, screaming when Madsen suddenly appeared, ten feet ahead of her.

His face was pale, his dark eyes standing out on the sallow skin and the cut on his right cheek still oozing blood. There was another patch of blood at his hairline, presumably made by the car door. He looked positively gruesome. His hand was wrapped in what looked like the suit jacket he'd been wearing earlier and was cradled across his stomach.

"Told you I'd outlast you," he said, advancing slowly. The expression on his face was one of sheer hatred. She'd never seen anyone look at her that way and it was frightening. He took another step and she carefully stepped over the shoelaces she'd tied between the two trees. If he'd follow her just right . . .

"How will you explain my disappearance?" she asked, stepping over the laces with her other foot, walking backward, keeping her eyes locked with his. She didn't want him looking too closely at the ground. "People know me, they'll wonder where I went."

"I haven't decided yet," Madsen replied gruffly. "But maybe I'll get rid of Trevor and tell them you took off with him."

Sadie was horrified and felt her eyes widen. "He's a child!"

"He's another complication!" Madsen roared back, the veins standing out on his neck. "Just like you are. I'm tired of complications."

"Is that why you killed Anne? Because she complicated your plan?"

"If she hadn't betrayed me, she'd be alive, but she knew in those final moments that I am not a man to be crossed. You'll learn the same lesson."

"That's awful," Sadie said, moving backward at the same pace he moved toward her. "And you cleaned up the basement?"

"I had to. My fingerprints were everywhere. How would I explain that?"

"I find it odd that you feel so justified, and yet you know you have to hide it. Quite a contradiction."

"Do you even know who I am?" he suddenly shouted and started moving forward faster. It was all she could do not to look down at the trip wire. She'd kept it low to the ground and piled pine needles and leaves to conceal it. He was only a few feet away from her now. "My father runs this state, my father *is* the law."

He took another step and she couldn't help but look down, holding her breath and already picturing him falling on his face. He followed her eyes and then kicked at the pile of leaves. They fell away from the laces, exposing her pathetic attempt at stopping him. Her heart sank. They made stuff like this look so easy on TV.

He lifted one foot over the trip wire and then the other. He stood there, half a dozen feet from her, looking smug. "I wasn't about to let some whore like Anne ruin everything for me. Not after she used me to try to make things work with your pathetic brother."

Sadie didn't know she had it in her, didn't know that there was that much anger and that much aggression inside her— she'd always been such a gentle soul—but at the sound of such angry and foul words, she suddenly lunged forward, dropping her head and running straight for his chest the way she used to when she and Shawn played football in the backyard, only she'd never put so much power behind her tackles back then. She'd never wanted to hurt her son, but she very much wanted to hurt this man. She saw him, in the moments before impact, brace himself and reach out his good arm, a look of excitement on his face, as if this was what he wanted—hand-to-hand combat with a woman twice his age.

But he took one instinctive step backward—the one step she needed him to take. His foot hit the trip wire after all and he fell back, twisting in the air and putting both hands in front of him in hopes of breaking his fall, the suit coat falling away. Right before his mangled hand hit the ground, he cried out, realizing what the impact would do to it, but it was too late. Sadie veered right, away from him, as his crushed hand slammed into the ground. He howled as the rest of him fell on top of it. She had too much momentum by then and couldn't stop until she was a few feet past him.

He rolled on the ground, his feet already scrambling for leverage to help him up. She didn't give him a chance. Instead she pulled the handcuffs from her pocket, grabbed his good arm and managed to slap the ring on his wrist despite his clawing and kicking at her. Then, as if she too had been officially trained in this, she hooked the other cuff to a scrub oak, a type of brush that though small, was excessively strong. Above where the cuff linked to the tree, hundreds of smaller branches shot out in every direction. He'd have a hard time breaking his way free from the tree. For a moment he stopped struggling, staring at the handcuffs as if not understanding what she'd done. Then he started fighting again, cursing and kicking up leaves like a trapped cat.

She didn't stay long enough to even look at him, instead she ran for the car as fast as she could, accidentally—of course—stepping on his injured hand amid her flight. She felt the shattered bones slide beneath the skin as he howled in pain once more. It was really quite gross. When she got to the car, she picked up the speaker and pushed the button, her eyes trained on the section of woods where she'd left Madsen.

"This is Sadie Hoffmiller. Is anyone there, er, does anyone copy?"

What did *copy* mean anyway?

Her heart was thumping like a bongo drum in her chest. She kept waiting to see Madsen come out of those trees. She could hear him yelling, and that gave her confidence that he wasn't free yet.

"This is Sadie Hoffmiller," she said, and noticed her breathing was becoming even more shallow than before. Maybe the shock was catching up to her. "Please answer me!"

She waited. The wind blew through the trees and she noticed lazy snowflakes falling from the sky. She looked up at the gray sky above her and sent a silent thanks toward heaven. God had spared her that moment she'd asked for. Would he spare her another one?

The speaker continued in its silence and she wondered if perhaps the damage to the car had rendered it useless, though it had worked earlier. But there wasn't even the sound of static now. Just in case they could hear her, she gave her location before turning away from the car. Her face was swollen, her eyes still burned, and her chest was difficult to inflate, but she had to get back. She had to get Trevor, clear Jack, confront Carrie, tattle on Madsen, and . . . find someone to teach her Sunday School class on Sunday. Surely the kids would be terrified if they saw her like this.

Then she remembered her cell phone. She opened the back door of the car and found it on the floor. She immediately tried to call Breanna. The words "No Service" blinked back at her and she wanted to scream; she would have if her throat wasn't still burning. After pausing for a moment, she went into her messaging program and typed out a text message telling her daughter where she was. She sent it to her outbox where it would wait for cell phone service to return.

CHAPTER 37

Sadie followed a bend in the road, walking as fast as she could manage, trying to estimate how far in they'd driven—she feared it was several miles—when she heard a car coming toward her. She stopped in the middle of the road, unable to react before a white minivan came into view, slamming on its brakes to avoid hitting her. She lifted her arms up to block her face from the rocks and dirt thrown up as the van skidded sideways to a stop ten feet away.

"Sadie!"

Sadie lowered her arms and blinked as Mindy Bailey jumped out of her van and ran over to her. She was dressed in pink scrubs with little purple panda bears on the shirt. The panda bears were eating lollipops. Sadie felt as if her thoughts were moving in slow motion. Why was Mindy here?

"Are you okay?" Mindy asked in her usual hyper tone, the words all pushed together to allow as many as possible to follow after them. "You don't look okay, in fact you need to get to the hospital. We can be there in fifteen minutes. Oh, I'm so glad I found you, I got lost, see, and I've been driving around trying to—"

"What are you doing here?" Sadie interrupted, still staring at her neighbor.

Mindy looked confused, then seemed to realize she hadn't explained. She took a breath. "I came home for lunch." That was it. She'd use a thousand words to say something that only needed ten, but all she said now was that she'd come home for lunch. Sadie blinked again, unable to figure out what lunch had to do with Mindy being in the mountains right now. A gust of wind blew and both women shivered.

"Um, can we get in the van?" Mindy asked. "I'll explain on the way."

That sounded fine to Sadie and she headed toward the passenger door, reminded of her urgency once her feet were moving again. She glanced over her shoulder to make sure Madsen wasn't sneaking up on her, but the road was empty except for some autumn leaves blowing across the ground. It was lovely to sit in the plush seat of the minivan and relax for a moment. It would have been even better if there weren't two feet worth of fast-food wrappers, Dr. Pepper bottles, school papers, and crayons on the floor. For some reason the van smelled like cat litter, but Sadie was in no mind to be picky.

Mindy put the van into reverse and turned around to head back the way she'd come.

"So how did you find me?" Sadie asked again. "You came home for lunch?"

Mindy began nodding vigorously. "I did, I had the last of the Alfredo you brought last night—it was delicious, by the way. I usually make that kind that comes in the packet, you know the kind, right? But homemade is so much better, the kids noticed the difference right away."

Sadie was always glad to have her cooking complimented, but she didn't have the presence of mind to thank Mindy right now. She didn't need to worry, though, Mindy was still talking and it was all Sadie could do to keep up.

"I also just wanted to check on the house, ya know, I thought I might have left the basement door unlocked and kept thinking about what happened to Anne, wondering if maybe she'd left her basement door unlocked and that's how the murderer got in. I saw that in a movie once, where he came in and lived in the house for weeks, learning all about the family. He actually fell in love with the woman and decided to kill the husband, so one day he—"

"What happened when you came home from lunch?" Sadie interrupted.

A momentary look of confusion crossed Mindy's face, but she found the original train of thought and pushed forward again. "Oh, right, so I ate the Alfredo and was double-checking the windows and doors before I left again when I heard Jack's truck squeal out of the circle. I saw it go around the corner just as you got in your car and chased after it. I couldn't figure out what was happening, but then the detective—he was on your porch talking to someone—jumps down, runs for his car, and takes off too. Well, I just didn't even have time to think, so I ran downstairs to the garage and jumped into the van. I worried that something had happened to someone else in the circle, that you and Jack were rushing to the hospital or something, so I took off, but I was way behind the rest of you so I thought I'd lost you guys altogether, until I passed you getting handcuffed by that cute cop."

"Cute cop?" Sadie said, picturing Madsen's face the last time she'd seen him. He'd been swearing and kicking, his face contorted with such anger and hatred that he looked demonic. The words he was using were anything but cute.

"Don't you think he looks a little like Val Kilmer?" Mindy continued. "I love Val Kilmer, in fact I was watching *Willow* a few days ago—remember that movie? And there's this part where he takes his shirt off. Whoa. I'm a married woman and all, but Val Kilmer without a shirt on is about as good as—"

"You saw me getting arrested?"

Mindy came back to the present again. "Well, that's the thing, there was something funny about what he was doing. See, first of all he was alone and cops aren't supposed to do stuff alone, and second, he looked so mad—like weird mad— ya know? But there was nowhere to pull over so I drove through the intersection and turned around to come back. By then he had just parked your car. Now why would he do that? I wondered. So I drove past again and then turned around just as he was pulling back into traffic. I thought I'd follow for a minute, but when he started heading out of town I really freaked. I didn't know what to do, so I tried to call the police, but we have really spotty service once you get past Mountain

View Road and my call wouldn't go through and so I thought the best thing to do would be to follow you until I got service. I had to stay back though, 'cause I didn't want him to recognize my van or anything. Then I saw him take the Green Valley exit and I thought, 'Mindy, this is so bad.' But there were no other cars on the off-ramp and I just knew he'd see me, so I pulled over on the freeway—the shoulder, ya know—and waited until he went into the trees before I followed." She looked over at Sadie with a sympathetic smile. "That was a mistake 'cause once I got to the trees I didn't know where you'd gone. The snow had melted on the road and I couldn't see any tire tracks. So I drove around for what seemed like forever, taking different roads looking for you, and then I found you."

Sadie smiled and tears filled her eyes—both actions hurt her face terribly. "Mindy, you're an absolute angel."

Mindy beamed at the compliment. The van came out of the trees, the fork in the road half a mile ahead of them. "Well, thanks," she said. "Now we just need to get you to the hospital. What happened anyway? Did he beat you up? I saw that on the news a few weeks ago, how these cops beat up this guy. He was in bad shape, I tell you what, his face all big and gross. I could tell right away he'd have a scar where they—"

Sadie sat up straight. "Mindy," she said, turning toward her savior and putting a hand on her arm. "We can't go to the hospital."

Mindy glanced at her and her eyebrows lifted. "We have to, Sadie, you're badly injured."

Sadie shook her head despite the pain it sent through her neck. "We have to find Jack's cabin," she said, pointing to the fork in the road. "Carrie has Trevor there."

Mindy's eyebrows lifted even higher. "Trevor?" she repeated. "What do you mean?"

"Detective Madsen killed Anne," Sadie said, leaning back against the seat. "But I think Carrie told Jack she'd done it and took Trevor and now she's hiding him. Jack turned himself in and said Trevor would be found soon, and Carrie was going to give Trevor to Madsen, but Madsen is handcuffed to a tree. Trina's helping her mom and we have to find them. Trevor is Jack's son, see, and Carrie found out about Anne and . . . well, it's a bit complicated." Wow, she'd spoken almost as fast as Mindy.

"Carrie?" Mindy repeated as if that was the only word of substance she'd been able to grasp in Sadie's explanation. She glanced at Sadie again. "Jack?"

Sadie pointed at the fork just a few yards ahead of them. "Take the other road," she said. "Jack's cabin is up there."

Mindy was silent for a few seconds and Sadie feared she'd perhaps dropped such a bombshell that even the likes of Mindy Bailey was silenced by the shock.

She was wrong.

Mindy took a breath and began talking again as if Sadie hadn't just shared such a sordid secret. Mindy had never struck Sadie as particularly bright. "It is? I've never been there. Steve has, he used to hunt with Jack sometimes and he told me about it—said it wasn't much. But Steve's not much of a rustic man, ya know, despite the fact that he works at a sporting goods store. He's more the athletic type, not so much the outdoorsman. This one time . . ."

Sadie tuned her out, her attention riveted on the road. Mindy made the turn as Sadie instructed and Sadie leaned forward, scanning the trees on either side. She remembered a dirt road on the left, that was the first turn, but it was a ways up the road.

"Turn there," Sadie said a mile later, pointing to the dirt road, hoping it was the right one. She immediately saw a large A-frame that she knew hadn't been there the last time she'd been to the cabin. She hoped it had been built recently and that she hadn't chosen the wrong road. There was no time to wander aimlessly.

Mindy hadn't skipped a beat. "And they wanted to charge me eighty bucks when he wasn't even there for an hour. I told them, no way, not for something like this. Now if it were carpets, that's different, but then you pay by the room for carpet, not by the hour. My father-in-law used to lay carpet and he said that most people don't know that—"

"Right here," Sadie said, swallowing as the trees parted enough to show the small brown cabin set back from the road. Both Jack's truck and Carrie's car were parked along the side and Sadie swallowed.

They were here!

CHAPTER 38

As soon as the van door opened, Sadie jumped from the vehicle and ran for the cabin door, throwing it open. Carrie and Trina looked up from where they were sitting at the small table covered in papers. Sadie barely gave them a glance before scanning the room, her eyes taking in the black filing cabinet next to the table before resting on the small form curled up in a port-a-crib in the middle of the room. She took a few steps forward and seeing his small chest rise and fall made her feel as if her heart had just begun to beat again. A fire was roaring in the wood-burning stove in the corner and Sadie was relieved that he'd been warm. The last thing he needed after all of this was to catch a chill.

Both of the other women came to their feet and the three of them stared at one another across the small—but surprisingly tidy—room. Sadie held Carrie's eyes. "You were going to let him take the fall for it?" she accused her sister-in-law. "You were going to let him go to prison?"

Carrie didn't look away, raising her chin slightly in a display of arrogance. The room was silent, until Mindy came up behind Sadie in the doorway.

"Oh, hi, Carrie," she said in what sounded like a cautious tone. But it didn't take long for her to switch into her hyper-oblivion mode. "Hi, Trina. Aren't you supposed to be in school? Do you like it there? It's fun, isn't it? I remember college, wow, what an experience. I think all kids should go to college. That's where Steve and I met, you know, I was a freshman. Have you met any—"

"Mindy," Sadie said, still staring at her sister-in-law. "Please, for once in your life, shut up."

Mindy's eyes went wide but her teeth snapped together. Sadie had never talked to her that way and, under the circumstances, Sadie didn't even care—though she knew she'd be baking later to make up for her rudeness.

"Who's to say Jack didn't kill her?" Carrie said.

Sadie shook her head. "That's not why he's there, is it? He's there because he thinks *you* did it and he believes it's all his fault."

"It *is* his fault!" Carrie hissed. She placed her hands on the small table and leaned forward, her eyes narrowed and her jaw tight. Trina looked like a scared kitten and seemed to shrink backward, making Sadie wonder just how willing a participant she'd been in this whole thing.

"No, it's not," Sadie said slowly. "Detective Madsen killed Anne, Carrie; he's the one who belongs in prison. You knew it wasn't Jack all along. He's a good man, and you know it, but you were willing to let him take the fall for vengeance."

Carrie's nostrils flared. "He is not a good man," she said. "How can you dismiss what he's done? How can you let him get away with it?"

"He's not getting away with anything," Sadie countered, throwing up her hands to encompass all that had happened. "He's had to live with himself through this whole thing, knowing how many people he was hurting. Now Anne is dead. He'll carry that with him the rest of his life."

"It's not enough," Carrie said between clenched teeth as she shook her head. "Not nearly enough to make up for what he's done."

"Perhaps not, but then he's never been good enough for you anyway, has he?"

Carrie's eyebrows came together and Sadie continued. "What he did was wrong—horribly wrong—but you are not helping anything." She looked at Trevor and began walking toward him. "Especially in this."

Carrie hurried to get in Sadie's way, lifting her chin and looking defiant. "You aren't—"

"Yes, I am!" Sadie said slow and sincere. "You've done enough and if you think I'll be half as easy to roll over as Jack has been, you've made a grave error in judgment. Madsen"— she looked at Trina with sympathy—"the man you know as Randy Sharp—isn't coming, and there is no way to keep Trina or yourself out of this any longer." Trina's eyes went wide with confusion. "You are going to have a lot of explaining to do, but if you try to stop me from taking this little boy to his father now, you'll have more fight on your hands than you could possibly imagine."

Carrie lifted her chin higher and when Sadie took another step and Carrie moved forward to block her way again, Sadie raised both hands and pushed the other woman as hard as she could. Carrie was taken off guard and stumbled backward before tripping over the hearth of the wood-burning stove. She immediately stood and took a step forward, but Sadie lowered her chin and took a stance similar to the one she'd taken with Madsen not long ago, crouching slightly, shoulders up and jaw tight.

Carrie straightened and the fear finally entered her eyes. She'd realized she was literally in a corner.

"Just give me a reason, Carrie," Sadie said. "It's been a very trying afternoon and I could use the outlet." Wow, she sounded like a wrestler or something!

Carrie's shoulders slumped and she took a step back, instead of forward.

Assured that Carrie wasn't going to try anything, Sadie bent down and reached out a hand to smooth Trevor's hair from his face, tears rising as she realized it was over. Trevor was found, he was safe. He had a life ahead of him, though one without a mother, with a father he barely knew, and a history he would never be free of. She reached under him and lifted him in her arms. Thank goodness she'd come at nap time. He shifted and blinked his eyes open as she adjusted him against her shoulder, not wanting him to see her swollen face.

"But . . ."

Sadie turned to face Trina who began to speak. "We . . . we weren't going to hurt him. And Randy—what do you mean about Randy?"

Sadie smiled at her niece, sympathetic for her situation. "You're going to be okay, Trina, really," she said in comforting tones. "Detective Madsen *is* Randy Sharp. He tricked you because he was going to blackmail your father. It wasn't your fault, but you can still do the right thing for Trevor and for your dad by telling the truth when you get to the police station."

"You don't understand," Carrie said from the far side of the room, crying now.

Sadie turned and looked between the two of them, mother and daughter. "Maybe not," she said quietly, one hand holding Trevor against her and the other smoothing his hair. She tried to keep her voice calm for Trevor's sake. "But I know Jack was willing to go to prison for you, Carrie. I wonder if that means anything to you. All he can do is try to make a very big wrong a little bit right. I wonder if you will make that harder or easier for him to do."

She turned, surprised to find a quiet Mindy still in the doorway. She'd forgotten all about her. "I'm sorry for telling you to shut up, Mindy, but can you please drive us back to town despite my rudeness?" Not waiting for an answer, she headed outside, aware of Mindy pulling the door shut behind her.

Sadie was only a few steps away from the cabin when tires crunched on the gravel drive. She froze, unprepared for anything else.

"Mrs. Hoffmiller," Detective Cunningham said with a tone that caught Sadie's attention despite all the swirling thoughts and emotions in her mind. He was stepping out of a brown sedan and hearing his voice allowed her to relax. He sounded relieved and scared and a tad bit hyper all at once. In moments he was at her side, attempting to take Trevor from her arms as another officer headed toward the cabin. "Your daughter called us and said you might be coming to the cabin. Jack gave us directions. Let me take him."

She held on tight to the toddler as Mindy followed the second officer into the cabin, relaying their story as fast as she could. "He's okay," Sadie breathed. "Just let me hold him for a minute."

Cunningham nodded and led her to the sedan, opening the back door so she could slide inside. "What happened?" he asked, once she had leaned against the seat. He had one hand holding the door open, the other braced against the frame of the car. His eyes were so troubled, and yet with relief behind them.

"Oh," she said, shaking her head as she tried to imagine how to give the details. "I don't even know where to begin."

"You're hurt," he said as his eyes seemed to scan her face for the first time.

"I hit a tree, but I'm okay."

"A tree?"

"I know, I can't believe it either, I've never hit anything in my life; well, other than Shawn's bike, I guess."

Cunningham paused, looking a bit confused. "Where's Madsen?"

"He's handcuffed to a tree about, oh, three miles or so from here. He's going to need surgery on his hand . . . and maybe some stitches for his face, but I think he'll be okay, other than the fact that he's a very angry man and I'm not sure what the cure is for that."

Cunningham's face scrunched, his confusion deepening. "What?"

She shook her head slightly and placed a hand on Trevor's hair again, reminding herself that he was there, still sleeping, blissfully unaware of his circumstances. She looked up and met Cunningham's eyes with her own. Her tears overflowed as the tension finally drained away, her body finally accepting that she, as well as Trevor, was safe. "Can you please take me to see Jack? This boy needs his dad."

CHAPTER 39

Sadie stood behind the mirrored wall looking in on Jack once again. Detective Cunningham stood next to her; Trevor was in another office being tended to by a representative of Family Services. In a few minutes, once Jack had finished giving his official statement to the police, father and son would be reunited.

"A bittersweet reunion if ever there was one," Sadie whispered under her breath, almost not realizing she'd spoken out loud until Cunningham replied to her comment.

"But a reunion nonetheless. It doesn't always have this kind of ending."

Sadie nodded her understanding.

"Madsen?" she asked after a few more moments, still watching Jack.

"Fine," Cunningham said bluntly with a shrug of his shoulders and the faintest smile on his face. "He'd nearly broke through the tree you hooked him to by the time we found him—mouth of a sailor, that kid."

"Very poor reflection on his parents," Sadie said with a nod, "that's for sure. I wonder how his father will cover this one up."

A silence stretched between them, but not a silence of discomfort. Rather it was a pause laced with anticipation of what words would fill the space between them—a comfortable silence, a calm following the storm.

"Are you ready to go to the hospital, get yourself checked out? Air bags pack quite a punch."

Sadie shrugged. "It's nothing some ice, herbal tea, and Tylenol can't fix. I'd rather stay here."

The door to the little room they were in opened and a female officer looked around until she met Sadie's eyes. "Mrs. Hoffmiller, someone would like to talk to you."

Sadie wasn't sure who to expect, but after leaving the room and seeing Ron waiting, her steps slowed. He stood up from the plastic chair he'd been sitting in, one of a dozen pushed up against the wall. She stopped and let him approach her, bracing herself for what she knew had to happen next.

"Ron," she said when he was a few feet away. "I know what really happened, and though I also know you're not an evil person, I don't think that—"

He cut her off by putting his hands up, palms out, and facing her. "I know what you're going to say," he said, squaring his shoulders. "But I've thought about everything and come to the conclusion that whether you agree with me or not, I did the right thing and I have no qualms about what I did."

Sadie was stunned, reviewing the regret and what had seemed to be tortured tones of their conversation back at the house. She shook her head sadly, even more confused by this man she thought she knew. However, she was grateful to have learned the truth about him before they married, rather than afterward. That would have been horrible. "Well, if you have no qualms about the choices you made, then you've only proved my position that we're not well matched."

His eyebrows furrowed as if he hadn't expected that reaction, but he quickly recovered. "I think you're being unfair, judgmental, and pious."

Sadie's mouth dropped open and she blinked at him. "Me? Well, I think you're being arrogant, demeaning, and stupid."

"Well, I think you're—"

She put up her hand to stop the juvenile exchange. They were years from the playground that was the foundation for such petty arguments. "It seems we agree."

Ron straightened his shoulders again and nodded sharply. "It seems that we do. I can't see myself with a woman who can't forgive me when I make mistakes."

"Mistakes?" Sadie repeated. "I thought you had no qualms about the choices you'd made?"

Ron didn't seem to know what to say to that, so she spared him having to come up with anything. "If I had a ring, I'd give it back to you, and since we both care about Jack I hope we can function as acquaintances for his sake. He's going to need his friends."

Ron opened his mouth to say something, then looked past Sadie's shoulder, closed his mouth, turned, and stormed toward the doors of the station—though another officer called out to him and ushered him into a room. Apparently the police weren't finished with Ron.

Sadie turned to see Detective Cunningham standing in the doorway of the observation room. "Everything okay?" he asked.

Sadie looked back toward Ron, but he was gone, and then she turned her head to look at Detective Cunningham again. She tried not to look at it all too closely, but somehow it felt as though she were looking at her past and then her future. He watched her carefully and she felt her pulse increase by the protective look on his face. "I've been dumped," she said after several seconds, their eyes locked on one another.

"Or promoted to a whole new position of possibilities," he said. "It's all about how you look at it."

"Very true," Sadie said.

"They're about to bring Trevor in, I didn't want you to miss it."

Sadie smiled at him as she passed him in the doorway. "Thank you." Once back in the room, many of those possibilities he'd just mentioned began spinning cartwheels in her head. Perhaps she was jumping to conclusions—it wouldn't be the first time—but there was a comfortable air with Detective Cunningham that tingled with anticipation.

He held her eyes for a moment, then blushed slightly and looked back at the glass. They watched in silence for nearly a minute as the officer finished wrapping things up with Jack, who was still signing paperwork.

She tested the next thing she wanted to say, and decided to go for it. Her timing was probably terrible, and yet with everything over she realized she might not see the detective again. Even if nothing came of it, she wanted some of her curiosity satiated in regard to this man. "When did your wife pass away?"

Cunningham stiffened quickly, then slowly relaxed. When he spoke, his voice was soft and vulnerable. "How did you know?"

Sadie smiled slightly but didn't meet his eyes, allowing him his privacy with facial expression if nothing else. "The tapering of your finger where your ring used to be, the sweetness in your voice when you talked about your wife's applesauce . . . and you understood when I talked about Neil's death."

After a few more seconds, Sadie turned to look at him. She smiled even though it hurt a little bit. She'd been oddly excited to have him see her with her makeup and hair done so he'd know what she really looked like—now she'd have to wait for the swelling and bruises to go away.

He met her eyes and cleared his throat before he spoke. "Two years," he said quietly. "Pancreatic cancer. It's been . . . hard."

Sadie smiled sympathetically. "I wore my ring for almost three years," she said. "It was hard to accept the shift in my future."

Detective Cunningham nodded, absently rubbing his naked ring finger with his right hand. "I took mine off on the two-year anniversary last month—I'm not sure I'm the same man without it."

"I'm so sorry," she said sincerely. And she was; losing someone you loved was a horrendously painful experience.

"Me too."

The door of the room Jack was in opened and Jack quickly stood, his eyes wide, his expression scared as he wiped his hands on the front of his pants—the pants he'd come in with and that had been returned to him. She noticed he had his wedding ring on again and wondered if he still had hope in regards to Carrie. Part of Sadie rebelled against the idea—Carrie had done very little to deserve a second chance—and yet who was she to say what was and what wasn't big enough for love to heal?

A woman led Trevor into the room and Jack tried to smile though he looked very nervous. Finally he crouched down and reached toward the hesitant toddler. After a few moments, Trevor let go of the social worker and made tentative movements toward Jack's outstretched hand.

"Hi, Trevor," Jack said, smiling despite the tears in his eyes. "I'm Jack, your . . . I'm your dad."

Sadie felt a lump rise in her throat and wiped quickly at her eyes before turning to Detective Cunningham, afraid if she kept watching she'd lose all composure.

"It's been a long day and I was thinking of making a gingerbread when I get home tonight, you know, to take the edge off. I know I'm not much to look at right now, but I can still cook. Would you like to come over and share it with me?"

Cunningham regarded her for a moment, then smiled, his eyes crinkling in the corner just like Sean Connery. "Gingerbread? I hear it goes well with applesauce."

Granny's Gingerbread

½ cup sugar
½ cup butter
1 egg
1 cup molasses (mild)
¼ cup applesauce
2½ cups flour
1 teaspoon cinnamon
1 teaspoon baking soda
2 teaspoons ground ginger
1 teaspoon cloves
½ teaspoon salt
⅔ cup hot water
Whipped cream (optional)
Powdered sugar (optional)

Preheat oven to 350 degrees. Cream sugar and butter, add egg and mix well. Add molasses and applesauce—mix well. Add dry ingredients and spices—mix well. Add hot water—mix well. Pour into greased and floured bundt pan (don't cheat with cooking spray!). Bake 45 minutes, cool in pan before turning out onto a plate. Serve with whipped cream, applesauce, or sprinkled with powdered sugar.

Tastes better on the second or third day as flavors mingle. (Smells just like Christmas!)

Acknowledgments

As mentioned in my dedication, I must first acknowledge my gratitude to my mother and the many ways in which she has shaped my life. Not only has she showed me how to be the right kind of woman (though I'm still working on the application part of some of those lessons), but she taught me the difference between bread from the oven and bread from the store. It wasn't until I left home that I realized how priceless a gift that really was. Many of the recipes featured in this book came from her and are the taste and smells of my childhood.

Big thanks to Jeff Savage who a few years ago hosted a first chapter contest for a food-based mystery; without that contest this book would never have come about. Thanks to Willard Boyd Gardner for his insight into police procedure, although he certainly doesn't deserve the blame for any mistakes included here. Thanks to my writing group members who over the years have helped fine-tune this story—Janet Jensen, Carole Thayne, Ronda Hinrichsen, Anne Ward, Becki Clayson, and Jodi Durfee. Thanks to my sweet cousin, Melinda Rich, for finding time to do a last-minute edit amid all her new adventures, and to my dear friend Julie Wright who, once again, came to my rescue and buoyed me up every time I needed buoying.

Thank you to everyone at Shadow Mountain, your support and enthusiasm is priceless. Specifically Lisa Mangum, the assistant editor who first said that, despite this book being different from my others, she'd like to take a look at it; Jana Erickson, who orchestrated all the details, Shauna Gibby for the great cover, Rachael Ward for the typesetting, and the entire marketing team for getting the word out. A big thank you to Erin Crouse, assistant to Jana, who tested each recipe to make sure they were doable in a kitchen other than my own.

Thanks to my husband, Lee, who remains my sun, moon, and stars, and my children—the beneficiaries (and victims) of my baking obsession. I'd be in trouble if I had to eat it all myself, and it wouldn't be any fun to eat alone anyway. I love you guys and so appreciate each of you in my life.

And thank you most of all to my Father in Heaven, for this story, the others, and all things stated above. I am blessed.

Enjoy this sneak peek of

ENGLISH TRIFLE

Coming Fall 2009

CHAPTER 1

"Is it just me or does it feel like the staff wants us to leave?" Sadie Hoffmiller asked after the door of the sitting room shut behind them.

"It's just you, Mom," Breanna said as she sat on one of the damask-covered settees and kicked out one leg so that she slumped into the seat. She managed to look perfectly Bohemian in the elegant room. "They're probably anxious to get back to their regular routine."

"Hmmm, maybe," Sadie replied, but she wasn't convinced. If not for the fact that Breanna had a lot to deal with right now Sadie would have tried to dissect the situation a little more; however, she could sense that with their departure only minutes away, her daughter was on overload. Sadie didn't want to add to her stress.

Instead, she sat down across from Breanna as if being in the sitting room of an English estate was an everyday occurrence instead of an unforeseen shift in Breanna's future. That Breanna didn't know Liam was heir apparent to an earldom when she fell in love with him didn't make the adjustment any easier, but it *had* become the reason they'd traveled to England in the first place.

Liam's father—William Everet Martin Jr., ninth earl of Garnett—had been ill for several months, and Liam needed to attend to some matters of the estate, requiring him to travel to England a week before Christmas. Sadie and Breanna had been invited to join him for the week between Christmas and New Year's, while Breanna was out of school, in order to meet the earl and tour the country of Liam's birth. They'd only spent one night at Southgate before leaving to see nearly everything else in England, returning only the night before last. Sadie couldn't imagine how they'd have thrown off the staff's routine when they'd been at the estate for such a short time. "It just seems to me that they're in a hurry for us to go back home."

"Well, they've got their hands full with the earl. I'm sure having guests—and foreign guests at that—is nothing more than an irritation."

Liam had had an extra week to adjust to his father's declining health, but admitted that he hadn't even recognized his father; he'd aged tremendously in the four years since Liam had seen him in person. Breanna suggested they forgo the sightseeing, but Liam assured them that the earl wouldn't want them to spend a week hovering when there was nothing any of them could do.

"Is Liam okay?" Sadie asked. She'd seen very little of him since their return to the estate. When his father passed, Liam would inherit the title, and the weight of responsibility sat heavy on his shoulders now that the fun portion of the trip was over. He'd spent nearly every moment either at his father's bedside or poring over the history and accounts of the earldom in the library, wanting to learn all he could before he returned to his other life in Portland, Oregon, where he supervised the bat exhibit at the Washington Park Zoo.

Breanna looked at her hands in her lap. She was wearing a T-shirt that said Keep It Clean, Keep It Green. "I don't know," she said quietly. "He's not sure when he'll be able to come back. If he could, I'm sure he'd stay here."

Sadie wasn't so sure he *couldn't* stay—he was going to be an earl after all, why worry about something as inconsequential as his job? "It must be hard to leave with his dad still so sick," Sadie said sympathetically. Both of Sadie's parents were gone now, and losing them had been second in heartache only to her husband's premature death almost twenty years ago. Nothing quite compared to losing people close to you, even if, like Liam and his father, there had been half a world between you for most of your life.

Breanna let out a breath and nodded.

"And how about you?" Sadie asked, peering at her daughter in hopes of reading her expression should she choose not to be forthcoming. "How do you feel about leaving?"

Breanna flicked her green eyes up to meet her mother's, then stared back at her lap. She shrugged one shoulder like a thirteen-year-old girl instead of a twenty-four-year-old woman facing the decision of a lifetime. Would she one day marry Liam and live the rest of her life as the Countess of Garnett? It was a subject she'd avoided talking about. For Breanna—earthy, easygoing, and hardworking—to consider living a life full of social functions, obligatory friendships, and a lifestyle dispro-portionate to that of her neighbors, would be difficult. Her world was nothing like this one. For a moment Sadie thought her daughter might be ready to discuss it now that the visit was almost behind them, but then Breanna's face broke into a smile.

"Let's see," she said, a tease in her voice. "How do I feel about leaving?" She tapped her chin with feigned consterna-tion. "I simply can't wait to eat a freaking Ho Ho."

"A Ho Ho?" Sadie said, pulling back in pure disgust. "We've been surrounded by the finest of English cuisine for the last week and you want a Ho Ho?"

"The very phrase *English cuisine* is pretty much an oxy-moron. It's bland, it's weird—mushrooms for breakfast? Come on! They served pigeons for dinner at that one place in York, Mom. Can you honestly tell me that a Big Mac isn't screaming your name about now?"

"Those were Cornish hens," Sadie reprimanded. "And they were delicious. The rosemary sauce was nothing short of amaz-ing."

Breanna waved her hand, as if unwilling to even consider the possibility. "Hostess and McDonalds are not multi-billion-dollar companies for no reason." Breanna smiled as if she'd won the argument. "I did like the English trifle from the other night—that was delicious."

Sadie couldn't help but smile at the memory. She made the layered dessert every Christmas, but had never had it with real ladyfingers and custard pudding made from scratch. "It was excellent, wasn't it?" She couldn't wait to go home and make it to see if she could match Mrs. Land's tasty creation. Now that she'd actually had real English trifle, she knew what to shoot for.

Breanna looked up as the door opened. Sadie straightened in her chair, all things forgiven and all senses on alert because there was food on the tray! Scones, clotted cream, strawberry jam, and tea—a cream tea for which Devonshire was famous, to be exact. The scones—pronounced to rhyme with the word *gone*—were not the deep-fried American kind, rather they were like a sweet biscuit that fairly melted in your mouth.

Grant the butler placed the tea tray on the small table. "Your final tea," he said as he righted the teacups on the saucers. "As soon as you finish here, you'll be on your way to Heathrow. Your bags are being loaded as we speak."

Aha, more proof that the staff was practically pushing them out the door. Their flight didn't leave until ten o'clock tonight—nearly seven hours from now—and it was only three hours to London. Why the rush? But she simply smiled at the man, watching his expression carefully.

"We can pour," Sadie said when he reached for the teapot. It felt funny to be waited on all the time and she took every opportunity to be self-sufficient. "And I hope the driver is okay to wait for a little while, we'd hate to rush." She thought she caught a flicker of irritation in Grant's expression, but he nodded his head and took a step backward toward the door, as professional as ever.

"Of course," he said. "I'll let the driver know he can turn off the engine."

Grant nodded once more when he reached the door, reminded them to ring the bell by the fireplace if they needed assistance, and left the room. As soon as he was gone, Sadie leaned forward. "They weren't even going to shut off the engine," she said smugly. "They'd probably send us out there with Dixie cups and the scones wrapped in a napkin if they could."

"Mom, please," Breanna said, reaching for her scone. "Can we just enjoy these last few minutes?"

Oh, fine, Sadie said to herself. She was willing to put off nearly anything when there was food in need of savoring. She picked up, split, and jammed a scone before topping it with a dollop of clotted cream.

"Are you sure you want to bother with the scone at all?" Sadie asked, raising her eyebrows toward the treat in her daughter's hand. "Seeing as how they aren't loaded with trans fats or preservatives? I mean, they don't even have any artificial coloring, for goodness sake."

"The scones," Breanna said, pronouncing the word like an American, "I like. But that cream stuff is nasty."

"That cream stuff is called clotted cream," Sadie corrected as she put the halves of her scone back together, making a sandwich, which was how the English ate it. "And Devon is famous for it."

Breanna looked up and lifted her eyebrows. "The very words *clotted cream* makes my point; it even sounds gross. And talk about unhealthy—it's like pure butterfat."

"And what do you think butter is made of?" Sadie asked, but then she promptly ignored her daughter's reply, putting up her hand to block any further complaints as she took her first bite, allowing the cool cream, sweet jam, and smooth scone to combine perfectly in her mouth. She chewed slowly and carefully, savoring every moment. When she opened her eyes, Breanna was grinning at her.

"You're such a food junkie," she said.

"Agreed," Sadie said before taking another bite.

It was several minutes before she finished the second scone, set down her cup of tea—peppermint, since she thought Earl Grey tasted like wet socks—and let out a satisfied breath. "Our last tea in England," she said sadly. "And I never did wrestle the scone recipe away from Mrs. Land."

"Whatever," Breanna said dismissively. "You'll go home, spend two weeks baking scone recipes you find online and end up with a recipe that blows Mrs. Land's out of the water. You'll call them 'Sadie's Scrumptulicious Scones' or 'Scones to Die For' or something like that."

Sadie cocked her head and smiled at the compliment. "You know me too well."

Breanna nodded and leaned back in her seat. She looked at her watch—a waterproof, multifunctioning black monstrosity that was as feminine as a chainsaw. "Where's Liam?" she asked.

Sadie shrugged. He'd texted Breanna, telling them to wait for him in the sitting room, but that had been nearly fifteen minutes ago. Sadie eyed the two scones they'd left for him and wondered if he'd notice if she ate one. Would he even have time to eat both with the staff in such a hurry to be rid of them? And yet, when she'd put on her jeans that morning she found them a bit harder to button up than they'd been when she had arrived. At fifty-six she no longer had the metabolism of her youth and needed to have limits. But it was so hard! And how often was she going to have a cream tea in Devonshire? Sadie gave in and grabbed a third scone. Breanna didn't seem to notice, so Sadie quickly prepared it and then savored every bite. When it was gone, the last scone called to her, but this time she ignored it. She couldn't eat *all* of Liam's scones.

In order to distract herself from that last baked confection, she reviewed all the amazing things they'd done and seen that week. She and Breanna had made a list on the airplane from the U.S. and had diligently sought out places from some of their favorite books and movies set in England. They'd toured Tintagel, the ruins of King Arthur's castle in Cornwall, Ascot where Eliza Doolittle attended the races in *My Fair Lady*, Alnwick castle in Northumberland, which was used as Hogwarts in the Harry Potter movies, and they even took the Jack the Ripper tour in London—creepy. Sadie felt sure they'd gotten everything on the list, but reviewed it in her mind one last time, mostly to keep herself from the final scone. Suddenly, she sat up.

"We need to take a turn about the room," she said excitedly. She didn't wait for an answer, moving to her daughter's side and pulling her to her feet.

"What?" Breanna asked, looking at her strangely as she stumbled to get her balance, nearly dropping the scone in her hand as she did so.

Sadie was already tugging her toward the perimeter of the room. "Remember? It was on our list—taking a turn around the room like Miss Bingley and Elizabeth in *Pride and Prejudice*." She waved her hand through the air in a regal fashion. "I'll be Caroline Bingley and you can be Elizabeth—although with your bad attitude, maybe you should be Caroline."

"I don't remember us assigning characters when we put it on the list," Breanna said before taking a bite of her scone.

Sadie gave her a dirty look, ignoring the commentary. Breanna shook her head but fell into step beside her mother, standing nearly five inches taller than Sadie thanks to the genetics she'd inherited from her birth parents. They walked slowly, scanning the collection of paintings and antique furniture on the interior wall as they made their way toward the far end of the long, narrow room. They'd been in this room twice before, but hadn't inspected it too closely. It was only fitting that doing so should be part of their final moments at Southgate estate.

When they neared the far wall, they turned and found themselves looking out the window furthest from the door. It was one of three floor-to-ceiling windows covered in elaborate folds of the same fabric used on the settees scattered throughout the room. It had rained off and on all week, and had just started to sprinkle again, giving the view of the garden a watery look. Breanna popped the last of her scone in her mouth.

"I wish we'd had more time to walk through the gardens," Sadie said as they walked toward the window and she looked out upon the meticulously kept shrubs and bushes. "It's too bad it was so wet."

Breanna suddenly stopped, and since Sadie's arm was linked through Breanna's she was pulled to a stop as well, and none too gracefully either.

"Why are you being so difficult?" Sadie said, tugging on her daughter's arm again.

Breanna didn't respond. Instead she lifted a hand and pointed toward the curtain panel just to the right of the window.

The curtain was pushed out from the wall, nearly a foot. Poking out from beneath the folds of the heavy pleated fabric were the toes of two black leather shoes. A glass-fronted china cabinet stood between two of the windows kept that particular curtain panel from being easily noticed. It was a perfect hiding place for whoever had chosen to do just that.

"Hello?" Sadie asked after several seconds of silence.

No response.

She and Breanna shared a look and Sadie felt annoyance rush through her at the idea that they were being spied upon. They'd have overheard her suspicions about the staff wanting them to leave. How embarrassing.

"All right," she said in her schoolteacher voice, directing her comments toward the motionless shoes. "We can see you, so come out. Is that you, Liam?" Liam didn't strike Sadie as the practical joker type, but it was the only explanation she could think of.

No answer. Not Liam.

Breanna took a step back, pulling her mother with her, and although Sadie's chest prickled with apprehension, she refused to give into it. She pulled herself up to her full five and a half feet and raised her chin. "This isn't funny," she said. "So just make it easy on all of us and come out."

Nothing.

Taking a deep breath, and ignoring a new tremor of fear, she took a few steps forward and in one motion pulled the drapes back to unmask their uninvited guest.

Sadie sucked in a breath and didn't move.

Breanna screamed before clamping both hands over her mouth.

The man pinned to the wall by what looked like a fireplace poker did nothing but stare at the floor with his face frozen in shocked horror, a blossom-shaped bloodstain on his chest.

ABOUT THE AUTHOR

Josi was born and raised in Salt Lake City, attended Olympus High School and made an appearance at Salt Lake Community College before marrying her high school sweetheart, starting a family, and moving to Willard, Utah. In addition to her writing, she loves to bake, travel, can her own peaches, watch criminal justice TV, and study the oddness of human nature. *Lemon Tart* is her ninth published novel, and the first of the Sadie Hoffmiller mystery series that combines many of her great loves into one delicious book.

In her spare time, she likes to overwhelm herself with a multitude of projects and then complain that she never has any spare time; in this way she is rather masochistic.

She also enjoys cheering on her children and sleeping in when the occasion presents itself. She loves to hear from her readers and can be reached at Kilpack@gmail.com.